Before the Blossom F

Lucy A. Clarke was brought up in Surrey, England. She has lived in various cities in England and abroad, but has been settled in Newcastle Upon Tyne for the last ten years. She has a degree in Philosophy and Psychology. This is her first novel.

Lucy A. Clarke

Before the Blossom Falls

Copyright © 2018 L A Goy

All rights reserved. No part of this publication may be reproduced, transmitted in any form or by any means, electronic or mechanical, including photocopying, recording or any information storage and retrieval system, without permission in writing from the publisher.

The characters, incidents and dialogue herein are fictional and any resemblance to actual events or persons, living or dead, is purely coincidental.

ISBN: 9781729062098

To Jane

PROLOGUE

Suffolk County, New York
17th August 1957

Funny. She had expected his voice to be louder, but it was Gwen's that came up the stairs most vividly. His voice barely reached her—low and indiscernible, like a grumbling wood pigeon. Gwen's was more of a squawking sound, a trapped hen trying to escape the pot. She could pick out certain words.

"Sorry."

And then. "So sorry."

And not long after. "Madness."

Finally. "Forgive me."

Nothing like the Gwen she knew, or thought she knew, full of ironic amusement and controlled tones, unfazed by seemingly anything. How little we know a person until we see them in crisis, Laura thought, as she sat on the edge of the bed. They had lain there just a few minutes before, like a couple of scientists, unable to believe the evidence unraveling before them. First, there was the snap of the front door, and then the thud of a dropped case, and, as though that wasn't enough, there was his voice.

"Darling, I'm home," he had shouted up.

The first few things, her underwear and corset, she had put on in such a hurry, whipping them up from the chair. Gwen had pulled on her robe and rushed over to the door, grabbing for the handle. His footsteps changed from the hardwood of the hall to the carpeted runner on the stairs. She had moved to stay out of view, but his eyes met hers as Gwen opened the door, and Laura knew she had been too slow.

"John, you're back early," Gwen said, as she slid through and shut the door behind her.

Why had she bothered with the corset? Why hadn't she just pulled on her dress? That would have been much more respectable. As respectable as anything could be in this kind of situation.

Of course, thinking about it, she could have hidden in the bathroom or… She looked down. Yes, there had been space under the bed.

The sound of a door opening downstairs made her sit back up.

"Laura, will you come down please."

It was John. Although after this, perhaps she should call him Mr. Forest. Suddenly everything felt as formal as that first day in his office at Mount Sinai Hospital.

Outside the bedroom, the floral smells of bath salts, soap and perfume all vanished, replaced by the housekeeper's wax and polish. The landing seemed too wide, and she felt unusually small, unable to fill the large space between the papered walls and the long sweeping bannister. She really needed support from both, but held tightly to the rail, and took the first few steps. Below, Gwen stepped out from the study and closed the door. She leaned her whole body back against the dark wood, her hands behind her, still on the handle. She lifted her head, but her eyes were closed. Her chest rose and fell with quick breaths. Laura made the final steps along the hallway, crossing scattered silk rugs.

Laura reached for her hand, but Gwen stepped aside.

"You'd better go in."

A large teak desk dominated the room, its leather top secured down by large brass studs. She was reminded again of their first meeting, but there was no smile or handshake this time. And this room was much finer than his office at the hospital, full of expensive leather bound first editions and heavy drapes.

He tapped his glasses against the desk.

"Sit down Laura." A long, buttoned leather couch stood against the wall, and an upright high backed chair sat on her side of the desk. She didn't like either of the options and remained standing, feeling the smooth silk rug beneath her feet as she shifted slightly from foot to foot. Her shoes still lay carelessly near the front door—probably next to his suitcase. "What a mess."

"I'm sorry John, I…" She didn't know what to say. "I know you must be upset—angry." Looking at him it was hard to tell how he felt. Tired? Resigned? But she couldn't suggest that.

He rubbed his eyes. "I'm not angry. The first few times, yes, but now I just feel depressed about the whole thing. It's all so inevitable."

She pulled back the chair, sitting stiffly, her hands resting in her lap and her ankles crossed. He leant back and swiveled slightly from side to side.

"The first was the nanny, or at least the first I know of." He smiled at Laura's face and shook his head. "Not Mrs. Morris, the one before her. Obviously she had to go. Gwen was so ashamed that first time—promised me it would never happen again, but it did. It's a sickness I guess. We tried a psychiatrist, and it seemed to help, for a while at least, but… " He flicked his hand towards her. "Mind you've lasted a lot longer than the others. Usually it's over before I have an idea of what might've been going on."

"You had an idea?" The words caught clumsily and she tried to clear her throat. He lifted a large water jug from his desk and poured a glass, passing it to her.

"I thought if I just turned a blind eye it would burn itself out like the ones before. But now I have to do something." He smiled wryly. "I do have some pride."

Sitting forward, he rested his elbows on the desk. "It's a shame. You're a good doctor. I had plans for you, but you'll have to go."

She raised her head to object, but he was right; they couldn't work together after this, at least not in the same hospital, and probably not even in New York. Maybe she would move back to California. Gwen could follow her out there.

"Don't worry, I'll give you a good recommendation. I can even help you find somewhere. James—Dr. Mitchell. He's just come back from a sabbatical in London. Don't you have family over there? We've got good relationships with a few of the hospitals." He dropped his head and ran thick fingers through his Ivy League hair cut. "You'd better go now. Come to my office tomorrow and we'll talk some more. But think about London. It might be best all round. And in the mean time…" He pushed his glasses back on. " Stay away from my wife."

PART ONE

CHAPTER ONE

London
21st October 1957

The box was white leatherette with a thin gold line around its lid. He had fished it out of his trouser pocket, like a schoolboy pulling out a prize conker, and held it out to her.

Kate looked at the gift and wondered if it could be a proposal. Might there be a very definite question about their future inside that box? But surely David would find a better place, a better way? Not under the bright unsympathetic porch light of the nurses' home, blackened with the husks of ill-fated flies. The laughter of her friends, and the dampened sound of music, came through the glass-paneled doors.

"Well, take it then," he said, pushing it towards her.

The hinge was tight, and it almost snapped back. But as she pushed again, the lid popped open and there sat a silver fob, much like the one she wore every day to work. Except this one gleamed, it's surfaces polished and unscratched.

"Turn it over."

"The Twenty Second of October, Nineteen Fifty Seven." She read the inscription out loud. "Thank you, I love it."

Far from feeling underwhelmed, she was pleased by its insignificance. But she felt the word *love* as soon as it was said and thought that he had too.

It had been several months since David had first said *I love you*, and she had lost count of the times he had said it since. At least initially, as though, like dropping pennies into a fruit machine, the more he said it, the greater the odds might be of her rewarding him with a return of those words. A few times she had thought to push them out, to please him. But something stopped her, and she held on tight.

And then he had stopped, just recently, just in the last few weeks.

"I thought it might be nice, a memento of your first day. You know…of being qualified I mean," he said.

"I'll make sure I wear it tomorrow."

Leaning forward, he placed a kiss on her lips and then another, the second a little longer than the first. The third and final kiss was brief. They were three fairly simple, closed kisses, and that was how they had been since the night of the party. Again, she felt relief—an end to the gradual build up—no more wondering where things would eventually end.

On the first few dates they had held hands, with a final short kiss before saying goodbye. She had enjoyed the touch of his skin, feeling his smooth palm in hers and the soft press of his lips, but as the kisses became more persistent, and his hands travelled and pressed and tightened, and his breathing altered, she had been disappointed. She had hoped it would be different this time. She wanted all those feelings. She wanted to feel her own short hot breaths, the tremble in her hands, and that unsteady nervous smile she saw in David. Was she a prude? A tease? Maybe if they were married it would be different? Or maybe this was how it was for a woman and how it was for a man.

"Shall I meet you after work again tomorrow?"

"Yes. I'll see you tomorrow," she said, as she turned towards the door. "Goodnight David."

The music instantly became more defined; there were lyrics, a piano and string instruments. She stood in the doorway of the dayroom. Val sat with a number of other student and staff nurses. They had pulled their chairs around in a large circle, and a red Dansette sat at its center, surrounded by scattered record covers and sleeves. Peg knelt by the player, watching the shiny black disc spin round.

"Did David walk you home?" Val said, as she looked up from a stack of albums piled on her lap.

Kate nodded and perched on the arm of her chair, loosening off her cape. Val knew not to ask any more. On her first dates, Val, Peg, and some of the other women—whoever happened to be in the day room or in one of their bedrooms when she returned—would sit up or lean in expectantly, wanting to know every detail, breaking from their conversation or the magazines or books they were reading. But her responses had been brief, and she couldn't fill their curiosity with all the details they wanted. How had it felt to hold his hand in the pictures? Nice but unremarkable, occasionally a little awkward, she had wanted to reply. Had he kissed her yet? No, she had answered, and then a few weeks later, yes. They had pushed and teased, but she had just smiled or shrugged or said yes or no. So eventually, over the months, their questioning had tailed off. Instead they just smiled or asked her if she had had a nice time, but nothing more, as though she had just returned from the shops or tea with her aunt.

"Dot just got this on hire purchase. There was a choice of colors—blue, yellow, green—but she went for the red," Peg said, as she pulled a record from its cover. "And Val just bought this..." Lifting the needle she placed it down gently. A hiss came from the front of the record player and then a fast piano and drum beat. It was one of the new rockabilly tunes. Peg held the cover up. "Jerry Lee Lewis."

Kate had heard her younger half sister play it the last time she had gone home. Their mum had shouted up to turn it down, and then eventually off when she'd really had enough. Peg jumped up and grabbed Val. "Come on Kate."

Someone turned the volume up, and Val laughed, as Peg pulled her in and back out. "Yes, come on. Get that cape off," Val shouted across over the music.

"We've learnt this new move," Peg said, as she spread out her legs, sticking both feet out and wiggling her hips. She walked quickly towards Val to the beat of the music, one hand holding Val's, the other free and shaking in the air.

"You look like a duck," Kate laughed.

"But a duck with rhythm?" Peg said, as she glanced over her shoulder, and Val pulled her in.

"Oh most definitely with rhythm."

"I saw it on the Six-Five Special a few weeks ago. I've been teaching Val," she said, catching her breath between words.

A few other women were up. Some of them tried Peg's new move, while others stuck to more traditional swing steps. Kate sat and watched until the record ended, and they fell back into their chairs, breathless and laughing. Except for Peg, who fell to the floor and lay at Val's feet. But just as suddenly as she had dropped, she sat up. "Time for something a little slower," she said, pulling out a record from its sleeve. There was the brief hiss again, and then, this time, rather than drums, it was violins. The song was from a picture, a romance they had just seen the week before.

"Do you think you could play it on the piano?" Peg said, as she looked up at Kate.

"Go on Kate," Val encouraged. "Give it a go."

An old baby grand sat in the corner, left from a time before radio and record players. A framed photograph hung just above, showing a group of austere young women in long tunics and elaborate caps. They stared blankly out at the day room, as they stood around the piano's lacquered black bulk. Now the piano only shone in certain places, much of it dulled by the rub of bodies and hands. The legs carried most of the damage, scarred with chips and scratches from careless cleaners with mops and brushes, or the heels and toes of overexcited nurses, before and after hospital dances.

"I've still got unpacking to do," she said, standing from the chair arm. "Maybe tomorrow."

"How's your new room?" Peg said, playing with the laces of Val's sturdy black work shoes.

"Fine, I've just got a few more things to put away. Has anyone moved in with you yet?" She thought of her old room just along the corridor.

Peg nodded. "Susan Jackson—a first year. She's struggling with homesickness still and hates the dormitory. Matron thought a quieter environment might help."

The needle lifted, as the record came to an end. Val gently nudged Peg with her foot. "Out the way Peg. I'll come up with you Kate."

The corridor smelt of newly laid carpet. Both the ground floor and the next floor up had been refurbished. As well as new flooring and curtains, each room had been furnished with built in wardrobes and divan beds that stood on slim wooden legs and castors. Every fireplace had been pulled out and the walls filled in and smoothed over, so you would never know there had ever been a place to burn coal. Instead, solid iron radiators, heated by a central gas boiler, hummed out a steady heat. There was even a kitchenette at the end of each corridor where the nurses could make hot drinks or snacks and take them to their rooms.

But for some reason the workmen had stopped, and the second floor remained as it had been. There was talk of more pressing work required in the main hospital, and at some point the updates would resume, but nobody knew exactly when. So Kate's room had been a compromise. Rather than wait, she had taken the room on the second floor when it became available, minding only a little that she would have to settle for a metal frame bed with springs that squeaked at each turn and worn dark wood furniture. At least there was a sink, a proper chest of drawers, and a desk that she didn't have to share anymore.

Val hummed the tune that they had just been listening to, a small smile on her lips. She leaned against her doorframe and stretched.

"Do you think that's how it is?" Kate asked.

"What?" Val said, as she yawned.

"Being in love. Like in that film—that song."

"What? Staring wistfully out of the window at the moon? Your heart playing like a violin?"

Kate nodded. "And the quickening of your heart."

"More of a rapture, a thundering of your heart." Val pressed her hand to her breastbone.

"Really?" Kate stood straight. "That's how it is for you? When you're with Johnny?"

"Oh Kate, you're serious. Sorry, I…Love's so many things, and I'm sure it's different…I mean…it's not the same for everyone. But you'll know. When you're in love, you won't need to ask the question." Val pushed herself away from the door and came forward a little. "Is everything okay with you and David?"

"Oh yes, everything's fine."

"Because…I know your mother expects it…but if it's not right…"

"*Everyone* expects it—a handsome doctor—I'd be mad wouldn't I?"

"Forget everyone else, and I'm sure your mum would understand…eventually anyway," Val said, and then smiled, leaning back again. "Tell her it could be worse. You could be going out with a lad from a skiffle group."

"Have your parents still not come round yet? Johnny's so nice. I don't know how they could dislike him."

"Mum's not so bad, but dad's still furious—says he should get a proper job—that he could get Johnny something at the Milk Marketing Board just like that." Val snapped her fingers and they both laughed. "How about the new registrar? I think he's meant to be starting tomorrow. Your mum would love that. I mean, after all, David's only a junior."

"Oh, I think Peg's got first dibs on him," Kate said, smiling.

"She's heard a rumor he's coming over from California. Now she's convinced he'll look like he's just stepped out of some Hollywood film studio."

Kate turned the handle of her door and pushed it open. "Let's hope she's not disappointed."

Before hanging her bag on the back of the door, she reached in and pulled out the white box and placed it in her bedside drawer.

Small and isolated, the only thing in there, it slid from the front to the back, as she pushed the drawer shut.

The first time David had said *I love you*, they had been walking across Hyde Park, returning from a party. She had been granted a late pass, and the summer night was warm and still. So they had strolled, in no hurry, the path intermittently lit by lamplight. Unused to alcohol, she was enjoying the effects of the drinks from the party, which had settled hazily about her. But then, at one of the paths darker points, between the faded light of two lampposts, David pulled her away from the path and kissed her. She remembered the light pair of sandals she wore and the dampness of the grass reaching her toes. The kiss grew deeper, and she could taste the evening's beer and cigarettes. And just as suddenly as it had started, the kiss stopped. "I love you," he said hotly into her ear. At the same moment he placed her hand up against himself, hard and upright, and reached down for her lips again. So in that moment, she had felt what it meant to be loved and found it lacking, and every time he had said those words since, she wanted to feel a rush and a desire to say "I love you" back, but all she felt was emptiness and the stiff weight of him in her hand.

CHAPTER TWO

Her cap wouldn't sit straight. The pins at first feeling too tight and then too loose. She tried again, as she stooped to contain her reflection—two hairpins in her mouth and a third in her hand. She had hung the mirror on a nail. It had already been waiting there, above the mantle piece, coated with the same pale green paint as the paper lined walls. It was probably the right height for the previous occupant, Mary Parker, a short stout girl. She would be away now on her honeymoon or perhaps already setting up home somewhere in— where was it? Camberwell or Islington? She couldn't remember. They hadn't been close friends, but Mary had come out with them a couple of times to the pictures. That wouldn't happen again, now that she had married.

Everyone had said, at twenty-seven, how well she had done to marry James Green, a banker form the city. Mary's father had worked as a clerk at the Co-operative, but he had liked a drink, so her mother had spent most of her life charring in order to make ends meet. It was only Val that had disagreed, saying that she had met more interesting goldfish than Mr. Green. She was right. Kate had never seen him form a single word at any of the dances, just bubbles that seemed to collect gradually in the corners of his mouth, and then dry to a glistening white powder.

Kate swallowed and shifted her feet away from the small electric fire, as it buzzed fiercely on the hearth. There were three quick knocks at the door, but she carried on with her task, the final kirby grip pinched between her thumb and forefinger, only glancing back briefly as the handle turned.

"Having difficulties?" Val said, as she closed the door behind her. She wore the same uniform as Kate, except there was a slight tiredness to hers, some of the color washed away and the edges softened. She dropped her cape onto the back of the only easy chair in the room. The navy wool and scarlet satin jumped out against the tired upholstery. "Here, let me," she said, as she took the final pin from Kate and positioned it, so that it firmly caught the cap and her dark hair beneath. "There you are Staff Nurse Ford. We can't have you losing your 'dignity' on your first day can we?"

"Thanks Val." Kate smiled at the old fashioned reference, still used by Matron and many of the Sisters. "You go on ahead. I'll be down in a few minutes."

"Okay, but don't be too long…" Val pulled on the handle. "Sister Bates is on duty today." Kate let out a sigh, as the door clicked shut. "Oh and I've got some news too, about the new doctor." The words floated away in the open length of the corridor as her footsteps continued.

Kate stepped off the hearth and onto the brightly patterned rug, enjoying the warmth of its pile. It had originally sat between her bed and Peg's, but with only one bed in this room it was too small, an inadequate gesture thrown to a sea of linoleum tiles. But she had been glad to replace the tired bedside mat that had lain uninvitingly on her arrival, its corners curling up and the center pressed down by so many other nurses' feet.

Two small safety pins sat on top of the chest of drawers. She took the first one and secured the top left side of her apron and with the second, the right. She fastened the metal buckle of her belt and reached for her shoes, pulling each one on and fastening their laces. Breathing out, and with one final glance in the mirror, she reached for her cape and closed the door behind her.

"My watch." Opening the door again, she went to her bedside table and lifted the fob from its box. She clenched it in her hand and hurried down the corridor, trying to pin the thing as she walked, but both tasks at the same time were impossible, as she pricked first her chest and then her fingers. Finally, she stopped at the top of the stairs, fastening it securely to her pinafore.

From the corridor below there was the smell of cooked and cooling breakfasts; a mixture of wet bacon, eggs and porridge, hung in the air and grew heavier as she approached the dining hall. She walked its length, past the hot food counter, where Mrs. Thompson, the cook, used ladles and tongs to serve watery baked beans and pale rashers, to the table that held the cereal and toast.

She sat down opposite Val and reached for the butter dish. "So, what's the news?" Kate said, as she lifted the lid and began to spread the butter.

"News? Oh yes." Val sat up a little straighter. "It's the new registrar, you know, the one coming over from America."

She nodded, biting down on her toast.

"Well..." Val rested her elbows on the table and leaned forward. "*She's* arrived."

Kate swallowed her toast. "She?"

"Yes. We saw her earlier. Sister was showing her to her rooms. Peg overheard her saying she's staying here until her flat's ready. There's been some sort of delay."

"A female registrar?" Kate spoke more to herself than to Val. She had seen female medical students pass through the wards, but they seemed to disappear like wraiths, she assumed through to the safe walls of general practice or the remaining women's hospitals.

"I know. Isn't it marvelous?"

"If you ask me I think it's rather strange." They both looked up, as Peg placed her bowl down and took her seat. "And it's all right for you two. You've got David and Johnny. That's one less eligible doctor."

"Poor Peg," Val teased. "She was hoping for Rock Hudson and got Grace Kelly instead. She is beautiful though, isn't she Peg?"

"Well, if you find rangy attractive, then yes...I suppose so." Kate smiled and shook her head, as Peg sprinkled salt with a small frown on her face. "One less eligible doctor and extra competition." She looked up from her porridge and began to chuckle when she saw the faces of her two friends. "What? Okay, she's not bad looking. More like Eva Marie Saint though, I would say. Looks like she's worth a bob or two as well."

"Oh, yes Kate. Her clothes were something else, the cut, the fabric."

"You don't think she runs up her own dresses?" Kate joked, as she thought of her recently unpacked case, filled mostly with clothes her mother and Aunt Mable had made for her from various Vogue patterns.

Val put down her knife and fork, noticing the new fob. "What do I spy here?" She reached across, lifting it lightly in her hand.

"David gave it to me yesterday."

Peg twisted round on her chair, and as Val dropped the fob, she lifted and turned it, showing the simple inscription on the back.

"Today's date." She released the fob and turned back to her porridge. "Well I suppose his sentiments were limited to a small space."

"Has this replaced the one Kenneth gave you?" Val asked, amused, as she took a drink of tea. Kate nodded. "What about the one before? What was his name?"

"Derek." Kate thought back to the skinny young boy she had first started to date in grammar school, and had stayed with a few months into her nurses' training. "Yes, the pin broke."

"She's collecting them like medals," Val said, placing her cup back down in its saucer.

But medals for what? There was nothing very victorious in any of those relationships. They had bumped and bumbled along, burning low and then out like damp tinder. No heroism, more of a puzzled shake of a young man's head, as he eventually walked away.

With a final gulp of tea, she began to stand. "I'd better go." She looked down at her watch. "I need to get the breakfasts sorted before Sister comes up for the morning report and prayers."

"I think you're in luck." Val gestured towards a table at the far end of the hall. "The doctor's arrival must have delayed her a little."

It seemed odd that the clock should say quarter to eight, as Sister Bates placed her usual bowl of cereal down and smoothed the back of her uniform, before taking her seat. The hands looked out of place, as they sat above her head. The larger of the two quivered slightly, forcing its way very gradually forward. Every morning, since Kate had first arrived, Sister Bates had sat in that seat as the large hand rested above the six, pointing directly at the top of her white starched cap. She watched uneasily while the Sister lifted the milk jug, as if someone had slightly altered a familiar painting.

As she stepped back from the table, she began to fasten her cape. "Look at you—like a shiny new penny," Peg said, waving her empty spoon. "You should be on the cover of the nursing times. That shade of blue suits you. It matches your eyes."

Looking down at her new uniform, Kate smiled and made a small curtsy. "Thank you." She glanced back at the clock. "Shouldn't you be coming too? There's the—"

"I know, I know. There's the breakfast to sort out." Peg scraped the last of the porridge from her bowl and stood. "Come on then."

It was quickest through the underground tunnels. They were originally meant for the transportation of waste and laundry, with their narrow dimly lit corridors leading to every corner of the hospital, although nurses and doctors would often chase down their paths, when in a hurry to get from one part of the hospital to another. Today though, Peg had persuaded Kate to walk through the grounds to the main entrance. So she pressed along the path, only half listening to Peg's talk, and unable to enjoy the low mists lifting from the damp grass or the pink and orange of the new morning sky.

A large area of the grounds had been cleared during the war to grow fruit and vegetables, and some of the beds still remained, looked after by the grounds men and sometimes some of the longer stay patients. Many had been dug over ready for the winter, and they followed the path alongside half empty rows of onions, sprouts, and wooden supports holding the last of the runner beans. Up above, the nurses had already opened the balcony doors and were beginning to bring patients out in their beds to try to gain some benefit from the fresh air.

***

The rectangular windows stood tall and high along both sides of the nightingale ward letting in the midmorning sun, still weak compared to summer days, but strong enough to warm the places where the windows directed it, so that each patient would get periods of sunlight resting across their beds. Some welcomed it as an addition of warmth to the erratic furnace driven radiators, but to others it was an annoyance, as they squinted their eyes, trying to read books or do puzzles.

It was just at this time of the day that the sun settled quite centrally on the nurses' table, and Kate sat down next to Peg, enjoying its envelope. She pulled a newly laundered bandage out of a basket beside her, stretching and rolling its long length, then pinning the tight ball in place. Both sat silently, concentrating on the task, occasionally observing the two nursing students at the far end of the ward as they completed one of Mr. Martin's two hourly turns. She had already walked the length of the ward several times, double-checking all the beds and lockers, pleased with how the morning had gone. Breakfast had been finished and cleared before Sister had arrived to lead the prayers, and she was satisfied that everything was ready for the doctor's round; Everyone was in bed, their sheets and blankets straightened and tucked in. The tops of the lockers were tidied and cleared, the curtain screens ran parallel, and all the wheels on every bed were aligned with one another.

As she picked up another bandage, she thought of Sister Bates and her forewarning of the new doctor's arrival. How had she put it? "In case you haven't already heard, the new registrar, Dr. Harrison, is a woman." She had waited, seemingly for the information to sink in. "She's already been mistaken for a medical secretary by one of the junior doctors, so I thought I had better make you aware." It had taken all her concentration to keep a straight face. "Anyway, she's collected her white coat from the sewing room, so it shouldn't happen again." It was only as the Sister turned to go to inspect the sluice that Kate dared to look at Peg, and they had smiled at one another.

The basket beside her was still almost full. The dozen or more balls that sat neatly in front of her had made little impact. As she dipped her hand in again to pull out another, the doors cracked open and the usual mix of doctors and medical students entered, led by Sister Bates and Mr. Clarkson.

"Here's Eva Marie." Peg whispered as they both stood.

Sister gave a small nod and they sat back down. There seemed to be a buzz on the ward. Even though they had moved away to the first of Mr. Clarkson's patients, she could feel a pulse of energy within the high ceilinged walls, as they all flittered about the new doctor, like fish around a coral reef. Mr. Clarkson, always affable, seemed younger today, gently laughing or nodding like an eager schoolboy. Even Sister Bates occasionally gave a flicker of a smile.

Dr. Harrison returned their smiles, but hers were long and easy, and her body seemed relaxed underneath her new stiff white coat, as she turned to Sister Bates, probably to ask questions about Mr. Johnson's fracture. Both wore their hair up, but their appearance couldn't have been more different. Not a single length of hair escaped the hold of a dozen Kirby grips at the back of Sister's head, but the doctor's blond hair was pulled up in just one large clip. Some of it had fallen loosely at the front, whether through the course of the morning or by the doctor's arrangement Kate couldn't be sure, but it softened further the even features of her face.

Were the temperatures still high in California? Kate imagined they must be. All the others looked like ghostly figures in comparison, any color from summer days at Southend on Sea or Brighton beach long washed away. Even Mr. Clarkson's holiday to Majorca had left no trace on his pale October skin, and his neck and hands merged into his white coat, which seemed as grey as an overcast sky next to the new doctor's.

"Come on slow coach." Peg said, nudging Kate, her own basket empty. "Do you want me to sort the tea urn out?"

Kate nodded and reached for another bandage. The task was one she had done so many times that she could easily perform it and watch the group, as they continued to make their way down to the very bottom of the ward. The letters her friend, Maggie O'Donnell, had written from Boston came to mind. Letters that told of a hospital with sliding doors and private rooms, and vending machines in every corridor. She could picture Dr. Harrison there, in fact much more easily than on Dickens ward, even though she stood only yards away—as clear as a freshly inked stamp. Maggie. She had only intended to go across for a year to earn some extra money for her family, but she had met a doctor and married and stayed.

"Ah, so that's the new registrar." The hushed voice caused her to straighten up and turn. David stood beside her, his hands hanging onto either end of his stethoscope.

"Please tell me it wasn't you who mistook her for one of the secretaries." She breathed out the words quietly, trying not to draw any attention.

"Ah no, that was Chummy. I think he asked her if she could type up a letter for him."

"And how did she take that?"

"Quite well apparently—said something about her typing not being up to much and her shorthand even worse."

"What are you doing here?" She said, glancing over to the back of the Sister's nodding white cap. "Sister Bates is just over there."

He shrugged and grinned, leaning down on the table, his arms lightly brushing hers. "Oh, I think I can handle Sister Bates." She knew he probably could. Like many of the young doctors, he had a sense of self-assurance, where nothing and no one seemed to be taken too seriously. She even saw it with some of the younger nursing students and cadets, occasionally catching them rolling their eyes or pulling a face before standing for Sister or Matron.

So instead of moving to leave, he leaned in closer, his eyes remaining on the group. "I wanted to see you, see how things were going on your first day…and then when I heard the new doctor was down here too, well I thought I'd come and take a look. See what all the fuss is about. Chummy hasn't stopped going on about her all morning and Morris has declared he's in love."

She looked at the group again—Mr. Clarkson, Sister Bates and the small cluster of junior doctors and medical students—every one of them unremarkable. Like extras on a film set, they blended into each other and into the background, as ordinary as the metal-framed beds and curtain screens that surrounded them. Dr. Harrison stood with them, but there was something that made her stand apart. Not as strong as a spotlight, but as though someone had snapped a clapperboard, and it was apparent to Kate that she had the most lines, the best lines. She supposed that this was what the girls had meant when they had compared her to those Hollywood stars. She stood out as someone far from everyday, far from ordinary.

"So, I was wondering if you fancied meeting up." She took a moment to register David's words. "There's a new teashop on the corner of Baker road. I've heard they do great cakes. The coffee walnut comes highly recommended," he continued. "When are you next off?"

Kate started to answer, but she was too aware that the group was now heading back up the ward, with only a few more patients to see. They had stepped away from Mr. Davidson's bed, so there was only Mr. Campbell, and there would be no need to stop by him. He was all tied up in a Balkan frame and likely to stay that way for several more weeks. "You'd better go," she said, her attention now fixed on Sister Bates, who was clearly watching the two of them. She couldn't decide if perhaps it was better for David to stay and explain his visit himself.

"So, when?"

"The day after tomorrow." Kate didn't look at David, but instead watched their progress up the ward.

"Do you fancy it then?"

"Dr. Richards." Kate stood as Mr. Clarkson called out David's name, and Sister approached them both.

"Continue with what you were doing Nurse Ford," Sister Bates said.

Reaching for another length of bandage, she sat down again and pulled the long piece of cloth tightly, watching her hands as they began to wind it round and round.

"This is Dr. Harrison, our new registrar," Mr. Clarkson said. "Dr. Richards is one of our junior doctors. You're not working here are you Richards? I thought you were over on Austen?"

"Bronte, Mr. Clarkson," Sister Bates said. "And might I ask why we find you down here?"

Hardly daring to, she glanced up and saw David look briefly at her and then across to Mr. Davidson, whose arm lay extended on the bed, as it slowly received a pint of blood.

"Drip stand," he said.

"Drip stand?"

Opening a safety pin, Kate looked back down at the ball in her hands and stabbed the soft cloth.

"Yes, we seem to be short of them. No idea where they all could have got to…so I popped along to see if we could borrow one."

"And none of the other wards, the closer wards were able to help? Austen? Hardy?" She didn't wait for an answer. "Nurse Ford, take a drip stand down to Bronte ward. The student nurses are about to start stripping the beds."

"Yes Sister," she said, looking behind her towards the sluice doors, where they were usually kept. The rolled bandage in her hand wasn't quite as neat as the others, and it sat rather loosely as she placed it down. Mr. Clarkson had stepped away and was addressing the others, but the new registrar seemed to be watching with what looked to be slight amusement, as though there was a joke there that Kate couldn't quite grasp.

Sister Bates turned back to David. "You might want to make better use of your time in future and send a cadet for this sort of errand."

There were four stands, and Kate pulled out the nearest one. But as she made her way quickly up the ward, she heard the squeak and drop of one of the five wheels. She pushed it further and it came again, squeak drop, and then again, squeak drop. But as she turned to go back to change it over, she heard Sister Bates. "Come on Nurse Ford. We haven't got all day, lunches will need to be sorted soon."

A few from the group—David included—looked across, and then Mr. Clarkson said "Right then," and they all began to move towards the door. "We won't be returning again today. Thank you Sister."

Grasping the cold metal stand, Kate followed behind them into the depressingly long corridor. She pushed again, and the noise only seemed to grow louder as she followed them. A few turned, but Mr. Clarkson seemed to be in no hurry, as he talked and gesticulated his way slowly up the corridor. Kate thought to try to pass and go ahead, but she could hear the Sister's reprimand as clearly as if she walked beside her. "Do not pass anyone that is your senior, Nurse Ford." But just as she was wondering whether to pick the whole thing up and carry it, Mr. Clarkson stopped and turned.

"Would you care to pass?"

"Thank you Mr. Clarkson." Kate dipped her head and hurried by, briefly noticing David's smile as she passed him. She looked straight ahead, wondering what she would say to the Sister on Bronte when she arrived with the unwanted stand.

***

Visiting had just finished, and the last family members had been ushered out by Sister Bates. A large bunch of fresh cut flowers lay on the table, brought in by Mr. Martin's daughter. Peg began to unwrap them from the newspaper. Bright yellow chrysanthemums and pink cosmos spilled out onto the wooden top, his allotment's last offerings.

"I'll get a vase," Kate said, as she stood. Just as she reached for the doors, one flew open and she moved away to avoid its swing, only remembering the oxygen cylinder when her stocking snagged against its metal carrier. "Blast!" How many times had she done that? She reached down and ran a finger along the thin jagged line.

"Ouch, are you okay?"

The bare calves were slim and tanned, following up to a pale blue pencil skirt, and then of course there was the crisp white coat.

Kate wondered if her eyes would be green or blue as she stood back up.

"Sorry, we've not been introduced," the doctor said, as she held out her hand. "I'm Dr. Harrison—the new registrar."

Kate rubbed her hands down the sides of her pinafore, as though she had just been kneading floury dough or planting bulbs in the garden. "Staff Nurse Ford."

The hand remained extended and so she took it. Surprised by its softness, she wondered how her own must feel, heated and hardened by the daily cleaning and sterilizing. Like pouring honey on toast.

"So, are you okay?"

"It's just a ladder, occupational hazard, I—"

It was the sudden sound of chair legs on parquet flooring that caused her to step away, and for them both to look across to the nurses' table. Sister Bates stood, but Peg remained seated, a bright orange dahlia held aloft and her mouth set in an 'O' of surprise.

"Dr. Harrison. I wasn't made aware of your intention to return to the ward today," the Sister said, as she walked towards them, her lips forced to a tight smile. "I'm sure you're still finding your way around, but it would be helpful if you could let me know in advance when you plan to visit."

The doctor smiled, although, with a little less assurance than earlier. "I'm sorry Sister. I've come up to check on Mr. Thompson." She turned briefly back to Kate. "I was just going to ask Nurse Ford how he'd been during the day."

Kate had stepped away slightly and stood quite still, close to the wall—as dumb as a maidservant—unsure whether she would be given an order or dismissed, by either of the two.

"I see, well in future I'd rather you spoke with me. I will find a nurse if there are any questions I'm unable to answer. If there is anything that needs to be passed on, you can leave that to me. It's best if all communication comes through me. It avoids misunderstanding. One of the nurses can come to find me. I'm never very far away." Sister Bates punctuated each sentence with a short pause and then turned her attentions toward Kate. "Nurse Ford. I think Mr. Davidson will have finished with his bedpan."

Kate nodded, lowering her head, relieved to walk away.

***

"…And then she just went straight up and introduced herself to Kate. Sister nearly burst a blood vessel—" Peg turned as Kate approached the table with her tray. "Oh hello, I was just telling the others about your encounter with Dr. Harrison. Very queer."

There was an empty seat next to Val, and she sat down slowly. "Oh, I suppose things are just a little different in America, a little less formal," she said quietly, trying to dampen Peg's talk. She wasn't sure why, but the encounter had knocked her a little off balance. She glanced around the hall, wondering if the doctor would come down for her supper. There was quite possibly a small kitchen in her rooms or she might choose to eat out. Certainly, there would be no shortage of offers from the other doctors. Or perhaps she had discovered the doctors' dining room and preferred to eat there.

"Didn't she Kate?"

"Sorry?"

"Sister Bates. Didn't she go and make you empty Mr. Davidson's bedpan? Even though there was a student nurse not ten foot away who'd only just handed the thing to him!"

Kate smiled. "Yes."

"And on your first day as well." Val said.

The main events and people of the day played over in her mind—David, Sister Bates, the drip stand and the stockings, and Doctor Harrison—small things that today somehow seemed much bigger.

"I think I'm going to the dayroom. Anyone coming?" She pushed back her chair and stood.

"You've only just sat down," Peg said, pointing at her plate. "And you've hardly touched your supper."

"I'm not hungry." She stretched and then lifted her tray. "Too much bread at teatime."

"Will you play the piano?"

Kate nodded.

"I'll go and fetch those records I bought the other day," Val said, as she moved her chair away from the table.

There was no red Dansette tonight, so Val walked across to the large wooden radiogram and lifted its lid. Kate sat down at the piano, as Val pulled the record out of its cover and then out of its sleeve, carefully placing the record onto the turntable, mindful not to touch anything but the very edges. The needle jumped very slightly as she placed it down, and violins came through the speakers. It was the same song from the night before. Kate already had most of the tune in her head and easily began to pick out the notes.

How old had she been when she first realized she could play by ear? Possibly about eleven or twelve. She remembered how surprised her piano teacher had been when he came through from the kitchen and found her playing along to the radio, slowly at first, but in no time she had come up to the same speed. She hadn't even really been aware of what she was doing, half listening to him rummage through music sheets in the next room, trying to find the scales for her grade three exam. Although impressed, and to play by ear he told her was a gift — something that eluded himself—he discouraged her from it. Yes, it was good to feel the music, but she must learn to read the music. Playing by ear wouldn't get her to grade three. So she had followed the teacher's instructions, never playing by ear again, as though it were some primal instinct that could undo all those lessons, the lessons her mother always reminded her were a luxury she couldn't really afford. It was only when she first came to the nurses' home she had begun again. The dayroom was deserted, but the radiogram had been left on, and the baby grand invited her from its corner. So she had sat down and listened to the music, and played.

The ringing started, and Kate stopped and turned to its source. The bell's metal arm battered down on its round casing above the doorway. Dr. Harrison stood below, leaning against the frame, holding her folded coat in front of her and seemingly unperturbed by the alarm for lights out. How long had she been standing there? Kate tentatively returned her smile before the doctor slowly turned to leave, and she followed her until she was out of sight, the bell still trilling above. She looked back at the others, but no one else seemed to have even noticed her, too busy pushing records into reluctant sleeves and picking up stray magazines. She was surprised at their activity, like an audience putting on their coats and standing to leave before the very end of a play, missing the best part.

"Come on, don't forget to shut the piano lid." Val called back, as she hurried towards the door, her arms full of books and records. The bell stopped suddenly. Kate sat a moment longer, running her fingers over the smooth piano keys, before closing the lid. The laughing and chatter ahead grew quieter, as the women found their rooms or climbed the stairs.

Her room was cold, and she danced about as she put on her pajamas, hopping from foot to foot to keep warm, only stopping when there was a light tap at the door and Sister Bates popped her head round, nodded and then closed the door again behind her.

Kate looked at the mirror over the fireplace and frowned slightly. It still hung in the same place as it had that morning. Tomorrow, she would see if one of the porters could raise it. She turned and picked up the fob watch from her dresser. Pulling back the covers of her bed, she moved a hot water bottle and put herself there in it's place. She rested her head back on the pillow and held the watch up in front, studying it properly for the first time, enjoying the cool weight of it, the smooth unscratched surfaces. Only the small engraving caught slightly beneath her fingers.

She turned it over and read the date out quietly. "The Twenty Second of October, Nineteen Fifty Seven."

CHAPTER THREE

The reflection was definitely hers, but she looked tired and pale. Almost all evidence of the California sun seemed erased. Laura washed her hands and then her face in the small sink. A slight smile moved across her face, as she remembered Sister Bates' expression earlier in the day. "Wow," she murmured, thinking of all the English hospital etiquette she was clearly still learning.

An English doctor at Mount Sinai Hospital had run through some of the differences between American and British Hospitals, and she recalled his final words of caution. "Sister runs the ward. Whatever you do, keep on the right side of her, and Matron too of course."

And what about Nurse Ford? No—Staff Nurse Ford. She smiled as she corrected herself and lowered her eyes, thinking of some of the doctors in New York and their flirtations with the nursing staff. Most of it had been harmless. Often the nurses seemed happy with the attention, even welcomed it, and sometimes it had led to courting, occasionally marriage. But she had also seen unwanted comments and touches, hands brushing casually or sometimes more pointedly against thighs and backs.

"You're really no better than them, flirting with the pretty nurses," she said, shaking her head.

As she moved from the mirror, she turned her attention back to the room. Laura had stayed with Moira for the first few days and she probably could have stayed until her flat was ready. But she had known Moira a long time and knew she liked her own space. Besides, her one bedroomed flat couldn't comfortably accommodate another person for more than a few days.

She had asked the hospital about the doctor's accommodation, but the bathrooms were shared, so a room in the nurses' home had been suggested. And, as fortune would have it, a Nurse Tutor had recently vacated one of the two attic rooms. It had recently been renovated, and was just as good, she had been told, if not better, than most of the doctor's quarters.

And she had been pleasantly surprised, as her footsteps had echoed across the parquet flooring. There were only a few pieces of furniture, but they were new and in modern lightwood. A single divan bed sat in the corner, and a bedside table with a small lamp stood by its side. There was a fitted wardrobe, a chest of drawers, and a desk with a matching chair. A further comfy chair sat in one corner, in another stood a small washbasin. The smell of fresh paint and newly cut wood was a welcome change to the carbolic soap she had been surrounded by all day.

Her landlord had promised that the flat would be ready in no more than a fortnight's time, so she had only brought the essentials across from Moira's, mainly clothes and cosmetics. It was only when unpacking that she realized she hadn't brought anything to pass the time, and without Moira to talk to, and no books or magazines to read, she was stuck for something to do. There were the journals that she had pulled out of the library earlier that day, but their academic style required more attention than she was willing to give that evening.

So she had picked up her coat and taken a walk around the grounds as far as the lamp lit paths would allow. As she walked back, she remembered the shelf of books in the dayroom. It had been a fairly sorry display, with coverless hardbacks and faded paperbacks. Many had flopped onto their sides, as if they had taken advantage of the empty spaces and decided to take a rest. But as she pulled on the bar of the front door, there was the sound of a piano, and of women's chatter and laughter. She stood in the doorway of the dayroom and watched for a moment, enjoying their free and easy manner with one another. She was used to groups of women, but she hesitated to go in. These were different. These were women enjoying that short period of time before marriage and children separated them, only briefly united by this shared time and space.

Then there had been that awful bell, sending them all packing their things away. Except for Nurse Ford. She had stayed seated at the piano, and Laura had felt unable to enter and just pass by and look for books, so she had turned away instead.

On the way back to her rooms, at the top of the final small flight of stairs, she had noticed the bathroom with its deep enamel tub and the toilet next door to it. These, she assumed, would be shared with Sister Bates, whose rooms were just opposite hers. She looked at the faded yellow light that slipped slightly under the door and thought briefly to say hello, to try to make amends for this morning, but she wasn't even sure if she wanted the Sister as an ally. It had been easier just to return to her rooms.

So she found herself getting ready for bed at only ten o'clock. When was the last time she had been to bed so early?

A firm knock on the door jolted her from her thoughts like a mistimed dinner gong. She looked in the mirror, checking her freshly washed face, and ran her fingers through her hair.

It was Sister Bates, still in uniform. "I hope I'm not disturbing you? I just wanted to check you were settling in all right." The words were warmer than her tone, which remained as cool as it had been on the ward.

"Yes, thank you." Laura glanced back into her room. "I seem to have everything I need."

"This arrived for you." She held up a pale blue airmail letter and handed it across to Laura. It felt so insubstantial, as though it was barely there in her hands, something imagined. She pushed her thumb and fingers into the thin paper, immediately recognizing the careless looped handwriting, the cross of the 't' and the circle of the 'o'. She flipped it over to the return name and address. It seemed to rise off the page, like a corpse standing up from its coffin.

"Is everything all right?"

Laura looked up at Sister Bates. "Yes, thank you."

"Very good." She moved towards her own room, but her hand hesitated on the door handle, and she turned back. "I usually take a small glass of sherry before bedtime…It's my one vice." Her eyes flickered and settled on Laura. "You would be welcome to join me."

"All right…that sounds lovely," Laura said, trying to cover her surprise.

Sister Bates gave a small smile and a nod. "Good. Why don't you come across in ten minutes? It'll give you time to read that letter, and I can get myself sorted out a little."

With the door closed, Laura looked down at the envelope. She pushed her finger a little way under the lightly gummed paper, but stopped. She wouldn't read it now. Her hammering heart told her that she shouldn't ever read it, that she should screw it tightly into a ball and throw it into the waste paper basket, or more certainly, tear the letter into a hundred pieces.

Instead, she propped it up on the dresser, picked up her book, and tried to imagine what Sister Bates would do in those few minutes. Tidy? Recover her thoughts from the day? Get changed into civilian clothes or even her bedclothes? She smiled at the thought of sitting opposite Sister Bates in her night things, sipping sherry. Looking briefly back at the letter, she opened a journal and tried to read.

***

To Laura's relief, she found the Sister unchanged, except for the removal of her apron. Her cap, dress, belt and shoes all remained in place, as though she were ready to leave for a shift rather than returning from one.

"Please, take a seat."

Sister Bates gestured over to a small upright settee, before walking through to the kitchen. It was brown tweed with five tight buttons running along its back. The straight wooden arms and legs made it look as though it were standing to attention, much like the rest of the room, which was a mirror image of Laura's in size and shape. But there was little else that was recognizable. There was no casualness or gratuity to anything placed within those four walls. Everything seemed to have a well thought out place and purpose; a painting was hung because that was where a painting should be hung, to break up a large expanse of bare wall. Even the two ornaments and the photograph sitting on top of the fireplace seemed to have been put there for the sole purpose of providing some relief to the bare line of the mantle piece. The photograph was of a young woman in uniform. It sat quite central in its silver polished frame, with the two ornaments either side, equidistant from it.

Laura looked at the door towards her own room, with its half unpacked suitcase, a coat draped over the back of a chair, and a toothbrush carelessly sitting in a cup. It seemed far more lived in and comforting than here. She thought to stand and go to the kitchen, to somehow make her excuses, but she heard the short squeak of a cork being pulled from its bottle, and soon after the sister reappeared carrying a tray with two full sherry glasses and also the bottle.

"How are your rooms? They're renovating the whole home slowly. Most of the hospital actually."

"Very comfortable. Very modern." Laura looked back at the fireplace and the electric bar heater buzzing on the hearth.

As if reading Laura's thoughts, the Sister looked around. "I'm still undecided. I've told them not to bother at the moment." She handed the small glass to Laura. "It's what I'm used to."

"Thank you Sister."

"It's Evelyn," she said, as she readjusted the cushion in the fireside chair and sat down.

"Evelyn," Laura repeated. The word left her reluctantly, and she wished she could catch it back and continue to call her Sister or Sister Bates. She watched the woman sitting opposite her lift her head and hold her look, her navy uniform buttoned up high around her neck. To call her Evelyn felt uncomfortably familiar.

"How old are you?"

"Twenty nine."

"And you're not married?"

Laura smiled at the familiar sequence of questions. "No." She felt the warmth of the sherry on her chest. "Perhaps we've both made the decision to pursue other things?"

The Sister took a sip of sherry and then twisted the stem. Glints of the cut glass came and went, as the syrupy liquid travelled back down the glass. "I think I've heard about women like you."

Laura shifted slightly in her seat.

Sister Bates lifted the glass again, taking another, larger swallow. "I think the term you Americans use is *career woman*." She leaned across and reached for the sherry bottle. "Is that what you are Dr. Harrison? A *career* woman?" She pulled the stopper. "Another one?"

Laura nodded as she sat forward, knocking back the remains of her glass.

"We are nothing alike." Sister Bates spoke as she poured. Then there was silence, as if she were deciding whether or not to elaborate. "My fiancée died at Dunkirk." She nodded over towards the mantelpiece. Laura turned to look again at the photograph and realized that of course it couldn't be a woman. The uniform was wrong. The peaked hat was flat and straight, none of the soft folds that the women usually wore. It was indeed a man, or more like a boy. The uniform was the only mannish thing about him. But it wasn't just his youth that gave him such a feminine appearance. It was the full lips and thick dark eyelashes, a gentleness that wasn't just from the softer focus of the camera.

"After I got the news, I wanted to help in some way. So I joined the women's nursing core. When the war ended, continuing with nursing just seemed the natural thing to do. No other man came along, and I took the position of Sister when it was offered to me. From that point, I feel my future was pretty much sealed." She took a large swallow and hung her arm over the side of the chair, gently swinging the empty glass. It was the most relaxed Laura had seen her. "It wasn't ambition that led me to where I am today. It was circumstance. I have just adapted to circumstance. I am a dedicated Sister, Dr. Harrison, just as I would have been a dedicated wife and mother if fate had dealt me a different set of cards. I think some people think they have the right to choose to be or do whatever they want, expecting the world to adapt around them." She leaned forward and picked up the bottle, holding it up towards Laura.

Shaking her head, Laura took a sip from the glass. The Sister poured herself another sherry.

"Do you think you'll use your kitchen? It is modest, but the facilities should be enough for you to make a decent meal."

"Yes it's fine. It should only be for a few weeks. Actually, I do need to stock up on a few things. Is there a store nearby?"

"Just off Harts Street. I forget that maybe you're unfamiliar with London?"

"Well, a little maybe but—"

"I should have thought. I'll ask one of my nurses to help you to find your way around the city. A guardian angel, if you like." As she paused for a moment, Laura leaned forward. How could she somehow decline the offer?

"I don't want to trouble you or your staff. I'm sure I can manage—"

Sister Bates shook her head adamantly. "Nonsense, when the nurses joined us from Jamaica a few years ago I did just the same thing. It's good for them too, to understand how things work in America, your culture. I know it's not the Caribbean, but I'm sure there are many interesting differences. It's good for my girls to broaden their minds."

Laura opened her mouth to protest again.

"I could ask Nurse Ford." She looked pointedly at her. "I believe you've already met."

Was that an attempt at humor? Laura really couldn't decide, and her neck warmed a little at the feeling she had in someway been caught out.

"She's an exceptional Nurse, a different caliber from most."

She waited for the Sister to continue, but nothing more came. "In what way?" She asked, before the topic changed.

"She excelled at everything at school. Head Girl, captain of the tennis and hockey teams, top of her class for most subjects. She would make an excellent Sister."

"Yes. I'm sure she would."

"Unsurprisingly, she's caught the eye of one of the doctors, so marriage seems a more likely prospect now. We're lucky to have held onto her for this long. Many of the students don't even make it to registration."

"No?"

She shook her head. "Either the hours are too antisocial, they miss their homes too much...they fail their exams, or they marry...mostly they marry." Another thought seemed to catch her attention as she spoke again. "Actually...maybe Nurse Jackson would be a better choice. She's still single, more time on her hands perhaps than someone whose courting...and she could certainly do with the experience." She looked up at Laura and smiled, apparently pleased with her plan. "I'll send her up to you tomorrow."

With finality, she drained the last of the sherry from her glass and set it down on the table.

***

What could she say to Nurse Jackson? Laura Kicked of her shoes and sat on the edge of the bed. She would simply tell her that there had been a misunderstanding. That she did know people here, and actually, she had a very good friend whom she had grown up with and now lived in London, not more than twenty minutes away. She could certainly get any help she required from her. The nurse would probably be as relieved as her to be freed from a day of awkward small talk.

The letter caught her eye, and she looked at the time. It would be nearly seven o'clock in New York. She thought of Gwen. What would she be doing? Probably helping the housekeeper with dinner or maybe spending a little time with the children before she handed them back to the nanny. If John were due back from work, she would most likely be upstairs in her bedroom, reapplying her make up, resetting her hair, perhaps changing into a more formal dress. But if he were away on a conference or travelling for research, what would she be doing then?

Laura would often get a telephone call. "Darling, John's away. Can I come over?" And she would be straight over. At first it would be just for a few hours and then the whole evening, even the whole day. A little more time led to her not returning home until the following morning. Laura assumed there must be an understanding between Gwen and the nanny, extra money maybe, and she wondered if this wasn't the first time. She never seemed to feel guilty that she wasn't there to make the children's breakfast and see them off to school. But over time Laura realized, even when she was at home, it was rare for her to be up, dressed and in the kitchen before the children left for school, let alone have their breakfast prepared. Unless John was there, then that was quite a different matter. Then she would be up before either him or the children stirred. She would make herself up, comb and style her hair. Occasionally she would allow herself to wear her gown, but usually she would choose a dress. Then she would go to the kitchen and make fresh coffee, before Mrs. Mooney, the housekeeper, arrived. She would place it on his bedside table and wake him with a kiss. A little later she would bring him the paper, and if he wanted his breakfast in bed she would bring that too.

Laura knew all of this because Gwen had told her, laughingly, their first morning together. She had tried to explain, as she came form the bathroom and stood with her hair perfectly placed and fresh lipstick. It was a very different sight from the tousled hair that had lain across the pillow, and the pale lips that had rested slightly apart in the dark blue light. Laura had pulled her back into bed, and she reluctantly agreed that in the future she wouldn't rise before her. And the next time, in the bright morning light, Gwen had shyly pushed her hair back from her face and rubbed her naked eyes. Gradually those self conscious actions faded, and she would lie smiling, her head propped up by her arm, looking down at Laura, or if Laura woke first, she would find her stretched across the bed, and upon stirring, she would smile lazily and reach for Laura and pull her close.

When they had become bolder, Laura had stayed over at Gwen's. She would lie there in the morning and hear the children's chatter and the nanny telling them to hush. She could never sleep through it—too guilty. Not like Gwen, who would occasionally turn, hardly waking.

CHAPTER FOUR

"Thank goodness," Val whispered to Kate. "The world has righted itself again."

Sister Bates sat in her usual place, the big hand of the clock pointing down at her like an arrow. The two Nurse Tutors sat either side of her, and for a moment Kate felt dulled by the ordinariness of the scene, as though a colorful dancing kite had been pulled from the sky. Was there any evidence of the doctor's existence? She found it, or rather Dr. Harrison herself, standing at the table with the toast and cereal.

"Do you see what I mean about her clothes? Classy." Val leaned in and whispered. Kate was only half listening, puzzled by a desire to meet the doctor again, but at the same time an almost stronger desire to avoid her. Like coming across a favorite teacher outside of school, half hoping for acknowledgement and half afraid of it. "Peg's over there." Val waved across to a table at the far side of the hall, as she walked towards the small line of nurses waiting for a cooked breakfast.

Tucking her hair behind her ears, she walked across to where Dr. Harrison still stood, apparently undecided between the different cereals on the table. Kate looked firmly at the toast, picking up two slices and placing them on a plate.

"Ah, good morning Nurse Ford. Maybe you could help me." Her voice was soft as though she were about to share a secret. "I'm a little scared to try the hot breakfast. What do you think?"

Over the other side of the hall Mrs. Thompson slid a glistening fried egg onto Val's plate. "If you've never had an English cooked breakfast, here probably isn't the best place to start."

"Really?"

Kate nodded. "There are some good cafés. Even the Lyons restaurants do a reasonable breakfast."

"I'll have to try it sometime."

"There's porridge." Kate looked towards the large metal vat. "It's not bad if you get here early enough. It needs to be nice and hot."

Dr. Harrison wandered over and peered into the steaming container and then walked back across. "I think I'll stick to toast and cereal today. Maybe in a few days I'll feel a little braver." She picked up a slice of toast, poured some cornflakes and then lifted her tray. "Well, maybe I'll see you on the ward later." She readjusted her hold and leaned in a little. "But don't worry. I shall definitely be following protocol this time."

Kate gave a slight smile. "Actually, I don't think Sister Bates is on duty today."

"Really?" Dr. Harrison turned towards the Sister, dressed in her full uniform. "She looks ready for the ward to me."

"She always does. Although there are rumors she's been sighted in a twin set." Kate immediately regretted her indiscretion, but the doctor just laughed as she walked over to join Sister Bates.

"What's the joke?" Val said, as she placed her tray down and took a slice of toast.

"Oh nothing, it wasn't really funny."

"Well Dr. Harrison certainly seemed amused."

Kate smiled and looked over at the doctor, as she sat down opposite Sister Bates and one of the Nurse Tutors. She looked up at the clock. "Come on."

"Good morning ladies." Peg said, pushing the butter dish over the white tablecloth towards them.

As Kate sat down, a Nurse Tutor stopped at their table, her finished plate on her tray. "Nurse Jackson." The student nurse sitting next to Peg looked up. "Sister Bates would like to speak with you."

Nurse Jackson looked over at the Sister and then turned back to the Nurse Tutor. "Now?"

She blew out a breath of impatience. "Yes, now."

Kate shrugged, as Nurse Jackson looked at her and then the others before standing. She stopped in front of Sister Bates and Dr. Harrison, nodding her head and looking back and forth between the two. She couldn't have been up there for more than a few moments. Not even enough time for them to start up a new conversation or to speculate why Sister Bates had asked for her. Before Kate knew it, she was back with them and glumly taking her seat.

"Come on," Peg said. "What was that all about?"

Looking into her porridge bowl, she pushed the grey oats around slowly with her spoon. "Sister's asked me to help the new doctor—show her where the local shops are, the underground, that sort of thing."

"Goodness is that all?" Peg said, sitting back in her chair.

"Well, that's okay. I've talked to her. She seems nice," Kate said.

"It's just that…I was so looking forward to going home."

"I'm sure you still can," Val tried to reassure her. "Your family only live at the end of the Piccadilly line. I'm sure it won't take more than half a day, and you've got a few days off."

"What exactly did Sister say?" Peg said.

"Just that I could finish my shift an hour early and go up to see Dr. Harrison to make arrangements."

"Heavens." Peg said. "What are you complaining about? That'll only take five minutes, and then tomorrow morning you can take her to the market and the local shops, maybe show her the nearest underground station and bus stop. I don't think she'll be expecting you to show her the Tower of London and Buckingham Palace."

"I'd help you out, but I'm working." Val offered.

"Aren't you off tomorrow?" Peg said, turning to Kate, but Val spoke before she had a chance to answer.

"She'll probably be seeing David. Won't you Kate?"

They hadn't firmed up any plans, but he would be expecting them to spend the day together. "Yes," she said, picking up her teacup. "Sorry." She took a mouthful of tea and placed the cup back down. "Besides, it's probably best not to mess with Sister's plans."

"Exactly," Peg said, standing up from the table. She pointed at the remains of Nurse Jackson's porridge. "And if you're not going to eat that we might as well get up to the ward." Nurse Jackson stood slowly and lifted her tray. "We'll see you up there."

Kate nodded. "Yes, I'll be up soon." She pushed her half empty plate away, and took another drink of tea.

***

There was a loud noise of wood against metal, as the domestic opened the doors with her wheeled bucket and pushed it slowly up the ward, her hands on the long mop, propelling it forward like an old tin ship.

Kate turned back from the distraction and kicked the second block away, as Peg held up the end of the empty bed.

"Where's Nurse Jackson?" She asked, picking up the two bits of wood.

"She's in the sluice. I think she's finishing off the bedpans and bottles."

"I'll go and fetch her. Will you help Mrs. Simpson move the beds across so she can get started on the floor?"

She found Nurse Jackson looking more wretched than she had at breakfast. "I mean, what will I say to her? What on earth will I talk to her about? We'll have nothing in common. She must be very intelligent too, to get to where she is. And she's from America. What do I know of America?" It seemed to Kate that she must have spent most of her day tormenting herself. "And she's so much older."

Kate kept hold of the words she felt bound to say. Earlier, at breakfast, she had almost offered to take her place, but something had held her back. There was David of course, but more than that, there was how much she wanted to do it. She was surprised that it didn't feel as though it would be a chore or a hardship. And there was Sister Bates too. Could she make changes to her plans? That final question ran through her head as Nurse Jackson continued to talk.

"I don't know what Sister Bates was thinking of, choosing me. She should have chosen someone like you Nurse Ford. Why didn't she choose you? You'd know what to say to her. You'd be more on her level—"

"I don't mind doing it," Kate said, quietly. The words that had been flowing from Nurse Jackson stopped, and for a few moments there was only the sound of dripping pans and bottles as they drained. "I'm off and I don't have any real plans as such…if you like…"

"Really? Would you do that?" Her face lifted and then fell again. "But what about Sister Bates?"

"I'll speak to Sister Bates," Kate said, with a confidence she didn't feel.

So, instead of going to the dayroom for bread and jam at break time, she went to Sister Bates' office and knocked on the large oak door, turning the handle when she heard "Come in."

Sister Bates sat behind her desk, made of the same dark wood as the paneled walls. She looked up and called Kate forward from the doorway. "Nurse Ford."

"Sister Bates."

"Is there something the matter?" She said, putting down her pen.

The words Kate had rehearsed flew from her mind like a flock of startled sparrows. How best to begin? "I don't suppose you were aware that Nurse Jackson had planned to go home for her days off?"

"She never said."

"No, naturally she wanted to help you and Dr. Harrison. It's just that…I don't really have any plans…and so I've offered to do it instead. That is, if you don't mind."

"And why isn't Nurse Jackson here making the request?"

"I'm sorry Sister. That's my fault. I said I'd speak with you."

For a moment Kate thought she might say no, as she peered over her reading glasses. Eventually she nodded slowly and picked her pen back up. "Very well, but you will have to do it all in your own time," she said, as she began to write again. "I can't allow a senior member of the nursing staff to finish their shift early."

"No, of course not." Kate stood and turned.

"And in future, please discuss any ideas you have with me first, before making arrangements with other staff."

"Yes Sister." She reached for the door.

"Oh, and Nurse Ford." Kate released the handle and turned back. Sister Bates pulled her top drawer open and lifted out a pale blue letter. "You might as well give her this. Whoever is writing to her keeps using an incorrect address. The post room has no idea where to send them."

"Yes Sister." She took the letter. Once on the other side of the door, she leaned back and let out a long breath.

***

The tiled floor of the main foyer had just been washed, and it slowed her pace. Sister Bates had given her a large pile of gloves to mend and sterilize not long before the end of her shift, and she had decided it would be judicious to stay until they had all been done. But it had made her late, and so she walked as quickly as she could, turning quickly through the revolving door, only slowing when she saw David waiting outside, leaning against one of the pillars. He gave her a wide smile and tossed his cigarette to the ground.

"So, about that coffee shop…and there's a great western on. I thought maybe we could catch that tomorrow too."

"I can't. I'm showing the new registrar around."

"Dr. Harrison?"

Kate nodded.

"Look, you're not mad at me about the drip stand are you? Because, I didn't…I mean if I'd had any idea—"

"Of course not." Kate shook her head and carried on down the large stone steps. David followed along beside her. "Well, I think it's jolly unfair to expect you to give up all that spare time. Can't someone else do it?"

"And expect them to give up their day off?"

David pushed his hands glumly into his pockets. "When are you meeting her?"

"I don't know." She pushed back her cape and looked down at her fob. "I'm meant to be going up to see her now. It's getting late."

"Well, can't we do something in the evening at least? You're not going to be with her all day."

Kate stopped and looked at David's face as he lowered it towards the pavement, his bottom lip pushed out, a slight crease across his brow. "Okay." She smiled, reaching for his hand and easing it out of his pocket. "We'll do something later in the day, in the evening."

He raised his head, and his face loosened into almost a smile as he took her arm, and they began again to walk in the direction of the nurses' home. "We could go to Lyons for a bite to eat and then maybe catch that picture I was talking about."

As they walked on, he told her what he knew about the film and how Gus had enjoyed it when he had seen it the other day. He went through which of the restaurants they might go to at the Lyons Corner Restaurant and that he could treat them to the A la Carte, as he'd just been paid—unless she would prefer the Grill and Cheese? When they reached the home he turned to her. "So, I'll see you tomorrow at six."

Kate smiled and nodded. "Six o'clock."

He leaned forward and caught her lips briefly. "See you then." He kissed her again before turning, and she watched as he strolled back along the path and gave his usual final wave. As she reached for the door, she looked at her watch. It was nearly quarter to ten.

The dayroom was fairly quiet, no music, just the murmurings of small group conversations. Peg had her nose buried deep in a Variety weekly, but Val looked up from her book and gave a brief wave, as Kate passed by to the stairs. She paused when she reached the final short flight that led to the attic rooms. A thin yellow light shone out below Sister Bates' door, and on the opposite side, a barely discernable orange light bled into the wooden floor of the hallway. She lifted and placed her feet onto each step, as lightly as she could, until she reached the small landing. Leaning closely into the door, she knocked quietly and waited. There were sounds, but she was uncertain what they were and where they came from. Nobody came to the door. She stood there, undecided as to whether to knock again, but this time there were footsteps that she felt sure came from the other side of the hall. She turned quickly towards the stairs.

"Nurse Ford, were you looking for me?'

It was Dr. Harrison's door that had opened, and her voice was hushed, seemingly as careful as Kate not to disturb the Sister. She stood in the doorway, trying to do a number of things at once—tuck in her blouse, tidy her hair, and smooth down the front of her skirt—so that none of the tasks were really effective. When she stopped, the blouse stayed mostly outside her skirt. The creases remained also, travelling up the skirt like an old accordion, and her hair fell again around her face. It was the first time Kate had seen the doctor anything other than composed.

"I'm sorry. I know it's a little late." She looked down briefly at the doctor's bare feet. "Sister Bates asked me to come up and introduce myself properly, but I got caught up on the ward."

"It's fine. I must have dozed off." Laura held up a folded journal. "The Lancet can have that effect. Although, I'm a little confused…I was expecting Nurse Jackson. Has something happened to her?" She leaned out into the corridor, as though expecting her to appear somewhere not far behind.

"She'd made plans to go back to visit her family. She still gets homesick." Kate pulled slightly on the collar of her cape, the wool itching against her warm neck.

"Oh, she never said."

"Well…it's difficult to refuse a request from Sister Bates."

"I can imagine."

"And you see, I'm off for the next few days and don't really have any plans…so, I offered to take her place…I hope you don't mind?

"No, not at all. And Sister Bates, was she all right?"

"I've told her." Kate looked down again at Laura's feet, at the lean curve of her ankle. "You must be getting cold. Shall I call back tomorrow?"

"Oh no, come on in." She stepped aside and pushed the door wider.

"Really, I can come back tomorrow."

"Please, I've had no company all evening." Laura gestured her in again and this time she followed. The room was sparse, more like a hotel room than any sort of permanent residence. Two suitcases sat under the windowsill. The top one open and only half unpacked. Kate had the same feeling as yesterday. That she was just passing through. "Besides, what sort of guardian angel would you be? Leaving your charge without a proper introduction. I'm assuming we're not going to keep calling each other Staff Nurse Ford and Dr. Harrison?"

"Guardian angel?" She looked around, unsure of where to sit. A coat lay across the seat of the only armchair.

"That's how Sister Bates described you, and actually, I'm beginning to think I could do with a little help." The doctor quickly lifted the coat, hanging it on the door hook. She sat down on the end of the bed and leaned back, stretching her arms out behind her.

"You could?" Kate sat down, perching on the edge awkwardly, as if tipped from a geometry set—a series of uncomfortable angles.

"Yes, there was a rather embarrassing incident where I dared to strike up a conversation with some poor unsuspecting nurse. I hadn't realized all communication needed to go via the Sister."

"It's Sister's way. It's meant to avoid any misunderstandings. Not all the wards are quite as strict, and Sister Jenkins and Sister Boyle—the other Sisters on the ward—they're a little more relaxed."

The doctor nodded slowly and played with the satin edging of the pink wool blanket. "So, what is your name?"

She moved back a little further into the chair. "Kate."

"Kate," Laura said, as she studied her face. "What a nice, straightforward name."

"It's Katherine, but nearly everyone calls me Kate."

"I'm Laura."

"Laura." She found herself repeating it, pleased that it suited her. Although she didn't say, feeling foolish that it mattered.

"Why don't you make yourself more comfortable. These radiators feel like they're permanently on. It's like a hot house, and that hat looks about as comfortable as perching a teacup on your head."

Kate stood and unfastened her cape, enjoying the sudden release of heat as it escaped with the heavy wool. She sat back down, but this time properly back in her seat and reached up, pulling out one pin at a time, enjoying the caps slow release, only aware of its tight hold on her scalp when she finally lifted it from her hair.

"So tell me. Am I the only female doctor here?"

"Yes. In fact we'd all just assumed…well, everyone was expecting a handsome eligible doctor from California. You'd been quite the talk of the wards leading up to your arrival."

"And even more so now probably." Laura said.

"Yes, I suppose so."

"Well, I'm sorry to hear that I've been a disappointment."

"Oh no, really you haven't." Kate shook her head and then smiled, leaning back in the chair. "Except maybe Peg, maybe she's a little disappointed. I think she'd been pinning her hopes on you a little."

Laura tilted her head and raised a brow.

"Peg's desperate to meet a doctor. She'd be the first to admit that it's one of the reasons she decided to train."

"A white coat chaser."

"A what?"

"A white coat chaser. That's what one of the doctors used to call some of the nurses in New York."

"Oh, I see." Kate wondered if that's what he would have called her. The truth was that she had hardly noticed David. He was just another in a brigade of overly confident junior doctors. In fact, the day he had asked her out was probably the first time she had really looked at him and noted the pleasing symmetry of his face, all the confidence gone from it as he waited for an answer. She looked back up at Laura. "So, would you like to do something tomorrow? I can show you the local shops—the grocers, the butchers. Do you have a kitchen through there?"

"Yes, it's pretty basic, but it would be useful to know where I can get supplies from."

Kate smiled. "Okay then, shall I call for you at about ten o'clock?"

"Perfect. Would you like some tea? That's the only thing I've managed to make so far, that and coffee."

Kate looked at her fob. "It's nearly time for lights out. I'd better get back."

"Lights out?"

"Yes, we're all meant to be in our rooms by ten. It's even stricter for the students. They're also meant to have their lights out."

"And does Sister Bates always check?"

"Always." Kate stood. "She's less strict with the staff nurses, but we're still meant to abide by the rules." She pushed the chair back under the desk and noticed a British passport lying next to a pile of journals.

"I've got dual citizenship. I was born in America but both my parents are English."

"So, how long will you be staying for?"

"Just a few weeks, my landlord—"

"Sorry, I meant in London, in England."

"Well, my contract's for six months initially."

"And then?"

"Who knows, six months ago I didn't have any plans to be here at all."

"And what made you come here? I know a few British nurses who have gone to America, but not the other way round. My friend, Maggie, she went to Boston."

"Well, I…" The bell began, and they looked at each other and smiled. "I wonder when my curfew is."

Kate laughed as she picked up her cape and cap. "I'd better go."

Laura opened the door. Sister Bates looked up from hooking a large bunch of keys onto her belt. "Dr. Harrison. Nurse Ford."

"Good evening Sister. I was just leaving."

"I see." She looked at Kate's cap in her hand. "Well, you need to go directly to your room."

"Of course Sister," Kate said, and began to walk away. "Oh, I nearly forgot." She reached into her bag and pulled out the letter. "I think it went astray."

"The address needs to be a little more specific, a little more than just your name and the hospital's. You're lucky it arrived here at all." Sister Bates added.

"It's always nice to get a letter. Particularly when you're so far from home," Kate said, trying to lighten the Sister's words. Laura studied the envelope, as though the address was in a code she was trying to decipher.

"Yes," Laura said, as she looked up. "Thank you." She tapped the letter in her hand and turned. "Goodnight."

***

The date on the postmark was just two days later than the one that stood on the dresser. She propped the new letter up against it.

"Have there been others?"

"None, none like this—none like you," Gwen said.

"But you've been with other women?"

"Yes, there have been women, other women"

"Many?"

"A few, yes." Gwen paused and buried her head in the pillow and then lifted it again. She reached for Laura's hand and intertwined their fingers. "But this is different. So very different, it scares me."

"Different?"

"I love my husband, and we have a wonderful life together…When I first met him, I thought, I could be happy with you. I could love you." She ran her free hand through Laura's hair, gently separating out the strands. "But over the years, no matter how much I've tried, I can't love him that way. So there have been women. But with all of them I was planning the end from the very beginning. Can't get too attached you see. We're not like men are we? We go to bed with our hearts. If not the first time, then the second or third…"

"And are you planning our ending?" Laura's voice caught against the words.

"That's just the thing. Imagining an ending with you seems impossible, and now John is someone to be endured. Not because he's changed in anyway. It's just that he isn't you, and I'm starting to resent him for it. Even the children—"

"Come away with me."

"Where to?"

"We could go to another state. I could get a job somewhere else—"

There was a click at the front door.

CHAPTER FIVE

The carriage had been busy, forcing them to take seats some distance apart and on opposite sides. Kate watched her companion as she studied the map of different colored lines overhead, her long legs stretching out into the aisle. She wore capris with moccasins, a contrast to the winteriness of the jumper and three quarter wool coat she had left unbuttoned. It was a strange combination, one Kate would never have put together, but it suited her. She looked down at her full skirt and wondered if she should have chosen something more casual, knowing really that she would never have thought to wear anything other than a skirt or a dress to go into the city. She thought of the one pair of trousers in her wardrobe, bought for camping a couple of summers ago and occasionally used since, usually when helping her stepfather in the garden, and also just a few days ago, the day she moved rooms.

Most of the passengers were men. The few women she could see were dressed similarly to her, certainly none wore trousers. Although, at the far end, two young girls stood, leaning against the end door. They had large flat cases with them, propped up against their legs. The sort you would carry artwork in. Both wore jeans, rolled up, with short white socks and penny loafers. One wore a sloppy jumper on top, the other a thick wool shirt that could surely only have come from her father's wardrobe. They leaned in and talked seriously, too seriously for their age. Laura had caught her gaze and smiled, and at that moment, although older, she seemed much younger than Kate.

The train slowed and then stopped, and she glanced out of the window to check the station. "Just two more stops."

Laura nodded, crossing her legs and pulling them in, as a crowd of people boarded and stood between them. She disappeared from view, only one elegant foot still visible, swinging casually just off the ground.

They had started off the morning a little awkwardly, as Kate began to walk with Laura towards the butchers and the fishmongers, telling her that perhaps she wasn't the best person to show her places to shop for food. There was no need to cook at the nurses' home, so she only visited the bakers or the green grocers on the odd occasion she needed to prepare a picnic or sandwiches for a day out. And it seemed a long time ago since her school cookery lessons, looking impatiently into the oven, waiting for bread to rise or a quiche to set. Laura had smiled and nodded, but didn't seem inclined to share her memories of school or her cooking experiences. She wondered if it was dodging pedestrians and crossing busy roads that made it so difficult to talk, but it was more than that. Laura seemed different from the relaxed woman who had leaned back across her bed and asked for her name just the night before. So she stuck to safe conversations, asking about the hospital in New York and telling her about her nurse training.

The butchers and the fishmongers were next door to each other. Laura had looked in the windows at the cuts of meat and whole fish and then beyond those displays to the rabbits, cows and pigs hanging unhappily on large hooks behind the counter. Kate asked if she wanted to go in, but Laura shook her head both times. She showed her the grocers, and Laura's face relaxed a little, as she glanced over the tins and packets stacked high behind Mr. Vincent's counter. They spoke for a little while with the shopkeeper, but left when he took hold of his stepladder for a customer who needed serving.

Stepping out onto the pavement, Kate watched Laura as she wrapped her arms around herself, her face distracted—not by the cars that pulled out and across or the large red double decker buses that groaned and then sighed as their doors opened, and not by the people who passed by. She seemed to be preoccupied by something, but Kate felt unable to ask her what the matter was. "The bakers is just a couple of streets away. There is one a couple of doors away, but he'll often sell yesterday's bread. There's also a greengrocer just a few doors along—if you want a better selection of fruit and veg than here."

"It's a little different," Laura said, as she looked up at the gold lettering on the front of the shop.

"Different?"

"Oh, I'm sorry," she said, as she turned towards Kate. "I guess I'm a little homesick. I think it's finally sunk in that I'm a long way from home. Waking up this morning to a couple of half unpacked suitcases was a little depressing."

"It is brave of you. To come all this way, and on your own."

Laura pushed a breath out and gave a small smile. "Not really brave. My hand was forced a little."

They were the first serious words Kate had heard from Laura, and she almost asked what or who had made her come, but Laura had turned away to look down the street, and the words were said so quietly that she wasn't sure if they had really been meant for her at all. "So…in what way are things different?"

"Well…usually when I shop, I just stick everything in a basket and go to the check out. I guess I just got lazy."

"Oh, well, we have self service shops." Cheered that she could at least settle Laura with something a little more familiar, she tried to think where the nearest one would be. "There's one about ten minutes away. I hadn't thought—I've never used one. My mother went to the one in Chippingfield when it first opened, but she's never been back."

"Really? Why?"

Kate smiled. "She said she didn't like doing the work of a shop girl." She started to walk on. "Come on. It's not too far."

As they entered, a woman reached to hand them a basket, but Laura smiled and shook her head. They walked along the aisles of cellophane wrapped meats and poultry. Rows of tins on shelves to shoulder height lined each aisle, and above their heads were signs. The first one read 'Jams and marmalades' with a neat stack of over a dozen different types below. Further along there was a sign for cake mixtures.

"Can't see me doing a lot of baking," Laura said, as she passed by the aisle.

There were large wire bins on stands dotted about with 'Bargain Buys.' Branston pickle was reduced to one shilling and seven pence, Nescafe down to two shillings and four pence.

"Is it like back home?"

"Similar." Laura picked up a tin of spam and then placed it back down. "This is great. I'll come back when I'm a little more sorted."

They squeezed past the queue of women, their baskets scooped under their arms or standing by their feet, and back out onto the street. "So, I think there's just the bus stop and the underground station." Kate said, unsure whether she was pleased or not that the task was almost complete.

"Do you fancy going into London?" Laura said, and Kate was surprised at the suddenness of the invitation and the way it was delivered. Quick and sharp, as though uncertain whether she would say yes.

"Of course, what did you fancy doing?"

"Nothing in particular, just seeing the sights."

"Well, okay then. We could get a train to St Paul's and then walk along the river towards the Houses of Parliament."

"Sounds Perfect."

So, here they both were on the underground, the day suddenly extending ahead of them. The bright sunshine invited them out of St. Paul's station. The air was cool, but there was some warmth in the sun, and the sky was blue, no clouds at all. Kate pointed out St. Paul's. Its dome and spire loomed large as they approached, and Laura seemed like her old self—as though Kate would know who her old self was. But she felt strangely as though she did, as Laura listened to her talk about the fire of London, and asked questions in her own way—slightly playful, slightly teasing. They walked idly along the Thames towards the Houses of Parliament, stopping to look into its deep waters and watch the boats traveling through its currents.

"Are you hungry?" Laura looked at her watch. "I hadn't realized the time. Let me treat you to some lunch."

"The Tate Gallery is a little further up. They probably have a café, but you don't need to pay."

"It's a thank you for today. Actually, why don't we try somewhere a bit different? There's meant to be a new coffee bar that's opened up on Old Compton Street. Do you know it?"

"I've not been, but I've heard of it. Val goes there sometimes with her boyfriend."

"It's just, a friend recommended it. I thought it might be fun."

"Well, all right then. It's in Soho, not too far. We could probably walk." Kate smiled. "I thought I was meant to be showing you around London. And what friend is this?"

Laura returned her smile a little awkwardly. "Lead on and I'll explain everything."

***

The waitress placed two glass cups and saucers filled with frothy coffee down in front of them. Kate smiled at her and then turned back to Laura, her smile growing as she shook her head.

"So, you've had to suffer all this sight seeing with me?"

"I wouldn't say suffer, and I haven't exactly had the chance to do any real sight seeing. Moira's a local. We've eaten out, been to the movies, that kind of thing." She smiled. "Besides, I now know that St Paul's Cathedral is not only the tallest building in London but it's also built on the city's highest point."

Kate grinned and shrugged. "I did a history project at school."

"Well I am all the richer for it. I wish I'd paid more attention in my history classes."

"Did you enjoy school?"

"They weren't exactly the best years of my life. Not like you. Head Girl, Captain of the hockey and netball teams…"

"It was hockey and tennis. Sylvia Watson was the Captain of the netball team." She picked up her spoon and stirred in some sugar. "How did you know?"

"Sister Bates. She was singing your praises. I think she had hoped you might follow in her footsteps one day, become a sister."

"Oh, Sister Bates. She's an old friend of my mother's. I think she might be a little biased. They grew up on the same street together."

Kate looked around the small coffee bar and ran her fingers over the smooth Formica of the high counter in front of them, before picking up her cup. They perched side by side on two high stools. On the other side, the young woman handed them a plate of sandwiches and then picked up a large cloth and slowly polished up the large espresso machine.

"Do you like it?" Laura asked, scanning the place herself.

Kate nodded as she took in the crowd of mainly teenagers and young adults, talking over coffee, cakes and sandwiches. There was generally a vibrant, fun atmosphere. Little Richard came from a jukebox in the corner.

"Moira says that bands often play downstairs. We should come back one evening."

"Yes, yes I'd like that." Kate smiled at Laura and the idea that maybe there might be other times they would spend together. "So, how do you know Moira?"

"Oh, we go way back. We were at school together in America. It was one of those international schools, mainly for British families but there were a few others too."

"And when did she come over here?"

"About five years ago."

"What made her come?"

Laura sat back a little on her bar stool, as if to assess Kate a little before giving her an answer. "Things were difficult in America, particularly for someone like her."

"Someone like her?"

"Lets just say Moira's a little more political than you or me, a bit more outspoken. You can't do that kind of thing, especially if you're a teacher. Things are a little better now, but I doubt she'll go back."

"And you? What made you come all the way over here?"

"Well, after New York, I moved back to California. I had some plans to get a job there, but…well let's just say those plans fell through. So, I took up an offer of a contract over here."

Little Richard ended with a big bang and there was just chatter and laughter around the room. Laura's story had been brief, with each sentence dismissed as soon as she said it. The distracted look had returned as she twisted on her stool to look at the jukebox, as though encouraging the young man leaning over to hurry up and punch in the buttons and fill the room with guitars and drum beats again. "I thought you said you were forced a little? That something or someone had maybe encouraged you to come?"

The music began again and she swiveled back round. "That's a story for another time," she said, leaning against the counter and propping her head in her hand. "Tell me a bit about you. What would you usually be doing with your time off?"

"Oh, I don't know, visiting my family…spending time with Val and Peg… or seeing David."

"Where does your family live?"

"Chippingfield, in Harlow."

Laura looked blankly at her.

"It's about an hours train journey from here. It's in Essex. It's not where I grew up. I grew up in Oxford, but it's where my mother lives now."

"Just your mother?"

"And my stepfather, and a sister—a half sister."

"And your father?"

Kate paused, deciding on which of the stories to tell. Start with the truth she thought. "He never returned from the war."

"Oh, I'm sorry Kate."

Looking down at her coffee, she twisted the cup slowly. "He's not dead." She looked up at Laura, watching her take in the information.

"Missing in action?"

Kate gave a small smile. "No." She lifted her cup and took a sip, setting it down again carefully in its saucer. "His final posting was in France. He wrote my mother a letter explaining he had met someone and he wouldn't be returning." She always felt ashamed at the idea that while other men were fighting for King and country and for their families back home, her father had somehow found the time to apparently fall in love.

"And how did your mother react to that?"

"She fell apart, pretty much. In a way it was made easier because so many other husbands hadn't returned…so she let people think that, that he was missing in action, presumed dead."

"And you?"

Kate held her gaze for a moment and then lowered it slightly. "Oh, I worshipped him. I don't remember things very clearly. I was too young. But I do remember the sense of fun, and when he left for the war the fun stopped. I mean not completely, but he was the catalyst. And then, when I knew he wouldn't be returning everything just seemed rather empty…flat. I didn't know that he had chosen not to come back. I thought, like everyone else, that he had just never been found. It wasn't until we moved, when I was about sixteen, that I found the letter. I was helping my mother pack up everything for the move to Harlow. I think she let me find it, probably felt that it was time I knew."

"Didn't he love your mother?"

Kate shrugged. "It's funny how people's affections can turn on a sixpence."

"Not everyone's. Have you seen him since?"

"No, I don't even know if he's still in France, or if they're still together. Aunt Mable says he isn't capable of staying in love with anyone. Sorry. I don't usually tell people about my father. I usually just say that he was missing in action. I was so used to saying that as I grew up that it still doesn't really seem like a lie."

"I assume David knows."

"Yes, and a few others, like Val. She's a nurse too, but I've known her all my life. We were at school together."

They looked at each other for a moment and then Laura glanced at her watch. "Would you like to grab some dinner? I imagine there are some pretty good restaurants around here. My treat."

Kate smiled. "You can't keep paying. Besides, I've made plans. I wasn't sure…"

"Of course, I'm sorry. I've probably taken up too much of your time already."

"Oh no," she said, shaking her head. "Really you haven't. I've had a nice time. It's been fun." She paused. "It's just that I promised David."

Laura nodded and smiled. "Anything nice?"

"Oh just some dinner and maybe the pictures. Probably some western that I'm going to hate."

Kate looked at her watch. Where had the time igone? She knew she had been leaving it late to return to the nurses' home to bathe and change, but now that plan was hopeless. She would just have to go straight to the Lyon's Corner House. "I've got enough time if you'd like another coffee though? But you must let me pay."

"Okay, yes another coffee sounds great."

***

The Corner House and David were just in sight as she walked quickly towards them. He paced backwards and forwards in front of the entrance, occasionally stopping to look up and down the street. As he caught sight of her, she waved.

"You're late."

"I'm sorry. Have you been waiting long?"

"It's okay." He smiled, although his annoyance didn't quite drop away. "How's your day been?"

"Good—fine."

"Are you hungry?" Kate nodded, but really she didn't feel like eating at all, still full to the neck with tea and coffee. "And how was Dr. Harrison?"

"Oh fine."

"Did you put in a good word for Chummy?"

"No. Was I meant to?"

David smiled and shook his head. "Does she have a boyfriend?"

"No, at least I don't think so. It didn't come up in conversation."

"Good lord, what did you two talk about?"

"Oh, just things."

"Girls things no doubt." He pushed the door open and Kate walked through, greeted by one of the waitresses.

"Probably."

"So that's that then or do you need to do anything else for her?"

"I just told her to come and find me if she needs anything."

"Be careful, you don't want her to become one of those hangers on."

"Oh I don't think that would happen. Besides, she's nice. I wouldn't mind."

They stood before two sets of large glass doors, one leading to the grill and cheese, the other to the a la carte restaurant. Both had only recently opened, and Kate hadn't been to either.

"Grill and Cheese?" David said, not waiting for an answer, as he held the door open for her. "I don't think we've got time to enjoy a proper meal before the picture starts."

She thought of Laura. She had left her at the Central Line, on her way to see Moira. She could have said goodbye in the coffee bar, quite certain that she was perfectly capable of finding her way to Moira's, or back to the nurses' home, or anywhere else if it came to it. But she had offered to walk her to the station, and Laura had seemed happy to take her up on it. So they had strolled together, and she had told her more about Val and Peg, and Laura had told her some stories about her and Moira. The enjoyment was only jarred by the knowledge that she would be late for David. That through choosing to walk Laura to the underground, she had also chosen to leave David pacing outside the restaurant, waiting for her arrival.

CHAPTER SIX

It was her final shift. Kate held onto the bannister rail, taking one step up and then another, until she finally reached the top. The paracetamol seemed to be helping with her headache, but her feet were sore and ached to be free from her shoes.

Val's door was slightly ajar. Normally she would have popped her head in to say hello, perhaps talk a little about their day, but tonight she just wanted to go to her room, draw the curtains and lie down.

"Kate, is that you?"

She stopped and opened the door a little wider. Val lay on her bed, her head propped up by pillows. Lowering her book, she looked at Kate.

"Goodness, you look dreadful. Have you only just got back?"

Kate nodded, reaching down to undo her shoes and then slipping them off. "My head's been pounding half the day." She pulled out the desk chair and slumped down.

"That's for you. It might cheer you up."

A small Selfridges bag lay on top of the dresser. Kate looked from Val to the package and back several times before going over and reaching for it. She peered inside.

"It's not going to bite," Val said, tucking her legs under her and laughing.

The packet inside was wrapped in smooth cellophane. She ran her fingers across the gold lettering of the company name and the words 'Fully-Fashioned Stockings.' Finally, she looked up at Val, who was watching her with an amused expression.

"I heard someone knocking on your door a little earlier, so I went out to see who it was."

"Dr. Harrison," Kate said quietly, looking back at the stockings, a faint smile forming.

"I'm assuming this has got something to do with the incident the other week?"

"I suppose it must."

"She seems nice."

"Yes, she is nice." Kate looked up from the gift. "Do you think it's a little strange?"

"What? The stockings?" Val paused, considering the doctor's gesture. "I suppose it's just her humor. Maybe she wanted to thank you for showing her around the other week."

It had been nearly two weeks since she had taken Laura around the city. Kate thought that she might have come to her room or the dayroom to seek her help, or just for some company. But she had only seen her occasionally, usually at meal times. And that had become less and less, as, Kate imagined, Laura started to use the self serve shop. She would always, naturally, sit at the Sisters' table. On the ward it was the same, with Mr. Clarkson and the junior doctors holding her attention. Laura always acknowledged Kate, with a smile from the end of the corridor or across a patient's bed. Sometimes, if they came close enough, she would nod and say "Nurse Ford." To which Kate would nod back and say "Dr. Harrison," as she felt the tips of her ears warm.

"Do you think it's too late to pop up and thank her?"

Val shrugged. "What about your headache?"

"Oh that? It's fine. The tablets must have done the trick," she said, bending down and pulling her shoes across. She slipped them back on, refastening the laces. "I'd better go now though. I'll see you tomorrow."

60

The door opened as soon as she finished the last knock, a little at first, but then more fully when Laura saw it was Kate.

"Hello, I'd hoped you'd come up." She looked at the bag in her hand and smiled. "You got the stockings then." Laura leaned against the doorframe. Her body seemed made for leaning—not stooping, as some tall girls did, all hunched over with rounded shoulders. Laura always walked tall and upright, her shoulders square. When she did stand still, and there was a piece of furniture to hand— the nurses table or a patient's chair—she would reach out and lean against it, and the object somehow seemed strengthened, more solid. As though she were lending it extra support.

Her shoulders, and the way she leaned, had pulled at the neckline of her pajamas. Kate couldn't be certain if the top button had already been unfastened or if the pull had stretched it to a point beyond its hold, but the material had spread open, like a curtain might be thrown open to let in the sunshine or show off a landscape. Her eyes were drawn to the horizontal planes of her collarbone, and her breastbone below. Laura looked down and pushed the button through its hole, and Kate had a compulsion to return the stockings. That it somehow seemed an inappropriate gift to give, and just as inappropriate to accept. She held up the bag towards Laura. "Yes, but I really can't keep them."

"Of course you can. It's just a silly present to say thank you for the other day, and also sorry for getting you into trouble."

"But they're far too good to wear for work."

"Well then…wear them for dancing or…when you see David."

Kate lowered the bag slowly. "Were you about to go to bed?"

"Actually, it's my last night. I'm moving into my flat tomorrow." She nodded back into the room where one of the suitcases, the larger of the two, lay on the bed, half full with loosely folded clothes. "Just finishing packing."

There were voices from the floor below. They both looked silently at one another, listening as the sounds grew louder and closer. It was Peg and Val, and perhaps one of the other staff nurses. She walked down the short flight of stairs with Laura following behind.

"There you are." Peg called out.

"Is something the matter?"

"Far from it." Peg grinned. "Things couldn't be better."

"Sister Bates has been called away. Her mother's not well." Val spoke a little breathlessly. "Nurse Tutors in charge, but she'll be off home after lights out."

"Even if she wanted to, she can't stay over. Dr. Harrison's got her old room." Peg said.

As if conjuring up her spirit, Laura came further down the steps and leaned out from around the corner.

"Oh, hello Dr. Harrison. Looks like you might be in charge tonight." Val gave Peg a sharp dig with her elbow. Unperturbed, she continued on. "One of the staff nurses has just bought a Dansette and some others are bringing their guitars. We're all meeting downstairs."

Grabbing Kate lightly by the shoulders, Val gently turned her towards the direction of her room. "Go and get your night things on. She'll be doing the rounds soon."

"Dr. Harrison, you look like you're all ready for lights out. Though I imagine she won't be checking up on you," Peg said.

"It's Laura. For some reason I seem to be trusted to behave myself."

"Well, if you fancy proving them wrong you're welcome to join us. We'll all be in room twelve on the ground floor from about half ten."

Kate turned back to Laura, who looked over as though she might supply an answer to the sudden invitation.

"If you'd like to come," Kate said. "I'll call back for you."

"Well thanks…Okay…It'd be a nice change from all these early nights surrounded by the same four walls."

"We'll see you later then." Peg called as she started back down the hall with the others.

Kate smiled at Laura. "I'll come back in about half an hour."

"Okay." Laura looked at the stockings still in Kate's hand. "I'll see you then."

***

The door of room twelve was ajar, but Kate's efforts to open it any wider were met with resistance. Laura stood behind, her arms wrapped around her thin cotton dressing gown.

"Just a sec." The shout came from just behind the door. "Susan, budge over so we can open the door."

After a few moments the door opened wider. They stepped over several pairs of legs to get into the room, warmed with people and cigarette smoke. A short gust of cool night air blew through the window, resting on its latch. The red Dansette had been placed on the dresser, and music came from it so loudly that the women talked in small groups, even though the room was of no size at all. Kate looked around for any available places. The room was the same as hers, but two beds occupied the space. Val and Peg sat with another staff nurse on the one furthest away. "Come on, there's room for one of you over here," Peg said, as she shifted closer to Val.

"Go on." Kate nudged Laura across to the bed and sat down opposite on the floor, squeezing between two other nurses. One handed her a bottle of schnapps and she took a small drink before passing it on.

For a while she sat forwards, distractedly checking on Laura, but Peg and Val seemed to chat with her freely. So she relaxed and sat back against the valance of the bed and talked with the nurses who shared her space on the floor, only glancing across now and again when there was particularly loud laughter or shouting from that side of the room.

"Kate, Kate, I've told Laura she should come to the dance on Saturday. I was thinking her and Gus would be a good match. What do you think?" Peg called across in between records.

Kate and some of the others on the floor looked across. "Yes, I mean...I don't know...possibly."

"Well he's tall enough." Peg turned back to Laura. "He's about six foot three."

The music started again and the rest of Peg's words were lost, but she guessed she was telling Laura more about Gus. Kate thought of David's flat mate, strong and athletic, a keen rugby player. Peg was right; they would make a handsome couple.

A crate of Babycham was pulled out from under one of the beds and Peg opened each bottle and passed them around. Another box came out. This one seemed to be filled with screwed up newspaper, but it turned out that they were champagne saucer glasses, carefully wrapped. Susan, the nurse next to her, passed her a glass and nodded over to the woman unwrapping the last few, a final year student whose name she couldn't remember. "Her uncle's the landlord at the Dog and Duck. We thought it'd be a treat to drink from the proper glasses." Kate poured the bubbly liquid into her glass.

"Cheers." It was Laura's voice. She smiled directly at Kate and held her glass aloft, the deer motif dancing just under her thumb. At some point she had untied her robe and flipped off her slippers, allowing her long feet to dangle over the side of the bed. Her cotton pajamas pulled tightly around the lean shape of her legs. Kate raised her glass briefly, taking a sip and then turning her attention back to the small group she sat with.

The records kept playing, but eventually some of the nurses left for their beds, including Dot with the record player, and guitars were played instead. Kate tried not to look across at Laura, but she kept finding herself drawn to that side of the room. Laura just had to do something slightly out of the ordinary—lean over to accept a cigarette offered from Peg, or reach across to take an album cover from Val. Each movement would cause Kate to glance across and then regret it, as invariably Laura would catch her look, and smile.

"Come on you lot, I've got a shift tomorrow." It was one of the nurses from a few doors away, holding onto the door handle, calling the night to an end.

Peg drew on the last of her cigarette and dropped it into an empty bottle where it let out a short hiss and a final billow of defiant smoke. She stood and pulled Val and then Laura up from the bed.

"Come on then ladies."

Kate stood and pulled her robe tightly around her, ready for the chill of the corridor. They walked slowly, stopping when they reached Peg's door.

"You know that weekend away in Oxford we've been talking about?" Peg asked. "Laura might be able to get hold of a car. We could drop Val at her mum's and then stop over at a B and B—show her the sights," Peg said, as though stopping off in a Bed and Breakfast was something that they all did regularly, nothing exceptional at all.

Kate looked across at Laura, who smiled and shrugged, as Peg reached for her door handle. "Goodnight."

The door shut and Val turned to Laura. "Don't worry. We won't hold you to it."

"Well...my uncle does have a car, and my aunt said I was welcome to use it anytime."

"She'll probably have forgotten about it by the morning." Val said, as they carried on.

There was only Laura's final short flight of stairs to go. Val had got caught up with a small group of nurses ahead, and they continued slowly down the corridor. Val turned back and whispered "Goodnight" to Kate and Laura.

Laura looked briefly up the steps and then back at Kate. "You should come round to the new flat, once I'm unpacked and settled in."

"Yes, I'd like that." There was the short click of doors closing further down the corridor and then silence. "Well. Goodnight then."

"What about this dance on Saturday? Are you definitely going?"

"Yes, but I..."

"What?"

"I don't know...I thought you were maybe just being polite...that it wasn't really your kind of thing. Peg can be quite persuasive, and sometimes it's just easier to say yes."

"Maybe I'll see if Moira can come."

"Well, all right." Kate smiled. "Maybe I'll see both of you on Saturday."

"Okay."

"Okay."

They both stood and looked at one another and then laughed, neither saying goodbye. Then they briefly hugged. Just long enough for Kate to feel Laura's firm body pressed against her own, and to catch her scent; not sweet like Aunt Mable's or musky like her mother's, not even flowery like Val's. But it stayed with her as she walked along the corridor, fresh but familiar, like breathing air and earth at the same time.

CHAPTER SEVEN

"Any more?" Val asked, as she sat up from her magazine and lifted the plate of bread and jam from the coffee table. It was bright considering the time of year. The old wooden arched windows in the nurses' dayroom had been replaced with large rectangular, metal-framed panes, making the most of the subdued December daylight.

"No thanks." Kate shook her head and returned to her book.

"I thought I'd find you two here." Peg stood in the doorway and walked over to the plate still held up by Val. "Strawberry jam. My favorite." She turned to Kate. "You're late. Sister sent me down. One of the student nurses still hasn't had her tea break."

Looking up at the clock, Kate closed the book and put it down. "I must've got carried away."

Peg lifted a slice of bread and bit through the shiny red jam. "Dr. Harrison has just arrived on the ward."

"Did you ask her why she never turned up to the dancehall the other week?" Val joked, as she took a slice from the plate and placed it back on the table.

"No." Peg paused and smiled. "But I did ask her when she's going to blooming well take us all to Oxford."

"You didn't?" Kate looked at her amazed, and then laughed at the impossibility of it as she stood and stretched.

"Of course not. She'll be off hobnobbing with all of the consultants now she's a bit more settled. I heard Mr. Boyd had his eye on her."

"Mr. Boyd has his eye on everyone." Val said.

"What's she doing up here at this time of day?" Kate asked out loud, not expecting an answer.

"Some sort of tutoring for the medical students." Peg reached for another slice of bread and took Kate's seat.

"I'll see you both later."

"If you get the chance, tell her we're all off the weekend after next. Just so she can get the car sorted." Peg called after her.

Kate laughed as she walked away. "Will do."

The night of the dance, she had looked out for Laura from the moment she had given David her coat. Even as the evening went on, she was still hopeful that she might come, imagining her and Moira dropping into a bar somewhere beforehand, arriving late. But one dance followed another, and it had surprised her how the lightness began to fall from her steps. David had asked her what the matter was, that she didn't seem herself. She had almost asked him to walk her home, but his concern made her change her mind, and suddenly she wanted nothing more than to be held by him.

"Lets dance." She had said, and he had gladly led her to the floor, where they stayed for most of the night. And when she wasn't dancing, she chatted animatedly with her friends and tried to laugh away the foolishness of the last few weeks. These were her friends, good friends, whom she had known for years. And she had David, who cared for her more than she deserved. She felt rather like a fish returning to the familiar safety of its shoal after being tempted by a brightly feathered fly, just escaping its hook. When David walked her back, she pressed herself into him and returned his kisses so ferociously that he had pulled away eventually, saying in surprise. "Kate, I can't breath."

The ward was the only time she had seen her, usually during the doctors' rounds. There was little occasion when they could have started a conversation, but there had been moments when they might have shared a smile or just a nod of recognition, something she knew Laura would have normally felt comfortable with. But she seemed to go out of her way to keep her eyes on Mr. Clarkson or the ward sister. So in turn, Kate would look the other way, or, if it were practical, she would stand from the nurses' table, or leave the patient's bedside, and go to the sluice or run an errand that she would otherwise have asked a cadet to do.

It was silly to have thought that they might have formed a bond, some kind of friendship. As Peg had said, Laura probably wouldn't have given any of them a second thought once away from the nurses' home.

The dirty linen trolley was full of sheets and towels for the wash. Kate dropped the last two pillowcases in and went to push, but Laura sat straight ahead, pulling X-rays half out of their cardboard envelopes and then returning them, until she must have finally found the one she was looking for. She lifted it above her head, and then, finally satisfied, clipped it to the light box.

Kate had seen her earlier with the medical students. She had begun to walk from the sluice with a trolley full of jangling metal bedpans and glass urinals, but had slipped back in and pushed it to one side. Instead, she went to the laundry cupboard and began to fill a trolley with clean folded towels and bed linen. A student nurse caught up with her, and they walked past the small huddle leaning in around the illuminated images. She hadn't meant to look across, hadn't even realized that she had, until, like two sets of searchlights, their paths of sight caught. Kate quickly looked away and walked on, but she had heard Laura's voice falter slightly as she talked through the treatment for Mr. Gray's hip fracture.

"Nurse Ford," Laura said, her finger lightly tapping the switch of the light box. "Would you like to look at some X-rays?" When Kate didn't move, Laura looked over. "You're perfectly fine. Sister is well and truly ensconced in her office. Besides, I'm sure you're entitled to a little tutoring."

Annoyed that she had let Laura see her hesitation, she pushed the trolley to one side and walked across. "Should I fetch the nursing students?"

"This is more post registration level." She snapped a second X-ray onto the light box, filling the screen. "And no, you don't need to fetch Staff Nurse Peters either." She smiled at Kate's uncertainty. "Come on. It's a one to one tutorial."

Kate moved closer and Laura turned back to the x-rays. "You know, there's little evidence to show traction works at all. There's a doctor here in London who's experimenting fixing the bone with pins and plates."

"Mr. Garcia." Kate said quietly, as she continued to look at the X-ray. Laura turned and looked curiously at her profile.

"Yes that's right—Mr. Garcia."

Kate drew her eyes away from the light box, blinking slightly. Laura's clear green eyes were a dizzying contrast to the grainy black and grey images. "I attended one of his lectures a little while ago with David." She glanced down the ward, disturbed by footsteps, relieved that it was only a student nurse carrying a sputum specimen at arms length. Turning her attention back to Laura, she recalled the consultant who had carried out the talk. "He's a wonderful speaker, very inspiring. I read a few of his papers afterwards."

"Well, you already seem to know more than the medical students, and probably most of the junior doctors as well…"

She felt a small bloom of color rise up her face and turned back to the X-ray. "And you think Mr. Gray would have been a good candidate for such a procedure?"

"I do."

The clean break of the bone was illuminated as Laura's hand drifted in front, and Kate followed the white crescent of each cuticle, each neatly shaped nail. "He's going to be in here for months, lying in traction, waiting for the bones to knit back together." Delicate tendons flickered across the back of her hand as she moved her fingers over the image. "At risk of bed sores, thrombosis, chest infections, muscle wastage…" Kate looked up, as Laura's words drifted off. Sister Bates walked purposefully towards them.

Kate stood up straight and raised her voice slightly. "I'll arrange for a porter to take the light box back down to radiography."

"Still here Dr. Harrison? We'll be serving up dinner soon." The Sister turned to Kate. "We're rather quiet at the moment. You might as well take the light box yourself."

"I'll be passing radiography. I may as well just take it," Laura said, as she stood from her chair.

Sister Bates switched off the light box. "As I said, Nurse Ford can do it. I don't think it will do the patients or the staff any good to see you portering a light box around." She pulled out the plug, handed it to Kate, and walked away.

Laura unclipped the X-rays, following the Sister's progress up the ward. She looked at the two images in her hand for a moment and slowly put them back while Kate wrapped the cable around the machine.

"Thank you," Kate said.

Laura looked up from the envelopes. "For getting you into trouble again?"

"For the tutorial."

Laura looked back down and ran her thumb and forefinger along the edges of the thin cardboard. "When are you next going dancing?"

The door closed behind Sister Bates and Kate watched it swing slightly backwards and forwards before turning to Laura. "This Saturday. I think there's a few of us going."

"I thought I might come along…would that be okay?"

Kate looked over at Laura and smiled. "Of course." She glanced towards the doors again. "Why didn't you come the other Saturday?"

Laura dropped the X-ray back into its place. "I got a little tied up with all the unpacking. There was a lot more to do than I realized." She looked at Kate. "And Moira already had plans…and I didn't feel confident coming on my own. I'm sorry, I should have let you know somehow, after you've all been so kind to me."

"It's all right. I just assumed it wasn't really your sort of thing after all."

"To be honest, I'm not sure if it is my sort of thing either. I haven't been to a dancehall for quite a while." She smiled as she filed the envelopes away. "But it might be fun finding out."

CHAPTER EIGHT

They both stood at the top of the steps leading down to the dance floor. The couples dancing were mainly young men and women, but there were some who were older, perhaps married, and also the odd female pairing where neither had been able to find a partner. A band played on a small stage at the far end of the hall.

"Please remind me again what we're doing here," Moira said, crossing her arms and turning towards Laura. They had made a deal. One hour at the dance hall, definitely no more than two, and then they would go onto one of Moira's jazz haunts in the West End.

"Well...firstly, I thought it might be fun." Laura took her arm and guided her along the perimeter, scanning the hall. "And secondly, I don't think I've ever seen you dance anything but the Bop."

"There's a reason for that," Moira replied dryly. "And who exactly are we looking for?"

"Just people from work...doctors, nurses... I thought it might be nice to mingle outside of our usual social circle." Laura hadn't mentioned Kate. In fact she hadn't talked of her since that first time, when she had gone onto Moira's after that initial trip out with her. She couldn't hide her delight, the energy of the encounter still moving through her as she told her of the day. But it soon began to dissipate when she saw the troubled look on Moira's face, the small frown. So, she had kept away, never giving into the temptation of knocking at Kate's door or looking into the dayroom as she passed by. She would show Moira, and herself, that she had learned lessons; that she was wise enough to know that some things were best left alone. Until that last night, when she knew she would be leaving. And what would be the harm in a goodbye gift? A small thank you? But why had she bought those stockings? It was such a silly thing really. Why couldn't she just leave it? Why couldn't she just follow her head and walk away completely? It wasn't just Moira who should be asking why they were in this rather quaint dancehall.

Laura glanced around, looking up along the balcony and following its length around the four walls. A few clutches of women, but mainly men, leaned over, but no one she recognized. She looked back across the floor and her eyes finally fell on a group of young women. She saw Val and then Peg, but it took a moment for her eyes to fall and rest on Kate. She stood as part of the circle, her back to Laura. The light from the glitter ball jumped and fluttered across her shoulders, her pale skin meeting the dark red evening dress midway down her back.

"Oh boy, you really owe me," Moira said, as she pulled her arm away. Laura turned and watched her taking in the small crowd of women. Moira had dressed in a full skirt with petticoats and a blouse, but a compromise had been reached with the usual flat loafers still on her feet. "These look just like the kind of people I've avoided since school."

She looked over at the group again, and wondered if they had been those girls Moira referred to, the kind who had been carried effortlessly through their school years on the arms of charm and popularity.

"We won't stay too long, I promise," she whispered, as she waved across to Val and guided Moira over. Kate turned and smiled, but before either had a chance to speak, Peg grabbed Laura by the arm.

"Come on, you'll do, finally someone taller than me. We seem to have a dearth of available men tonight." Laura had no time to protest, as Peg took her hand and pulled her towards the dance floor. "Are you okay to lead?"

Laura nodded, feeling she didn't really have much of a choice. In truth, she was probably more confident leading. Her height had meant she had always been a natural choice for the men's steps when practicing in friends' living rooms or at parties if there weren't enough boys to go round.

It was a familiar swing number, and she moved Peg easily in towards her and back out again. Kate was watching, and Laura raised her eyebrows, briefly catching the beginnings of a smile, before the dance steps insisted she turn away. The dance went on, and she often found Kate following them amidst the chatter of the other women. Laura clapped the band, surprised at how much she had enjoyed the dancing.

Peg leaned across. "You're pretty good, better than a lot of men actually."

Laura smiled at the unusual compliment. "Thank you."

"Do you fancy another one? I can lead this time if you like?"

"All right." Laura nodded and allowed Peg to take the man's part. She was pleased to see Moira talking with Val. She also noticed that two young men had joined the group, and they were holding Kate's attention. One of them she recognized as David, and guessed the other, by his height, must be Gus. She turned her attention back to Peg and concentrated on the steps.

"Oh, there's Gus. They must have finished their shift," Peg said, as the dance came to an end. She took Laura's hand. "Come on I'll introduce you. David's taken, but Gus is single. I think I mentioned him. I've been chasing him for ages, but with no joy. Not much of a talker, but he's usually good for a dance." She led Laura across to where the two men stood.

They were handsome in a nondescript way, hair creamed back with a neat side parting; David's lay obediently flat but Gus's kinked and curled in a dark thick mass. Both of their suits were grey, one a slightly darker shade than the other, and their shirts were both white. The only real difference was their ties, although they were both long and narrow. David's was striped blue and white whereas Gus's was dark, almost black, with a small geometric pattern. David stood close to Kate, his hand resting on her waist each time he leaned in to talk to her.

"Good evening gentlemen," Peg said, as she approached them.

"Hello." They both turned and smiled at Peg and then Laura.

"Hello Dr. Harrison—always seems strange seeing someone out of their white coat. I hardly recognized you," David said, standing back slightly to appraise her. "It must be your hair. I've never seen it down."

"Yes, maybe. And it's Laura. Please call me Laura." She suddenly felt awkward with all the attention.

"And the dress," Kate added. "It's a beautiful dress."

Laura looked down at her evening gown. She usually wore pencil skirts and sheath dresses, but tonight she had picked out an evening dress with a full skirt. At one time it had come out at nearly every dance. Then it had sat quietly in her wardrobe, until finally being unearthed when she had left for England, flying like a ghost from between a series of pencil dresses and skirts. She almost hadn't brought it with her. The full skirt with all its lengths of material made it difficult to pack. She had seen it in the window of Saks, and when she had tried it on she had felt transformed. She stood in the changing room, moving from left to right and turning around. She wished at that moment there was enough room to dance, to properly feel the full flow of movement in the skirt, and the light catching the dips and curves of the silk. It had cost her nearly a full months pay.

She had certainly caught Mrs. Forest's eye the first time she had worn it. She remembered the appraising look she had received from across the hotel foyer, and again when she had later been introduced. It was a look she had seen from other women before, but usually at select private parties or small hidden bars in Greenwich Village, never before at a hospital function full of doctors and their wives, and never by a woman like Mrs. Forest. She was all rich lipstick and heavy perfume, but there was a vulnerability that immediately interested her. She seemed much older, but as it turned out there was only five years between them. The embracement of the role of wife to the Chief Physician, and the clothes, hair appointments and beauty parlor sessions that came with it, had lent her an extra maturity.

"Call me Gwen by the way. Mrs. Forest is so formal. Do you play tennis? You should come down to the club sometime." That was when Gwen had caught her later, when Laura had been collecting her coat. And that was all it had taken. A simple invitation that they both knew perhaps meant more.

She smoothed her hands down the narrow corset that hugged into her waist. "Oh this. I bought it with my first pay packet as a registrar. That was a few years ago. I think I might have put a couple of pounds on since."

"It fits you perfectly. It makes you look younger."

She looked up and smiled at Kate. "Well, when you get to my age—"

"Oh no…that's not what I meant…It's just the style of the dress…"

"I'm only kidding, I—"

"Would you like to dance?" Laura turned and found Gus standing closer behind. They had said no more than hello, and she felt a little surprised at the sudden invitation. He was easily the tallest man in the room. His height suited him, and probably made him seem better looking than he actually was. He shuffled uncomfortably, a drink in his hand.

"All right."

"Great." Suddenly aware of his glass, he looked around for a place to put it.

"Here, I'll take it." Kate offered. He passed the tumbler across with a smile and took Laura's hand.

As she had suspected, his frame was better built for the rugby field than the dance floor, and they began to dance a basic but passable waltz. The moves were slow and simple, inviting conversation, but nothing seemed to be forthcoming, just awkward smiles and a groan when he accidentally caught the edge of her toe.

"I'm sorry. I'm not the best for small talk," he said.

"How do you know David?"

"We share a flat, but we go back a long way. All the way through medical school."

Laura gestured over to Kate and David. The glass still rested in Kate's hand. "Have they been together long?"

"About six months, but he's completely smitten. I think he'd pop the question if he was sure she would say yes."

"Why would he think she wouldn't?"

The music ended, but the band started up again almost immediately with a fast, loud, swing number. "Do you want a drink? The bars just over there."

He handed Laura a small glass of orange squash and picked up his own drink of stout from the bar, taking a mouthful. "When you see two people together, sometimes there's a perfect equilibrium, and you think, yes, these two are made for each other. But then there are others where things are a little off balance—it's tilted one way or the other. You know, when the attraction…the love there, isn't completely equal on both sides."

"And you think that's the case with them?"

"Yes, and the thing is it probably won't change. It rarely does. These things are set pretty early on. I know—I've been there before."

"We probably all have." Laura took a drink. "So what do you think will happen?"

"Oh, she's a smart girl. He's handsome, clever, fun, good job…but she's honest too… She's got integrity. The worry for David is she might think herself out of it. I've no doubt she loves him, or in time could love him, but I don't think she'll ever be *in* love with him."

Placing his drink back down, he leant against the bar, offering a cigarette to Laura. She shook her head. "He'll always be hanging on by his fingertips, poor chap." He tapped a cigarette against the case. "Sorry, I told you I wasn't too good at small talk. Should we talk about the weather?"

"Are you in love with her?" She was surprised at the abruptness of her words.

He lit the cigarette and drew on it, smiling briefly before shaping his mouth to release the smoke, turning it into more of a grimace. "A little maybe."

Laura watched him carefully. "Would you ever do anything about it?"

He shook his head and released a more forceful stream of smoke. "No…I danced with her once, and I knew."

"Knew what?"

"Knew I would just be another David."

"You could tell just from a dance?"

He smiled and nodded, picking up his drink from the bar. "Come on let's go and join the others."

As they walked back across, Laura looked around for Moira and found her talking to Peg and Val and a few of the other women, who she could only assume were nurses too. She pulled briefly on Gus's arm. "I'm just going to check in on my friend. Thanks for the dance."

"Okay, maybe we could dance again before the end of the night?"

"Yes, that would be nice." She smiled as she walked away, turning from one side and then the other as she squeezed past people, finally reaching her friend. "I see I needn't have worried about you. Look at you holding court, charming all these women."

"Well, can we go soon? Because even my charm has its limitations."

"Hello." The voice was quiet but Laura jumped a little. Kate stood just to her side.

"Hello." She glanced over and saw that David and Gus still stood on the other side of the dance floor. A young man with a pompadour hair cut and a bright checked jacket had joined them. He looked as though he would be more at home in a jazz club or one of the coffee bars in Soho.

"That's Johnny, Val's boyfriend," Kate said.

"He looks a little out of place."

"I don't think Val even knows he's here. I think he's come to walk her back," she said, as she turned towards Moira. "I'm Kate."

"I'm sorry. I forgot my manners." Laura said. "Moira this is Kate. I think I told you, Kate took me around London when I first arrived." Laura tried to keep her voice light and natural, but she could tell from Moira's expression that something had clicked into place.

"Ah yes, Laura's guardian angel. I had a pretty impressive history lesson from you later that day." Moira's words were directed at Laura, but her eyes remained squarely on Kate.

"I think I probably bored her silly," Kate said.

"Oh, I doubt that very much…I imagine you would have had her full attention." Her eyes found their way slowly to Laura. "She's a big history fan."

Laura smiled awkwardly, trying to think of a way to change the conversation and remove the quizzical look from Kate's face.

"You're a good dancer," Kate eventually said, as Val came to join them.

"Thank you. I've not danced for ages, but it's amazing how it comes back to you."

"What were those steps? I've never seen them before," Kate said, looking down, as though Laura's feet might explain them.

"Just swing moves I picked up in New York. I can show you, if you like." Laura listened to the mid tempo music that had started up again. "In fact this would be good to dance to. Would you like to?"

Kate looked across the dance floor and then at Laura. "Okay, but I have to warn you I have two left feet."

"She's lying Laura. She's a fine dancer," Val said.

Laura took Kate's hand, almost certain that Moira and the others would be watching them, as she led her across to the edge of the dance floor. But when she stopped and looked back they were all talking, with their gazes directed only on each other. She relaxed a little and faced Kate, allowing herself the enjoyment of the smooth slender hand in hers, so different from Gus's, where wiry hair extended past each of his thick knuckles.

"So," Kate said smiling, looking at her feet and then back up at Laura. "Where should we start? I don't think I've danced with a girl since I was at school."

"Just pretend I'm David."

Kate laughed. "That could be difficult."

"Here." She took the hand she held and placed it just below her shoulder, and gently rested her own at Kate's waist. Kate looked back down as Laura took her other hand in hers.

It wasn't the places they touched, although those had an impossible itch to them, creating a desire for Laura to hold her even tighter. It was the spaces between them that were concentrated with a sudden awareness. The pockets of air between their palms, and the emptiness that fell between the end of a fingertip and the back of a hand felt charged with life. The full skirts of their dresses pressed lightly against each other. Kate looked down at her shoes, presumably waiting for her instruction, but her face held a look of concerned surprise as she lifted her head and raised her lids. The center of her mouth fell open slightly, as their eyes finally met.

"Oh no you don't." The voice and movement jarred like a dead cannon ball thudding to the ground, as David pulled Kate away from Laura's hold and swung her around. "Only old maids and wallflowers need to dance with each other." He placed his arm around her waist and smiled broadly, guiding her across to the center of the dance floor.

Angus crushed his cigarette and smiled at Laura, offering his hand. "Come on. My swing isn't up to much either, but I'm happy to give it a go if you are."

As they danced, Laura hoped to catch that look again. She wanted to be certain that she hadn't imagined it. But there were no glances, no indication that anything out of the ordinary had passed between them. In fact, David appeared to have her full attention. He seemed to be telling her a story, him mainly doing the talking, her nodding and smiling, an occasional laugh. And then it came, that look, over his shoulder. It was Laura who couldn't hold it—chose to break it. When she did look back David had turned her, so that Kate and the look faced another direction, and the moment, again, had been stolen away.

She danced with Gus long after Kate and David had rejoined their friends. He stopped asking between dances if she fancied another, and they just continued on. She was safe in his arms. She understood how she felt in his arms. She understood herself and she understood him, as he pulled her in a little tighter. It was only when a slower dance came on and he drew her closer still that she tugged herself away from his hold.

"Would you like a drink?" He asked.

David was over at the bar amidst the crowd for last orders. "Yes please."

"Are you two doing anything on Wednesday evening?" Peg's question was directed at her and Moira as she rejoined the group.

"Nothing much." Laura shrugged.

"How do you fancy the pictures?"

"Sorry, Wednesday's my marking night," Moira said, a little too quickly.

"It's fine." Kate shook her head. "Laura, don't let Peg push you into anything."

"Val and I were meant to be going to the pictures with Kate, but I'm covering a shift, and Johnny's asked Val to go and see a band with him."

"Look, I'll just not go. You don't mind do you Johnny?" Val turned to the young man beside her.

"Nonsense. You should go. I really don't mind giving it a miss."

"What's the movie?" Laura asked.

"An Affair to Remember," Kate said quietly.

"Wow, is that still playing?"

"Just at the Rex. I think this is its last week. Have you seen it?"

Laura shook her head. It was a lie. She had seen it about six months ago. She glanced over at Moira, unsure whether she maybe had mentioned it, but nothing showed on her face.

"Great, it's all sorted. Now is anyone going to dance? It's getting late," Peg said.

"What's all sorted?" David said, walking up behind the group. He rested his hands on either side of Kate's waist and glanced over her shoulder into the small cluster of women.

"Oh nothing," Peg said. "We thought we were going to have to cancel the pictures on Wednesday, but Laura's offered to go with Kate."

"This Wednesday? Well, I could've gone with you." He bent down slightly, resting his chin on Kate's bare shoulder.

"It's 'An Affair to Remember'." Peg raised her brow. "Would you really want to put yourself through that unless you absolutely had to?"

He leaned in further and pressed his lips to Kate's ear. Laura turned away as the bandleader called for the last dance, but not before she heard him whisper. "I don't mind. If that's what you'd like to see."

The song was a familiar slow number and had been in the hit parade a number of years ago. Peg pulled on the arm of her bespectacled suitor, who had been standing quietly beside her. "Come on." She looked over at Laura and nodded towards the dance floor. "Looks like you've missed your chance."

Gus was doing a rather awkward box step with a woman almost as tall as herself, her bright auburn hair bobbing, as she seemed to carry the conversation with fifty words tumbling from her mouth for every monosyllabic answer he gave.

"Unless you'd like to dance with me, can we go now?" Moira said.

Everyone had moved onto the dance floor, including Kate and David. She turned to Moira. "Come on then."

Laura thought of the dark cramped basement of the jazz club. The paint peeling off its damp walls, showing the wounds of pink plaster beneath, and the low sofas they would be slouched in soon, the material rubbed to a thin skin. Moira would be able to be herself there, holding half a pint of mild in one hand and a cigarette in the other. "I'll just say goodbye." She could see Johnny's bright coat amidst the different suits of grey, and made her way across. "We're off," Laura said. Val nodded. "I can't see the others. Will you say goodbye for me?" She hadn't looked for Kate. It was probably best just to leave her dancing with David.

"Promise me I won't have to do that again in a hurry."

"I promise," Laura said, pulling on her gloves and walking away from the dancehall, the music growing alternatively louder and softer as the doors opened and shut with people leaving.

"Laura." Kate stepped carefully down the stone steps, lifting her skirts slightly. "I thought I'd missed you." She approached them both. "Are you okay for the pictures then?"

"What about David?"

"Don't worry I'll speak to him. I don't think he was serious." Coatless, she hugged herself against the cool evening air.

"Well, yes then. I'd love to."

"It's at the Rex. Will you know how to get there?"

Moira moved closer to the conversation. "Don't worry, I'll give her directions."

"Is seven o'clock okay? We usually go to the tearooms before. They're upstairs."

"Kate, there you are." David stood at the top of the steps, Kate's coat over one of his arms. "Come on, you'll catch your death."

Kate turned back to Laura. "I'll see you on Wednesday." She touched her hand briefly and walked up the steps. He held the coat open and she stepped into it, giving a quick glance back before turning her attention to David and the others, as they came through the dancehall doors.

"Would you like to share with the rest of the class?" Moira asked.

Laura turned reluctantly from Kate to her questioning gaze. "I'm sorry teacher. Share what?"

"That moment there with you and the Head Girl. I thought we'd both agreed a while ago that it wasn't such a good idea pursuing that particular friendship."

Laura shrugged. "She's nice. She likes me. I like her. Is there a problem?" Moira raised her brows, seemingly unconvinced. "Look, I can spend time with an attractive woman and not necessarily want to sleep with her."

Relenting a little, Moira took Laura's arm as they began to stroll towards the underground. "Okay, well if you're not going to heed any of my advice…friends is fine…because, Laura…" She stopped and gripped her arm a little tighter. "She probably doesn't even know that two women *can* fuck."

Laura laughed and pushed her hands further into her coat pockets. "I hope you don't use that sort of language with the rest of your pupils."

"Only the ones owho're likely to get into trouble."

PART TWO

CHAPTER NINE

Women dress for other women not for men, her father had once said. Kate stood back and appraised the image before her. She had pulled open the wardrobe door to make use of the full-length mirror, and stood as far back as the bedroom would allow.

Memories of her father were usually poor sketches running disconnected from one to the other. She remembered celebrating her seventh birthday, not long before he left for the war. She could recall him in his uniform, all shining metal and leather, stiff cotton and wool. And there had been the photographs; photographs of him standing in her grandparent's back yard, and another one of him lifting her high above his shoulders. Her favorite was the one on Margate beach. She was about five. Her mother and father sat either side of her. She must have just come out of the sea. She had a towel wrapped around her shoulders, her damp hair falling in wet mats. Her mother wore a sundress, but her father was just in trunks, with his dark hair pushed back from his face. The photograph was black and white, but you could see that his eyes were blue, lighter and brighter, in contrast to his hair, although his hair was darker in the photo because it was wet, like hers, from the sea. Droplets of seawater danced and shone on his athletic body. She knew that she looked like him. *You're every bit your father, eyes, nose, hair, just about everything...except maybe your mouth, you have a Marshall mouth.* Her mother had smiled down at her. *Let's hope she hasn't got his restless spirit though. Let's hope she's got a more sensible head on her shoulders.* That was Aunt Mable's voice. A forewarning of what was to come perhaps. Handsome with a restless spirit, and that, it seemed, had been enough to seal his and her mother's fate.

She walked towards the mirror and studied her mouth. Her mother was right; her lips were much fuller than her father's. *You have lips that should smile more, and I'm determined to make them smile more.* That's what he had said the first time he had met her mother. Charmer, she thought, but mostly he had just made her unhappy. Her mother seldom smiled or laughed, except perhaps in a sad or sardonic way, usually accompanied by a shake of her head.

The thoughts she had of him were like snaps taken by a camera, not a proper cine film that could be played in her mind, and few words, just the odd ones, like those—*women dress for other women not for men.* Those were as clear as if she were sat in their old front parlor in Oxford, her mother just finishing applying her lipstick and giving a final nod to the mirror, as she snapped her purse shut. They had been off to a party, leaving her to the care of her Aunt Mable and Uncle Harold.

Kate puzzled over exactly what her father had meant. Did he think that women saw each other as competition, and that they had a desire to impress one another? Was jealousy and reluctant admiration a much more powerful influence than the less critical judgment of men? She supposed any dress she chose to wear for David would have received the same careless appraisal, one of pleasure, but quite probably pleasure at whatever she wore or how she looked. Did women judge each other? Was she going to so much trouble for fear of being judged by Laura and falling short? Did she want Laura to envy her hair that she had so carefully styled or reluctantly admire the dress that pinched tightly in at her waist and fell in full soft folds? Did she hope that Laura might note the color of her eyes, as she had her father's, and jealously wish they were hers? And did she envy the clear green of Laura's own eyes?

A jumble of discarded clothes lay on the bed and across her chair. Earrings, necklaces and bracelets spilled over the jewelry box and onto the dresser. She looked in the mirror and ran her fingers through her hair and down the bodice and skirt of her dress. She didn't know exactly what she wanted, but she did know it was important to her how she looked tonight.

When she went to the pictures with Val and Peg, she would carelessly pull out a dress, or skirt and blouse, and looked forward to a treat of tea and idle chatter, followed by a film, usually a romance or a comedy. The amount she looked forward to it depended on the picture they were to see and how much there was to catch up on. She also thought of her first dates with David, the tightness in her belly that she had felt as she dressed before seeing him, an excited expectation. But this was stronger, a more ferocious tumbling, like live eels in a market stall barrel, uncomfortable, almost like fear. It was a feeling that made her drop her earrings and tear her first pair of stockings.

***

Kate chose the middle of the three glass paneled doors, feeling the cold of the brass bar through her gloves as she pushed it open. She loosened her scarf slightly and glanced briefly around the entrance of the Picture House, not expecting to find Laura there yet. She smiled at the young girl behind the confectionary counter.

"No friends tonight?" She called over.

Kate shook her head.

"A date?"

"I'm waiting for someone," she said, and walked slowly around the tiled expanse of the foyer, glancing across the displays and placards for future features. She had always loved the pictures from being a child, when she would attend the Saturday matinees with Val, allowing their mothers a break. They rarely missed a weekend, following all the serials from one week to the next. They would try to get there as early as possible to avoid the long queues, and to be as far in front for the dash to get the best seats.

She could still feel a taste of that old excitement as she walked between the white marble columns and looked up the sweeping staircase to the minstrels' gallery. Then, she had a thought. They hadn't agreed exactly on where they would meet. The tearooms had a separate entrance outside the picture house. Would it be better to wait outside in case Laura went straight up? She looked around again and then walked back towards the doors.

The air was cool but still, and at first she didn't mind the cold that lightly bit the tips of her ears and nose, but as the minutes passed she began to feel a small ache in her toes. She made her fingers into tight fists and then released them, dancing slightly from foot to foot. She looked at the clock suspended over the Jewelers shop on the opposite side of the busy street. It had just turned twenty past seven. The picture would be starting soon. She looked up and down the street once more before hurrying up the steps. Once inside, she felt her cheeks pink up. She looked over at the three ticket windows and the small queues at each one, and then turned to the confectionary stall where a few couples stood with popcorn, ice cream and drinks. There was no sign of her. She walked up the staircase, missing every other step, stopping at the minstrels' gallery, and looking down at the foyer below.

Outside again, she stood on the steps and then the pavement. She pushed her hands into her coat pockets and stepped out into the street. Looking up and down, she wondered how long she should wait. She would stay just another ten minutes. But when those ten minutes had passed and they had turned into fifteen and then twenty, she still remained under the lights of the Picture House, somehow unable to walk away.

"You are ridiculous." She breathed the words slowly into her scarf. Looking up and down the street had now become almost habitual and she did it once again, with only half a heart and little thought. So her chin lifted from the warmth of her coat when she saw the figure that bobbed up and down and weaved in and out, one moment on the pavement, the next on the road, and then back on the pavement again, trying to avoid pedestrians. The speed of travel was so fast that it quickly became Laura.

"I'm so sorry." She halted breathlessly in front of her, pinching her right side, at what Kate could only presume was a stitch. She wanted to pinch her too, to be certain she was there. She looked less put together than all the times Kate had seen her before—no hat, gloves or scarf, her coat unbuttoned. "God Kate, you look absolutely freezing." Laura placed a hand in the small of Kate's back, guiding her towards the Picture House entrance. "Let's get inside."

Once in the enveloping warmth of the foyer, Laura stood, her hands resting on her hips. She pushed her coat behind her, and moved her legs as far apart as the narrow dress would allow, rather like an athlete might stand after running the one hundred meters. She composed her breathing and smiled. "I'm amazed you're still here. I felt sure you'd have gone."

Kate shook her head and returned the smile. "Where's your hat and gloves? Is everything all right?"

"They're on the ward. I left in such a hurry. It wasn't until I came out of the hospital that I realized." She took a breath. "And then I didn't dare go back in case I got entangled in something else."

"I didn't think you were working today."

"I wasn't. I went back to the nurses' home to drop off my keys. Actually, I thought I might catch you. I thought we could've come in together, but you must've already left." She shook her coat off. "I knew I'd left my gloves on the ward the other day, so I thought I'd just pop up to get them. Boy, that was a mistake." Laura looked down at her watch. "We'd better get the tickets. I'm sorry. There's no time for the tea rooms, and the movie's probably started."

"I don't think the main picture will have started yet."

They walked towards the small queue at the ticket office. "So, what happened on the ward?"

"Mr. Potts pulled his catheter out, and no on call junior doctor to be found. He turned up eventually."

"And did you mange to drop off the keys?"

"Yes, directly to Sister Bates." Laura shook her head. "I'm sure that woman doesn't like me."

When they reached the front of the ticket booth, Laura stepped in front. "Let me get these. It's the least I can do after making you wait so long."

There wasn't enough time to protest, as Laura stepped forward and bought two for the front circle. "Thank you." She said as she took the ticket and led the way up. Their feet fell quickly on the red carpet that ran along the wide marble staircase.

Only the light of the screen lifted the theatre from complete darkness. The usherette guided them, showing them two seats with her flashlight. They smiled at each other as the opening credits ended, and the screen panned out to a New York skyline. The Empire State Building dominated the center of the screen. Laura hung her coat over the empty seat in front of her. There was only a single chair arm between them. When Laura sat down their arms brushed against each other. They both pulled away quickly. Laura ran her fingers through her hair and then placed her hand in her lap. She leant across in the dark towards Kate.

"It's all yours."

But during the course of the film, as if Laura were made from steel and Kate were the magnetic north, their bodies slowly pulled towards each other. First, Laura's legs, which were crossed away from Kate, became uncrossed and then crossed towards her. Not too long after, she did the same, and felt Laura's hip and thigh against her own. A little later, she felt the hardness of Laura's elbow, as it rested again on the chair arm, gradually followed by the softer flesh of her shoulder. All the time Kate looked straight ahead, but the film had become a blur of impossible sentences, and the actors and actresses just meaningless figures. Everything that was happening was happening right next to her. The screen seemed very far way.

Didn't Laura feel it too? Could such a sensation just pass one way? She thought it impossible, but Laura looked straight ahead, seemingly absorbed in the film. She thought to move her arm, but it felt like such a colossal task. How could it be done in a measured way? It felt impossible. Like removing a leg from a table and hoping it would remain somehow standing. And truthfully, it was the last thing she wanted to do. Each raised bump of her skin seemed to dance with life, and she pressed her arm a little closer. Their knees touched.

She had a desperate need to swallow. All the feelings sat in her mouth like a large boiled sweet. But the film was at a melancholy part, and she longed for a dramatic scene, for loud music, for one of David's action filled westerns. She was sure that if she swallowed at that moment, Laura, perhaps the whole audience, would hear and turn and know (even though she didn't really understand it herself), and look at her in horror. But even if the film were to make everyone laugh or cry out, it wouldn't drown out the sound of her trying to swallow down her feelings. Even if someone were to suddenly shout "Fire!" and the whole audience rose from their seats in a rush of panic, it wouldn't be enough.

She did swallow, a heavy, labored swallow. And Laura did look across, but only to share a moment of the film with her. Kate smiled back, unable to hold her gaze for more than a brief moment, before looking back at the screen.

***

A light dusting of snow had fallen and settled firmly everywhere like a thick frost. Kate almost lost her footing on her way down the steps from the picture house, and she reached quickly for the handrail.

"I think we need to be careful. It's almost like ice," Laura said, as she reached the bottom first. She turned and took Kate's hand to help her down the final steps. With both of them safely on the pavement, Laura blew into her bare hands and then thrust them into her coat pockets.

"Damn that junior doctor." She pushed out her elbow towards Kate. "Here, link in with me. It'll be safer."

Kate paused for a moment and then took Laura's arm, instantly feeling more secure. To everyone, they would just look like two friends, holding each other up on a treacherously icy night. Which after all, she reminded herself, was all they were.

They walked slowly and carefully.

"Isn't it beautiful?" Kate said, as she stopped at the top of an avenue. Trees formed a long tidy line along either side. They were cherry trees, planted uniformly apart, and Kate had seen them blossom over many years. Once the blossom fell, they became as ordinary as any other tree, but tonight they dazzled. Snow covered the side of every trunk and every branch with sparkling fragments. There was no breeze. The branches remained completely still, but the snow on them danced and flickered under the lamplight.

"Isn't it perfect?" Kate paused for a moment, looking up before she spoke, hesitantly at first. "On evenings like this…when there's not a soul in sight, no traffic, and the air is perfectly still, nothing is moving…everything seems rather unreal, too perfect. Almost like I'm walking through the set of a film…" She looked down, shaking her head. "I'm afraid I'm not explaining myself very well."

Laura smiled and turned to her. "So…what would that make us? Are we the stars of this movie?"

"Well…" Kate gave the question some thought. "You would be the heroine. That's for certain." She smiled at her. "But I think I'd be lucky to even get a walk on part."

"In that case." Laura said decisively, reaching for Kate's hand and slipping it back through her arm. "I don't think I want to be part of this movie. Come on lets go grab a drink." She pulled her in a little closer and Kate felt her feet slide away. She clung to Laura, but it was like clinging to a sinking ship as she felt Laura begin to go down too. Just as she braced herself to plunge to the pavement, she was pulled back up. Laura had managed to grab onto some railings. With a secure hold and her footing regained, Laura pulled Kate upright with her other arm. She released the railing and pulled her in tight with both arms. Kate rested her head into Laura's shoulder, as grateful as if she had saved her life. The avenue was still perfectly quiet. Only their heavy, relieved breaths broke the silence. The panic over, Kate felt the full length of Laura against her. She was aware of enjoying every place they touched, as their breathing began to slow. It was Laura who finally shifted away slightly.

"Are you okay?"

Kate nodded, stepping back and beginning to laugh, her hand still in Laura's. "You?"

"Good thanks." Laura began to laugh too as she carefully linked Kate in again and they set off gingerly, past the remaining cherry trees. "How about a nice cup of tea, and a couple of sugars for the shock?"

Laura stirred her coffee and tapped the spoon against the cup, encouraging the foam to fall back, before placing it on her saucer. As she lifted the cup she blew gently, raising her eyes to Kate. "Did you ever think to train to be a doctor?"

Kate looked at her, a little surprised. "No." She shook her head. "Should I have?"

"Well, I'm sure you could have got into college."

Kate swallowed her tea and leaned back in her seat. "I'm just pleased to be a nurse. I spent a year at the telephone exchange trying to persuade my mother."

"Didn't she want you to be a nurse?"

"No." She leant forward and twisted the teaspoon that lay in the saucer. "I was with someone, had been since high school. Everyone assumed we would get engaged and married. My mother couldn't understand why I would want to train for a vocation."

"So, what happened?"

"Nothing really. I just knew it wasn't right. I told my mother I wasn't sure, that I didn't think I was ready." Kate looked at Laura with a half smile. "I told her how useful nursing would be for preparing me for marriage. All those domestic duties."

"Domestic duties?"

"You know, cleaning, making beds, preparing breakfast. They even teach you the correct way to ring out a dishcloth. So, eventually she gave in and agreed. I think she thought that once I realized how much hard work it was I would change my mind—and Derek too."

"Derek?"

"The boy—my boyfriend. Even after I told him I was going off to train, he still wanted to make a go of it… I was a coward. It was my way of saying goodbye, but he just couldn't see it. At least not for a while."

"It's not too late you know."

"Too late? For me and Derek?" Kate laughed.

"To retrain. If you wanted to be a doctor."

Kate placed her elbows on the edge of the table and leaned forward a little. "I admire what you've done, but it's not for me. Besides, by the time I qualify I'd be nearly thirty."

Laura placed her cup down and looked at her. "And you should be long married by then I suppose. Probably even started a family?"

Kate looked down, as she ran her fingers along the table edge. "Yes. I suppose so."

"To David?"

"Maybe, I don't know. He hasn't even proposed."

"I suppose I have to take my hat off." Laura's tone had changed.

"To David?"

"To David, to men." She leaned forward and stirred her almost empty cup. "I mean they've really got it worked out haven't they? Have women running around after them at work, their secretaries, their nurses…and then they go home to be looked after by their wives."

"My priority is the care and comfort of the patients. All of those jobs are done for them."

"But you said so yourself; all that practice you must be getting—cleaning, making beds, serving breakfast and dinner. David must be able to see right in front of his eyes what a good wife he has in store for him."

Kate shook her head. "That's not fair, besides, what about Matron and the Sisters? They're more in charge of the wards than any of the doctors."

Laura drained the last of her coffee and set the cup down. She shrugged. "Just substitute mothers."

How had the conversation turned so quickly? Kate stared at Laura, her mouth slightly open. She shifted in her seat. "It must be so easy for you," she said slowly.

"Easy?" There was a challenge in Laura's voice.

"To make the right choices. I suppose your parents were supportive of you going to university?"

"Well, they didn't discourage me if that's what you mean."

"And I'm sure there was no hesitation about fees?"

Laura shook her head. "No," she said, more quietly.

"I imagine your father's salary has probably always been paid straight into his bank account." She rubbed the side of her cup with her thumb. "My father, when he was around, got a weekly pay packet, and very little of it, if any, wasn't spent by the end of the week. It was the same for my stepfather too." She drank the last of her tea. "And you're right. I probably will be married in a few years time, and I will care for my children and my husband. That's what we do isn't it? Is there anything so strange about that? I think you'll find that's how the majority of women feel." She pushed her empty teacup and saucer away from her. "Don't try to make me feel stupid or something less for that."

"The majority isn't always right." Both cups were empty now, and Laura stared into hers.

"But it's what's important."

"Is it?" She looked straight at Kate.

It seemed that Laura had been tapping away at her beliefs with a small toffee hammer from the first day they met, and tonight she had given her final decisive blow. Kate wondered if she would be able piece everything together again.

"I'm sorry. I didn't mean to make you feel uncomfortable." Laura looked around for the young woman that had served them. "Could we have the bill please?" She turned back to Kate and kept the smile she had used for the waitress, but her eyes had lost the intimacy they had held at the pictures and under the cherry trees.

As they stepped outside, Kate wrapped her arms around herself as though trying to stay warm against the cold night air, but it was more a protection from the chill that had dropped between them. The easiness seemed all but gone, and she couldn't fathom why. Perhaps they had shared too much; their differences now opened up and very apparent.

"Are you getting the bus?" Laura said.

Kate nodded.

"I'll walk you to the bus stop. It's on my way."

They made light conversation as they walked. Laura mentioned that Peg had been talking about the Oxford trip again at the dance, but Kate doubted anything would come of it now. She felt that this might be the last time she saw Laura, except perhaps awkwardly in pale green corridors, feet stopping and starting on linoleum floors. She could see the lights of the number fifty-seven.

"That's my bus." She looked both ways for traffic, the queue quickly shortening. The last person stepped up, but just as Kate started to move away, Laura grabbed her arm, pulling her back.

"I don't think you're stupid at all. I think you're wonderful." Laura's words rushed out like punctured air.

The bell from the bus sounded, and a surprised smile and a nod was all Kate could give before she ran towards the bus. Quickly climbing up the narrow steps to the top, she took a seat and looked down. Laura stood where she had left her, scanning the bus, smiling when she found Kate.

"Ticket Miss."

She reached for her purse as the bus jolted briefly and moved off. Taking her ticket, she watched the lamps along the Thames, and tried to recall if anyone had ever told her she was wonderful before.

CHAPTER TEN

The two women turned at the sound of the horn. The car seemed impossibly long to Kate, almost twice the length of her uncle's Ford Anglia. And there were four doors, no climbing awkwardly over the back of the front seat. Everything was polished to a high shine—the cream bodywork, the chrome, even the windows—producing a distorted reflection of themselves and the nurses' home behind. The red leather seats shouted unapologetically through the glass, as Laura pulled over and wound the window down.

"Good morning, where's Peg?"

Kate leaned down; her eyes level with Laura's. "She's coming, running late as usual."

"We think she might be moving to Oxford," Val said, turning at the sound of a heavy suitcase dropping down behind her.

Puffing a breath out, Peg smoothed her hair. "Don't you find it's just as hard to pack for two days as it is for two weeks? You still have to pack for all possible eventualities."

Their three cases stood by the roadside as though they were part of a set, each one slightly larger than the next. Laura climbed out of the car and unlocked the boot. "It's December and it's England. I predict it is going to be cold and probably wet, with a slight chance of snow."

"Not those sorts of eventualities—I meant men. Preferably ones who're just finishing their law degrees."

Laura laughed and nodded towards the car, as she and Kate lifted the luggage. "Hop in, it's open."

"It's a beautiful car," Kate said, as she reached for the polished chrome handle.

"My uncle cleans it every Sunday, but never drives it, not since his heart attack. Aunty Betty wanted it to get a bit of a run out, although I'm not so sure he was too thrilled when she made the offer." The leather was as soft as butter, and Kate ran her hands along the sides of the seat. Laura climbed in beside her and turned the keys in the ignition. She had never seen a woman drive before, not close up like this, sitting beside her. Laura took hold of the steering wheel and gave her a brief smile. "Are we all set? Peg, have you definitely got everything? Toothbrush?" Peg nodded from the back seat as she wiped a smudge of lipstick from her teeth and then snapped her compact shut. "Okay then, let's go."

Leaning forward, Peg rested her elbows on the back of Kate's seat. "Game of eye spy?"

Laura laughed as she pulled the car out. "Let's get out of London first."

The Bed and Breakfast was set back from the leafy road that it shared with other, similar, detached Edwardian properties. Except it wasn't really a Bed and Breakfast, at least not like the one Kate had experienced on a long weekend away in Kent several years ago with her family. Here there was a large radiator that warmed the room comfortably, not a small gas fire that needed spare change left by its side to feed each time the meter ran down. And the lady at the reception desk—and it was a proper desk with a telephone, a bell and a signing in book—seemed genuinely pleased to see them and assist them in any way she could; Quite unlike Mrs. Parks, who had greeted them like unwelcome relatives who had invited themselves to stay, never risking enough congeniality that they might feel they would be welcome again. But the best difference was the en-suite bathroom and toilet. That meant no queuing in the morning or the worry that all the hot water might be gone. It must have been someone's home at one time, a large home, probably with servants and grounds men. The drawing and dining rooms were now converted to a bar and a dining room for breakfast, and evening meals too if you chose.

"It's a family room. I hope you don't mind. I thought you two could share and I'll take the single." Laura looked at her as though it was important that she liked the room.

"Not at all. It's lovely. Peg and I are used to sharing. We used to be roommates."

Peg popped her head round the bathroom door. "Luckily neither of us snores. Do you remember Patricia Grady? You could hear her through the walls."

Laura looked at her watch. "Right. It's nearly four o'clock. Shall we unpack, have a look round the city and then get a bite to eat?" She looked over at Kate. "Any school projects on the Bodleian Library or Magdalen College?"

Laughing, Kate shook her head. "No, I'm afraid not. It's one of those cases of too close to home. I can guide you around, but I probably can't tell you a great deal about any of it. But…" She opened her suitcase and pulled out a small guidebook she had found in the local library the previous day. "I do have this."

"Okay…" Peg lifted her head out of her suitcase and held her hands up. "Put the book down. Why don't we just have a wander today? Soak up the atmosphere? Tomorrow, when Val's here and we've got the whole day, I'll let you bring the book."

Kate put the book back in her case.

"Thank you though. It was a nice thought." Laura said.

"Peg's right, we should just go out and see where things lead us. It's probably more fun."

"Free spirits." Laura suggested.

"Something like that." Although, not at all really. Kate wasn't like Peg. She found it hard to just run with things. She wanted to walk behind that book—a focal point for their trip out. She looked at her case and then at Laura, and gave her a slightly uncertain smile.

***

All four of them leaned over the bridge in silence. The mist sat low over the river, and the morning sun caught its rise where the breaks in the trees allowed.

"It's beautiful."

"Like a movie?" Laura said, and Kate nodded. A large group of empty punts clonked against each other directly below. A young man had caused the disturbance. He stood with one foot on the deck of a boat, and the other on the stern of the next. Busily, he hopped from one boat to the next, linking a long chain through each one. Warmed by the activity, he had removed his jacket and rolled his shirtsleeves as high as they would allow. His arms were slim, and knotted tight with muscle.

"Do you fancy a punt?" Laura said.

"Oh, they'll be closed for the season. He'll just be checking them over," Kate said, as she watched.

The man continued to jump from boat to boat. Laura looked at her and smiled and then looked back down. "Hello," Laura shouted—a loud crack in the early morning air.

The young man stood and raised his head towards the bridge. His hand shielded his eyes from the thin yellow sunlight. He smiled up. "Hello."

Encouraged, Laura leant a little further over the bridge. "We were wondering how much it was for a punt?"

"Punting's finished for the year. I've just been sent down to count them. Make sure they're all secure."

Kate nodded along to his words and tried to pull Laura away from the bridge.

"But it's such a glorious day." Laura called down, holding on and leaning further. Kate reluctantly looked back over.

He seemed to be considering the day's weather. "Don't you find it rather cold?"

"A little maybe, but we'd soon warm up if we take it in turns."

Another smile formed on his lips, as he paused and looked back at the boats, and then again up at them.

Laura pushed off from the bridge. "Come on." Kate and the others followed down the steps behind her, like dutiful foot soldiers, until she reached the bottom and stopped. "So?"

"Okay, but I'll have to come with you."

"Fine."

He smiled and held out his hand. "George."

"Laura," she said as she took it.

The other two stood slightly behind Kate, unusually quiet. It was normally Peg who led the way. Although she doubted that even Peg would have been so bold as to speak to a stranger in that way, and ask such a favor.

He loosened the chain and released the first boat. It drifted slightly away from the others but then settled. As he stepped lightly onto its bow, Kate couldn't help but admire his grace.

"Ladies." He took a small bow and extended his hand out in an invitation for them to board. Laura took a firm grasp and jumped across. Steadying herself slightly, she turned and held her hand out to Kate. "Come on."

Kate held tightly onto her hand, and tighter still, as she swopped the solid stone path for the less certain wooden boards of the boat. The movement was far less than she anticipated, but Laura placed her hands on Kate's hips, pinning her lightly until her footing became sure. She could feel the warmth of Laura's breath through the damp air "I forgot to ask if you could swim."

"If I know Kate she probably swam for the county," Peg called, seemingly finding her voice.

"Just for a term, then I got dropped," Kate said quietly, looking down at the hands that still held her.

"You don't look like a swimmer." George turned to her as he helped Val onto the boat and safely navigated her to a seat. His gaze moved to Laura. "Now, you look like a swimmer."

Kate knew what he meant. Although reasonably strong, she was slight compared to Laura. The sports that she had excelled at had required agility and speed rather than a particular strength. Her arms had developed through the serve of a tennis ball and her legs from running the length of a hockey field.

"Yes, and rowing," Laura said.

"Really?" He said. She nodded and guided Kate across to take the seat opposite the other two. "Well, you'll have no problem with this then." He lifted the punt. "Come across and I'll show you."

"I'd rather sit and watch for a while." She turned and lowered herself down next to Kate. The boat was narrow, and Kate felt their shoulders, hips and knees all bump together, as Laura settled herself on the cushion. She tried not to think of last night, when she had watched Laura through the gloomy darkness, wondering what all of these feelings meant, and wishing Laura could always be there, drawing those reassuring breaths.

"Just a moment." He hopped off and disappeared into the boathouse. Within moments he reemerged, his arms filled with an assortment of wool blankets. "Here, you might get cold," he said, handing a blanket to each of them.

Laura took hers and shook it, allowing it to open and fall onto both of their laps. Kate lifted her own and did the same, and they both pushed the thick wool around their hips and under their thighs. The action of tucking the blanket either side of them brought their bodies in closer still. She felt Laura's thigh press up against her own and the length of her arm brush gently against hers. She felt it through every single layer of wool and cotton.

"My don't you two look snug?" Peg said, as she tucked a bright green rug under legs. Val was also arranging her own tartan blanket around her knees. Kate shifted herself slightly, loosening the rugs and allowing a little space between them.

George smiled and pushed off. He balanced easily. His long legs stood far apart across the bow of the boat. His eyes rested on Laura. "Have you ever been punting before?" Kate asked.

"No, how about you guys?" Laura said.

Val dipped the tips of her fingers in the water and quickly brought them back out again. "Do you know, I never have. It's more for the tourists and students I suppose. How about you Kate?"

"Only once."

"Really? Who with?" Val said.

"Derek."

"How terribly romantic." Peg said.

He probably had hoped that it would be. That had been the idea at least. But she could only remember feeling awkward, as he struggled to lift and guide the pole, his youthful frame at sixteen still gangly—yet to fill out into the athletic young man he would become when she left for nurse training. She had returned his smiles as they had travelled down the river Cherwell. He had tied up the boat, and they had sat together eating the sandwiches and cake their mothers had made, and she had thought, *I am playing at being somebody here, at being a young girl in love.* And that was rather how she had felt from that day forward, always playing at being in love. He had kissed her later as they lay on the square of Macintosh, the remains of apple cores and crusts of bread lying around them. She tried to remember that kiss, but it felt like a photograph. Something held up from a distance, far removed from her. She could remember the cake though, almost taste it—the tart soft cherries bursting on her tongue and the buttery crumbs that had fallen onto her lap, before she brushed them away.

Peg looked behind and then turned back round, leaning forwards towards Kate. George was showing Laura how to hold the pole, pointing out its metal shoe. He stood close behind and directed her hands with his own to the correct position on the pole. "Do you think he could be any more obvious?"

So it wasn't just her. Peg had confirmed her thoughts; George was much closer to Laura than he needed to be. He leaned into her again. His smile was a continual presence, only altering by degrees. There was that same twinge of jealousy she had felt when Laura had danced with Gus. Then she had convinced herself that it was Laura she was jealous of. Gus had always had a soft spot for her, so it wouldn't have been too unreasonable to feel slightly put out. She had tried to ignore that he had danced with dozens of other girls at lots of dances, and it had never bothered her before.

She didn't even try to fool herself this time. She was jealous of George. She was jealous of how freely he touched Laura's hands and arms, even her waist and hips, under the guise of tutoring her in the art of punting. She was just imagining ways to tip him in without everyone following suit, when he turned his attentions to the whole group.

"So, where are your boyfriends? I can't believe they've left you all to punt alone."

"We thought we would manage," Kate said, still watching the two of them. Her eyes finally rested on Laura's smile, which was pleasingly directed at her.

"So," he said, quieter this time, his words directed just at Laura. "Do you have a boyfriend?"

"Peg's single." Laura said, throwing her answer back into the group.

"Yes, she's far too choosy," Val said. Peg gave her a small shove.

Why Peg was so often overlooked had always puzzled Kate, and when she did get asked out, it only seemed to last a couple of dates before they didn't call anymore. *She's got a little too much to say for herself. Men find that off putting. She needs to let the men do a bit more of the talking. Men like to be listened to, not talked at.* That had been her Aunt Mable's observation.

Paying her the first real attention, he looked over at Peg and smiled. Caught slightly off guard at the sudden interest, she sat up a little taller.

"Here Peg. Why don't you have a go?" Laura said, handing the pole back to George. "Thank you."

Peg stood, a little reluctantly, as Laura negotiated past her.

"So...what do you do when you're not punting?" Laura asked, as she sat and pulled the wool rugs back over her legs, and, in doing so, moved a little closer to Kate.

"Oh, I'm at St Catherine's—studying Law."

Kate tried to laugh with the others at the coincidence. She would have to control these thoughts about Laura. But she couldn't control the swell of her heart or her increased pulse as Laura smiled and gently squeezed her knee under the blankets.

***

Kate answered the knock at the door. "Come in. We're still getting ready."

Closing the door behind her, Val looked at Kate and then over at Laura. "We are just going to the hotel bar for food?"

"Yes," Kate said. "Why?"

"Well. It's just suddenly I feel rather underdressed."

"Oh." Kate looked across at Laura standing at the mirror. It was the first time she had dared to look at her fully while they had changed. She wore a light blue sheath dress. A short set of pearls rested against her throat. They matched the earrings she clipped to each lobe. Kate smiled as Laura looked across.

"You look wonderful," Kate said, before she had fully realized the words.

Laura repositioned her earing and smiled back. "Thank you. So do you."

The bathroom door opened, and Val turned to Peg as she stepped out. "These two think it's a black tie dress code downstairs."

"I know, I'm sure I saw pie and mash on the menu, not lobster."

Kate picked up her shrug and put it across her shoulders.

"You all look great," Laura said, reaching for her clutch bag. "Come on, we don't want them to run out of oysters before we get there."

As they came down the stairs, the receptionist called over, a telephone receiver hanging from her fingers. "Are one of you ladies called Margaret? Peg?" She lifted the telephone onto the raised counter as Peg moved forward from the group. "There's a call for you."

The other three watched, as her worried face became full of smiles. She put down the phone and made her way back across. "That was George. He must have remembered where we're staying. He's invited me out—for a meal." She glanced between the women. "Do you three mind?"

They all shook their heads. "Far be it for us to stand in the way of true love," Val said.

Peg beamed and squeezed her hand. "He'll be here in half an hour." She looked down at her blouse and skirt. "I need to go and change. Thank goodness I brought that black dress." She started back up the stairs calling behind her. "See, what did I tell you? Always be prepared."

"So, a table for three then?" Laura said.

Their bowls were empty except for the last scrapings of custard, which patterned each one. Val pushed hers away and sat back in her chair. "Do you think you might stay on in London, Laura?"

Laura looked at both of them and considered the question. "I don't know. Maybe. I guess it's a little early."

Kate had started to forget that Laura might only be temporary. Over the weeks, she had become such a real, solid thing; it seemed hard to believe she might at some time not exist—at least not in her world.

"Another drink?" Val asked, as she stood and picked up their empty glasses.

They both nodded. Kate watched as she went up to the bar, and then turned back to Laura. "Why did you give George the impression you weren't single?" It was a question she had wanted to ask since that morning on the punt, but she tried to deliver it casually.

"George?" Laura shrugged. "I just had a hunch that Peg rather liked him."

"How very noble of you."

Laura looked at Kate and leaned back in her seat. "Besides, he's not really my type."

"Your type?"

"No." She shook her head.

"And...what is your type?"

"That would be telling." Laura smiled up at Val, as she took her drink. "And there's no point in guessing." She placed the glass down and rubbed her thumb against the corner of the beer mat. "David. He's your type I suppose?"

Kate gave a small shrug. "I'm not sure if I have a type. David's just David."

"Just David?" Val leant across as she sat down, and nudged her gently with her arm. "There's no need to go over board."

"I mean he's…" Kate started but couldn't think of any words to describe him.

"Handsome, clever, tall…" Val suggested as she smiled at Laura.

"Yes…yes. He's all of those things." She took a mouthful of her drink. "So, what about you and Johnny?"

"Me and Johnny?"

"You know. Is he the one? Do you think you'll marry him?" She knew the answer. They'd discussed it hundreds of times up in their bedrooms.

"Eventually—we talk about it. But he needs to concentrate on his music. Besides, I like living in the nurses' home—the independence. I don't really want to give that up yet. I enjoy nursing, and I've only been qualified a year. I'd like to work a little longer."

Kate tipped her drink from side to side, watching the one small piece of ice finally disappear. "You might not have to give it up, at least not straight away. There's a girl over at Queen Mary's who's just married, and they've allowed her to stay on. Maybe if you spoke to Matron."

Val looked a little surprised.

"I know, I only heard about it recently," Kate said.

"It's not that Kate. I've heard about it. It's just I wouldn't have expected you to suggest that sort of thing."

"Would you do that?" Laura turned to Kate. "I mean, if David were to propose?"

"I don't know. I've never really thought about it. I've never thought it was really an option."

Val shook her head. "I don't think David would like it. What about you Laura? Will you carry on when you get married?"

Kate tried to imagine Laura as a bride. What sort of dress would she wear? What sort of man would she marry?

"I've never given it much thought. Kate's right though, times are changing. It's a real possibility."

The bartender rang the bell for last orders.

"I'd better get going. I don't want to get locked out. Mum doesn't like to leave the door unlocked before she goes to bed." Val said, as she pulled her handbag from under the chair.

"Are you sure you don't want us to walk back with you?"

"I'll be fine. The students will all be walking home too." She pulled her coat on as she stood. "Besides, it's freezing outside. There's no point in all of us getting cold. I'll see you both tomorrow."

"Bye," Kate said, a small heat rising in her as she turned to Laura. It was just the two of them. She hoped the blush in her face would be attributed to the coal fire beside them.

"Would you like another drink?" Laura said.

"Just a lemonade, but it's my turn—"

"The gentleman at the bar asked me to bring these across." The bartender began to arrange two coasters. Kate and Laura looked at one another and then at the two young men, as they raised their glasses to them.

"It's okay, thank you," Kate said. "We were just leaving." She stood and picked up her shrug, and then remembered her manners "You will thank them though?"

Kate led the way through the bar door, turning back to Laura once they were in the small reception. "Did you mind? I couldn't be bothered with all that small talk."

Laura shook her head and smiled. "No, not at all." She looked up the stairs. "Come on. I wonder if Peg's back."

The room was in darkness, and Kate felt up and down the wall for the light switch. Peg hadn't arrived back, and she couldn't decide if she was pleased or not that it was just the two of them. Part of her wanted Peg to fill the room with talk of her evening, for there to be a pleasant dance of conversation between the three of them, instead of the silence that hung thickly as they looked around the room, and then at each other. "Do you think she's all right?"

"Oh George seemed harmless enough. I'm sure she wont be long," Laura said, as she dropped her bag onto a chair. "Do you want to use the bathroom first?"

Kate nodded and slipped off her shoes, picking up her wash bag and pajamas and closing the bathroom door behind her. She applied cream to her face and began to remove the rouge and powder, revealing the pale skin beneath. Her lips were softened by the loss of red lipstick, her eyes stark without the black kohl and mascara. She unbuttoned her dress and let it drop to the floor, and then her petticoats. She loosened her corset and unfastened her stockings, rolling each one down and then off. At once she felt lighter, freer. She stood in front of the mirror and watched the slow rise and fall of her breasts, noticing the smooth curve of her collarbone with its two small boney prominences, and the small pelvic bones that sat either side of the dip and curve of her belly.

"Do you have a pen?" Laura called from the other side of the door.

Kate quickly reached for her pajamas. "I think there might be a pencil in the dresser drawer," she said, quickly buttoning her top. Kate opened the bathroom door and Laura looked up from a newspaper, the pencil in her hand.

"Any good at crosswords?"

"So-so."

She dropped the paper and pencil onto Kate's bed. "I've made a start. I thought I'd have a bath now. It'll give you two more time in the morning. I think we have to be out by ten." She stopped to study Kate's face. "You have lovely skin."

Kate touched her own cheek briefly. "No make up."

Laura smiled. "I won't be long."

Picking up the newspaper, she adjusted the pillows before sitting up on the bed. She started to read each of the clues, trying not to listen to the sounds beyond the bathroom door. Each one created a picture, which try as she might, she could not discard. The sound of a zip, and there was Laura loosening off her dress and slowly stepping out of it. The sound of taps turning and the sudden rush of water, and there was Laura, feeling the temperature, skating the waters' surface with her slim hands. Kate tried to concentrate on the crossword, reading the clues over and over until they became meaningless. She heard the quiet splash of water and a slight gasp, and there was Laura, lowering herself into the hot water, letting it pool around her as she sank further, gradually stretching out into the full length of the bath—her body adjusting to the heat——resting her head against the cool enamel. Kate put down the paper and shut her eyes, trying to clear her thoughts. The occasional sound of water lapped through her. She kept her eyes closed, hoping to be released into sleep.

There was someone else in the room. Kate slowly opened her eyes and found Peg pulling back the covers of the single bed. Remembering where she was, she sat up and looked to where Laura lay next to her. The crossword sat between them, almost finished. "You're late. Nice night?" She whispered, feeling Laura move at the sound of her voice.

"Hello sleepy heads. I was trying not to disturb you."

Peg slipped under the blankets and called across to Laura. "I was just going to take your bed if that's okay. Save you from having to move." She leaned over and switched off the bedside light. "Besides…She might not snore, but Kate's a definite blanket thief."

Kate smiled uncertainly and lay still in the dark. The room was now quite chill.

"Come on," Laura whispered, as she stood from the bed and pulled back the blankets on her side. Kate swung her legs round and sat on the edge, slowly untying the belt of her dressing gown. She let it fall from her shoulders and heard Laura's own gown fall onto the back of the chair. The mattress moved slightly as Laura climbed back into the bed.

"Aren't you getting in? You must be freezing."

"It's okay, I—"

"Will you two sort yourselves out? A girl needs her beauty sleep," Peg shouted across.

Kate stood and folded the robe and then turned back towards the bed. The lamplight cast silhouettes around the room. Laura lay on her side, her back to her, but she reached behind to pull the blankets. Kate slid in, bracing herself against the cold sheets, just able to sense the warmth from Laura's body. It reminded her of earlier that morning when they had sat together on the punt, underneath the blankets. But this time there were no boots, hats, coats and gloves. She moved a little further in and caught one of Laura's feet against her own.

Laura took a sharp breath. "Your feet are freezing."

"Oh yes, she has very cold feet too. Sorry Laura," Peg called over. Kate moved her feet back across to the edge of the bed.

"Goodnight. Sweat dreams," Laura said.

"Goodnight. Don't let the bed bugs bite." Peg said, rolling over and away from them.

"Goodnight." Kate said quietly. She pulled the blanket up and turned on her side, feeling its satin edge rest against her chin. For a while she watched the shadows dance against the curtains and listened to the wind intermittently blow through the small gaps between the window and its frame, eventually she closed her eyes.

"I thought she didn't snore?"

Kate opened her eyes at the sound of Laura's voice. A faint, but consistent snort and wheeze came from Peg. She moved across to the very edge of the bed. "She must have had a few drinks with George." She leaned further. "I think she's lying on her back. Do you want me to poke her? I think I could probably reach her from here."

Kate began to reach across, stretching her fingers out, but Laura pulled her arm back and tucked it down at her side. But she didn't remove her hand, leaving it resting gently on top of hers.

"Don't disturb her." She spoke quietly into her hair. "Are your feet still cold?"

"A little." Her voice was barely audible, but she was surprised that she had spoken at all. Her chest felt so tight that she was sure it must be airless.

She felt the shift of Laura's body and the gradual warmth where they now touched. Her heart pounded, like a band of marching drums, beating up from her chest and then falling out as a dull quick thud against her pillow. Small breaths fell against the back of her neck and she felt the warm arch of Laura's foot move backwards and forwards against her own. The movement was slow, and with each stroke she felt her stomach lift and fall. She felt the brush of something against her neck. Her hands? Her lips? She waited for it again—alert to it now.

Peg breathed out, and rolled off her back towards them. It was nothing dramatic. Just someone who had woken themselves with their own snores, a catching of breath, but it might as well have been the last exhale from a man thought dead—the fright that it gave her. For a moment Peg seemed to be staring across at them, her mouth slightly opened in surprise, but the quiet rhythmical breathing showed she still slept. It was only the briefest second of fear, but it must have caused her body to change, to tighten or straighten, something to make Laura stop the pattern of her foot and pull away.

"There," Laura said, and this time she definitely did feel a kiss; a solid, single kiss, just below the crown of her head. "Sleep well." Laura squeezed her shoulders and moved back across to her side of the bed, lifting away the warm pockets of air.

She lay quite still as the thud of her body continued, gradually moving back to her chest, and there it remained, returned to her heart. A stammering, fluttering thing she could not control, and as long as its beat continued in such a way she knew she wouldn't sleep. So she lay there, and listened, and watched the shadowy walls that changed as a car passed by or the wind stirred the trees outside. Eventually, she felt Laura's breathing alter to one of sleep. She lay there a few moments longer, and then gently turned and watched the rise and fall of her back, relaxed and unaware. She shifted further across. Not close enough for their bodies to touch, but enough for her to capture her scent, and some of that warmth. She closed her eyes and thought that she would never sleep again.

When she woke the next morning, Laura was already in the bathroom. The curtains were still closed, and Peg lay on her front, her head turned away.

"Do you want me to run you a bath?" Laura said from the doorway, a toothbrush in her hand.

Kate lifted her head from the pillow. "Have I got time?"

"If you're quick. We need to check out by ten."

"Okay, thanks." The bath water started to run, and she lay there and listened for a while, eventually lifting the towel from the back of the chair. Steam drifted through into the cool air of the bedroom.

"Hi." Laura smiled, as she dropped her toothpaste into her wash bag.

"Hello." Kate stood in the doorway as Laura turned off the taps and felt the foamy water. Bubbles slid down her fingers, and she shook her hand, releasing them back into the mass of suds, although a couple lifted and drifted up into the air.

"Well I'll leave you to it. You might want to add a little cold."

The car journey home was a little quieter. The excited anticipation of the trip was gone, with only the nurses' home and their next shift to look forward to. Gales had been forecast, and sometimes they felt the sudden sway of the car, as a force of wind pushed against it. In an effort to hurry from the weather, they lifted the luggage quickly out of the boot, while Laura, upon Kate's insistence, remained in the car. They dashed, turning just to give a quick wave.

"Kate!" Laura called, leaning slightly out of the open car window. As Kate hurried back, the strong gusts encouraged the others to continue on to the shelter of the home.

"Have I forgotten something?" She stooped down towards the window.

"No," Laura said, trying to control the loose hair that blew across her face, catching in her eyes and mouth. "I'm having a house warming party on Christmas Eve." She shouted slightly above the wind. "It would be lovely if you could come. I don't know if you're free?"

Kate knew David would expect to see her. He was going to his family for Christmas, and they had loosely made arrangements to see each other before he left. "I'm working on Christmas day, so I'll be around on Christmas Eve. I could ask Sister for a late pass."

Laura smiled. "Great. You can bring David if you like, but it'll mainly be Moira's friends, mainly women." Kate nodded. Laura hadn't mentioned Peg and Val, but she knew the invite was just for her.

She stepped back from the car. "Well. I'll see you Christmas Eve then."

"Great, Christmas Eve," Laura said, slowly rolling up the window and giving a small wave from behind the glass. Kate stood, hugging her arms around herself, until the car was out of sight.

When she came into the lobby, Val was waiting for her. "Forget something?"

"Yes, my gloves."

Val looked down at the gloves on her hands and back up at Kate, but said nothing.

CHAPTER ELEVEN

She read the same lines half a dozen times, before dropping the book down on the bed beside her and finally allowing her mind to go to where it really wanted to be. Since their trip to Oxford she had tried everything to keep herself distracted, spending time with David whenever she could, or if he was at work, going to Val or Peg's bedroom. If they weren't around she would go down to the dayroom, or sometimes the dining room for a late supper. But even company didn't always do the trick; Laura somehow slid through her thoughts, like a paper knife, opening a letter she felt would most probably be best left unread.

Sometimes her thoughts were in context—of real events; like their evening at the pictures, or their weekend away in Oxford, or the night of the dance. Other times she thought of what was to come, of the housewarming party on Saturday, of what Laura's friends would be like, of what she might wear and how she might be with her. And then there were other times when there was no more than the sense of her, nothing clearer than the brief curve of her lips, the tilt of her head, or the arch of her brow.

She stood and walked over to the door and quietly opened it. Looking across the corridor she could see a light under Val's door. She slipped on her dressing gown and padded across the hallway.

"Val, are you still awake?" She leaned and whispered into the door.

The door clicked open. "I was just reading." Val opened the door more fully. "Is everything okay?"

"Are you all right for a bit of company for a while?"

"Of course."

Kate sat in the small easy chair. Its low seat encouraged a casual slouch, one she had adopted a hundred times, but tonight it felt unnatural, and she uncrossed her legs and sat up.

"Have you done anything with Johnny yet?"

Val placed the bookmark in her novel, closed it, and placed it down on the bedside table. "Done anything?"

"I mean…Have you gone very far?"

"Do you mean sex?"

Kate nodded, looking at the floor. Val sat down on the edge of her bed. "Making love…" Kate cleared her throat. "Yes. Sex."

"No, not yet."

"Will you wait until you're married?"

"Probably…I don't know. Kate you're not thinking of …with David?"

She looked up and shrugged.

"But you're not even sure if you're in love with him."

"Everyone assumes I must love him. Everyone makes me feel as though I should."

"Your problem is that you care too much about what other people think. You always have done. You can't love someone because you think other people want you to. Anyhow, I don't think we feature half as much in people's lives and thoughts as we think we do. They'll soon turn their attention to other things. The housework, baking bread…bills they have to pay…something. Kate, don't rush into anything. I've heard women say it's a messy business, painful mostly, the first time."

"So if I'm not going to enjoy it, does it matter who I do it with?"

"Especially because of that. Jane Davis said on her wedding night it hurt so much she wept." Val leaned back and gave a small smile. "Besides, it's meant to get better." She sat back up, serious again. "What's the hurry Kate? Has something happened? I can't imagine David's the sort to push you into anything. I always thought you'd wait until you were married, or at least until you were sure how you felt."

The bell sounded and Kate stood. "I'd better get back to my room."

"Don't rush into anything you might regret," Val called after her.

And then there was Maggie. She had begun to think more and more of Maggie. Maggie O'Donnell, who, unlike the other staff nurses, had been so kind to her on her first day as a student on the ward. Who had even come to her room, after she had dropped the tray of syringes that had shattered on the ground, and Sister Hunter had shouted at her. She came to her room to tell her, in a soft Irish accent, that she wasn't to worry, and that it happened to everyone. Maggie O'Donnell, who, two years later, had asked her to go to America, saying how much fun they would have, how exciting it would be—although her voice was serious and gentle. Maggie O'Donnell, who had said she would wait another year until Kate was registered, that she didn't mind waiting if she would come.

But Kate had shied away from the idea; the invitation so close to her ear that it had made her blush each time she thought of it. She lied about homesickness, but told Maggie that she should go—that the money was too good to wait. So she went, and wrote lengthy letters every week without fail. And when she first mentioned Doctor Matthews, Kate's heart had dropped, but in her letter back she encouraged her to tell her more about him. Then, only a few months later, she wrote of the marriage proposal, but Maggie also wrote that she hadn't given an answer, and had asked her what she thought she should do. Kate had written 'yes', that she should say 'yes.' If it had been another friend, if it had been Peg or Val, she might have written back asking 'what does your heart tell you?' or even 'do you love him?' But she knew best not to ask those questions. And after that, no more letters came.

It was Sally Peters, one of the nurses from Maggie's year, who confirmed that she had married—even had a photograph. It had been in color. Kate had forgotten the brightness of her auburn hair, and her skin—how pale it was. The photographer had been too far away to show the light dusting of freckles, or perhaps her make up had been heavier that day, for the wedding. She had always felt as though she could just blow those soft pigments away, with a breath, or a touch of her fingertips.

CHAPTER TWELVE

"I can't come tonight...I forgot David's off, and I promised we'd go to the pictures."

"Oh, okay...of course, if he's off ...then you should..."

"Yes, I feel as though I've neglected him a little lately. He's wanted to see some Robert Mitchum film—a war film. Not really my thing, but you know... "

"Yes... "

"If I don't see you before, have a good Christmas."

"Yes, you too. Merry Christmas."

That was how the conversation had gone just half an hour ago. Laura and Moira had been walking through the hospital gates, back to her flat, when Kate had chased them down, slightly out of breath, her cheeks pink from the run.

"It's probably a good thing she's not coming." Moira suggested from across the breakfast bar.

Neither had spoken much since they had arrived back at her flat. Like a closing lock on a river, Kate's words had shut down the flow of party preparations and easy conversation. Laura looked up from the kitchen counter where she was placing green and black olives into a long segmented tray. "Who?"

"God Laura. You know exactly who. I hadn't actually realized you'd invited her. Probably not one of your wisest decisions."

"What do you mean?"

"You know what they say. Loose lips might sink ships…"

"What do you think she would do? Report me?"

"Well, that's not entirely impossible. You do remember the main reason why you're here in the first place? Do you want that to happen again? Cos there are only so many places you can run to. Anyway, she wouldn't necessarily have to report you. It would only take a little idle gossip to cause you a great number of problems."

"She's not like that. Do you think I would've asked her if I'd thought there was any possibility?"

Moira picked up an olive from the tray and tossed it into her mouth. "Do you think she knows?"

"No—yes…I don't know. There's something…I get the sense of something between the two of us."

Chewing slowly, Moira pushed the stone out between her lips and held it between her thumb and forefinger. "Sounds dangerous…that is why I'm going to move onto the fact that Sarah is coming to your party. Have I told you about Sarah?"

Laura sighed and threw the last couple of olives into the tray. "Yes, you've told me about Sarah."

"Have I told you how attractive, hip, and most importantly, available she is?"

"Many many times." Laura smiled, taking the tray through to the living room

"And she's *dying* to meet you."

***

"Are you sure you don't want to go out? We could get a bite to eat, go for a coffee somewhere." David took Kate's hand as he sat beside her on the sofa.

"No, I'm happy just staying here, if you are. Where's Gus?"

"He's on a date. One of the girls he was dancing with the other week, the red head—quite a looker. He's seen her a few times."

Kate tried to remember the dance hall, the people. She remembered talking with Laura and her friend Moira, and Laura dancing with Peg, and how she had almost danced with her—just for a moment. She also remembered hurrying out of the hall to catch Laura before she left, to secure the date at the pictures. Did she dance with David? Oh yes, but she only remembered because it had been when she had seen Laura leaving and she had felt captured—fenced in by his arms. The only dance partner she remembered Gus having was Laura, and Peg had been right; they had made a handsome couple.

"Could I have a drink?" She turned her attention back to David.

"Of course, tea…coffee? I'm not sure what we've got in."

"Do you have anything a little stronger?"

"Oh…I think we only have beer, though there might be a little sherry left."

David returned with the sherry and a bottle of beer. They sat quietly as she drew quickly on the sweet liquid. Within a few minutes it was gone and she placed the glass on the table. She took the bottle from David and put it down, taking his free hands and pulling him towards her.

David reached across and cupped her face in his hands. "Oh Kate, I do love you." He exhaled a heavy breath and pushed himself forwards, pressing his mouth firmly against hers. The wetness of his lips covered hers, and she began to kiss him back. As she felt his tongue, thick and loose, push inside her mouth she leaned back and guided him, so that he was almost lying, although a little awkwardly, on top of her. She felt his hardness, as he groaned heavily and pushed further against her.

"Oh Kate," he sighed against her ear, moving his lips to her jaw, and then to the base of her throat. He lifted himself slightly away from her, and with trembling hands began to unbutton the front of her dress.

Reaching forwards, she closed her eyes and felt for his erection. David stopped for a moment and then reached down, feeling for the end of her petticoats. He pushed them higher, his hot hands catching on her stockings at intervals, as he moved them up to the tops of her thighs.

"Kate." His voice was thick. "Kate, look at me."

She opened her eyes. There was the desire still there in his face, but also a tenderness that she could not bear. Kate dropped her hand away.

"I'm sorry David. I can't do this." She pushed gently at his chest and his thighs, trying to release herself from his weight.

"God Kate. I'm sorry. I thought you wanted to. I thought you were ready to…" He lifted himself away from her and moved to the end of the sofa.

Kate shook her head, pushing the skirt of her dress back down, pressing it hard over her knees. "It's my fault. I thought maybe I was too."

His head slumped forward and he pushed his hands back through his hair. She knew she should reach out and tell him that everything was all right. But something held her back, and she hated herself for it, for her coldness, her disdain for his affection.

With the last button hooked through, she placed a hand on David's knee. "I think I should go. It's getting late." She stood as David looked up at the clock on the mantelpiece. It had only just turned nine o'clock, but he didn't argue with her. "Are we still all right for next Saturday? When you get back from your mum's?"

She tried to give him a reassuring smile. "Of course. I'll see you next Saturday." The suggestion to try to meet before then rested on her lips, but instead she just said "Merry Christmas." She turned to the door and closed it quietly behind her.

The voices rose over each other, as she paused at the bottom of the stair well. She had rung the bell of the shared entrance, and had been surprised to be buzzed directly in. As she slowly climbed the stairs, she began to doubt whether it was such a good idea to come.

Someone must have been changing records, as loud music joined in with the sounds of talking and laughter. The door to the flat had been left ajar and she stood hesitating, unsure whether to knock or not. Deciding that it was unlikely that anyone would hear, she slipped through the doorway.

There were a couple of young men sitting together, but the rest of the party seemed to consist of women. It was a very modern open plan flat, with the living room and dinning room all in one area. She could just make out Laura through the smoky air and dim lighting, sitting on the arm of a long sofa. She leant down to talk to a woman. Laura's hair was loose and fashionably curled under. It fell across her face as she leant a little closer. The other woman wore her hair up in a ponytail with a short fringe—beatnik style. She was all laughs and smiles. Laura only seemed to have to open her mouth for her to toss her head back and touch Laura's hand or push her away teasingly

"Oh, you made it. We didn't think you were coming." Kate turned to see Moira standing behind her. "Come with me to the kitchen. I'll fix you a drink."

Although most of the party seemed to be going on in the living room, there were still quite a number of women standing in the corners of the kitchen or leaning against it's counters. There was also a larger group that had congregated around the breakfast bar, some standing whilst others sat on tall stools. Moira gestured to the end one which had just been vacated, and indicated to Kate to sit down. The counter top opposite was filled with the widest selection of spirits and mixers she had ever seen in anyone's home.

"What's your poison?" Moira asked, picking up one of the cocktail shakers. "Martinis are my specialty, but I could make you a high ball if you fancy a longer drink?"

"Oh, well I've never had either, so I'll just have to trust your judgment."

Moira looked her up and down. "A highball, and maybe just drink it slow," she said, turning back to reach for the bottle of whiskey.

Kate let her gaze carry around the kitchen, allowing it to rest occasionally on individuals. A couple of times she caught the eye of someone and they smiled. One even raised her glass slightly in a sort of greeting.

She smiled back and turned on the stool towards Moira who had given the cocktail a final shake and was now pouring the concoction into a tall glass half filled with ice. The drink cracked and fizzed invitingly.

"Oh, I nearly forgot." Reaching to the back of the counter, Moira pulled out a small paper umbrella, pushed a cherry onto its end, and dropped it into the glass "Enjoy."

"Thank you. It looks wonderful." She took a sip as Moira watched expectantly. She smiled and took a larger mouthful.

"Good?"

"Yes, *really* good."

Moira smiled, pleased. "Remember it's stronger than it tastes so take your time."

Kate nodded as she took another drink. Moira placed her own glass on the breakfast bar and leaned towards Kate.

"So…what happened to your date?"

Looking down at her glass, she took another, larger mouthful. "Oh, David wasn't feeling too good." Not wanting to elaborate further on a lie, she tried to think of a way to change the subject. "That woman talking to Laura. Who is she?"

Moira's eyes widened slightly, and Kate felt her directness in the warmth of her cheeks. "That's Sarah…" She studied Kate's face as she continued. "She's a friend of mine—a writer. They only just met tonight but they seem to have hit it off."

"A writer?" She rescued the umbrella out of the half empty glass, and placed it in a dish filled with discarded olive stones. "Has she published anything?"

"Yes, mainly poetry, but she recently had a play running at Ovalhouse. At the moment she's working on a novel."

"Goodness. That's impressive." And Kate was impressed. It sounded highbrow and intellectual, quite a different world.

Moira looked at her, turning her glass slowly between her fingers. Kate reached for hers, about to take a mouthful of the syrupy liquid, but was surprised to find that it was empty of everything but ice.

"Let me fix you another one, and then I'll introduce you to a few people. Same again?"

"All right." She smiled, glad that the first cocktail had helped her feel a little more relaxed. As Moira picked up the spirits and mixers, Kate thought of Laura in the next room. A number of people had wandered into the kitchen to fix drinks, but there had been no sign of her.

"Hope you don't mind, but I decided to make you a mojito instead." Moira passed the glass over and then raised her voice slightly, seemingly for the benefit of the small group standing nearby. "Martha's got an allotment, and she's brought so much mint over I don't know what to do with the stuff."

One of them raised their head above the others. "You ungrateful swine. I'll not bother next time," she said, frowning at Moira and then turning her attention to Kate with a smile. Kate smiled back, and that seemed to be all the invitation Martha needed, as she headed across the kitchen towards them.

"Martha, this is Kate. She's a friend of Laura's. They work together."

"Another Doctor?" Martha looked at Kate incredulously.

"No, a nurse."

"Even better. Truth be known, it's you lot who do all the hard graft isn't it? Terri, Pat." Martha called over to the other two who had formed part of her original group. "Come over and meet Kate. She's a nurse. Terri, maybe she could look at those lumps on your chest." She turned back to Kate confidingly. "We're all sure they shouldn't be there."

They were the two young men she had seen earlier, but as they slowly wandered across, she realized that, although dressed as men, they were, like everyone else at the party, women. She could see that their features were too fine to belong to any man she had ever known, and their chins were as smooth as her own.

They both held out their hands to greet her. Kate looked briefly at Moira, who seemed unable to hide her amusement, and then shook both of their hands. Terri leaned forward, her voice soft and serious. "I haven't really got any lumps on my chest. Martha loves to make a joke…usually at the expense of somebody else."

"Particularly Terri. She's far too nice to fight back," Moira added.

"Are you suggesting I should pick on someone my own size?" Martha continued to joke, as she brushed her hands down her long skinny hips.

The second drink lasted a little longer than the first, as she consciously drank more slowly, aware that she was starting to feel a little lightheaded.

"Another one?" Moira asked, pointing at her empty glass.

"I should go and find Laura and say hello."

"Well hold on. I'll make you a Martini, and you can take it through." She turned towards the counter and Kate went to stand by her.

"All right, but will you show me how you make one?"

"Sure, first of all you take about half a dozen ice cubes and pop them in the shaker."

The top door of the refrigerator swung open as Moira pulled on the handle. It seemed to be a complete freezer compartment, packed with ice. They had a fridge at home, in fact they were one of the first families in the street to get one, due to the good fortune her stepfather had with the football pools. He had surprised her mother, who had claimed that it was an extravagance. Kate must have been about fourteen and she remembered the compartment on the right hand side—no bigger than a shoebox, and the small ice tray that sat inside. She had filled the tray, and the next day made orange squash. She pushed the first two cubes out and went to push the next row, but her mother had told her that two was plenty, as though they should be rationed like her sweets. They melted too quickly, but not before she felt the satisfying tap against her teeth and the chilled top layer of the sugary drink. Her mother still shopped every day for fresh meat and fish, and since Kate had left home, the tray was rarely used. Sometimes an aunt or uncle might have a Bloody Mary at Christmas, and her mother would allow two cubes to be dropped into the drink.

The ice clunked into the bottom of the shaker, and Moira picked up a bottle of vodka in her right hand and a bottle of vermouth in her left, but both became distracted by the woman who had positioned herself next to them.

"Well hello there. Managed to prize yourself away?" Moira said, as she placed the lid firmly onto the metal container.

The woman smiled and shook her head, her ponytail flicking from side to side. "I've just come for a couple of drinks. Don't worry I'm heading right back through as soon as I can." As she spoke, she glanced across at Kate.

"Sarah, this is Kate. She's a friend and work colleague of Laura's."

"Oh right. I think Laura mentioned you. You're a nurse?"

Kate smiled, inexplicably as pleased as a child that she had somehow been part of their conversation. "Yes. I work on the same ward. Moira was telling me you're a writer."

"Yep. I paint a little too. Are you into the arts?"

This wasn't the sort of party small talk Kate was used to, and she considered her answer carefully. "I sometimes go to the galleries—"

"I was just talking to Laura about the Jackson Pollock exhibition at MoMA. Do you like abstract expressionism?"

Kate felt that there was a challenge to the question. That to answer "yes" or "no" or "it's okay" wouldn't be enough, and would be met with a look of silent disappointment.

"The Museum of Modern Art—in New York," Sarah said. But Kate had known that, and it annoyed her that Sarah must have looked at her and thought that maybe she wouldn't; that she had perhaps put those words out there as a trip wire for her to fall and stumble over.

"I don't really understand a lot of the modern paintings."

"Maybe we could go to some of the galleries sometime. I can talk you through them."

"Thank you. Maybe sometime,' Kate said, although she could think of nothing she desired less. Not that she wasn't interested to understand the paintings better—she would have liked that. She just didn't want this particular woman explaining them to her.

Moira poured the Martini into two slender stemmed glasses. Rather than a cherry, she pushed a green olive onto two sticks and dropped one into each drink. "Et voila!" She handed one of the glasses to Kate and turned to Sarah. "So what can I get you?"

"Surprise me—and you know Laura's tastes better than I do. What do you think she would like?"

Moira looked up at the clock. "Hmmm, how about a Tom Collins for you? And I think, looking at the time, Laura would probably like a bourbon and ice."

"Great, maybe I'll get extra points."

"Anything I can do to help."

"Well, thank you—but no help required." She smiled as she popped a glacier cherry into her mouth before stabbing another one with an umbrella. "I always get what I want."

"I feel sorry for everyone else." Both women turned towards Kate, who realized that she must have said those thoughts out loud.

"Excuse me?" Sarah said, the pink paper umbrella held just in front of her opened mouth.

"I just mean…" Kate twisted the cocktail stick around slowly in her glass. "If you're busy getting what you want, where does that leave everyone else?" She looked towards Moira to see if maybe she had overstepped the mark, but Moira's eyes were fixed on the doorway, where Laura stood with an amused expression on her face.

"Lying in her wake by the sounds of it," Laura said.

Kate smiled back uncertainly, unsure if the comment was a compliment to the writer's character or not. Looking over at Sarah, it seemed that she was just as uncertain.

When she turned her attention back to Laura, she found her still looking at her. The kitchen felt much smaller. "I think this one's my favorite," she said, turning to Moira and tapping her glass.

Moira handed the glass of bourbon and the Tom Collins to Sarah. "Kate's been trying a few of my cocktails. Just to warn you, it seems she prefers the hard stuff."

"Thank you Moira. You're putting my hostessing skills to shame," Laura said, her eyes remaining on Kate.

Sarah handed Laura her glass, and with her newly freed hand took her arm. "Come on. Let's see if those two spots on the sofa are still free. I can never understand why parties always end up in the kitchen."

But before Sarah could fully usher her out of the door, Laura turned back. "Are you two coming through?"

Moira looked over towards the bottles of spirits. "I better stick around here and help with drinks. Kate, why don't you go on through?"

"No...thank you." She shook her head. "I think I'll stay in here and watch you make a few more cocktails—if you don't mind." She tried to give Laura a convincing smile. "I'll make sure I come through and see you before I go." She knew she was being petulant, but she would rather have gone back to see David than sit and listen to them discuss the latest plays and art exhibitions, or worse still, ask for her opinion.

"What can I say? I throw a great kitchen party." Moira smiled a little uncomfortably. Laura gave Kate one last look before leaving.

"You definitely won that." Martha had moved closer and spoke quietly into her ear.

"I'm sorry?"

"I watched the whole thing. She might have ambushed Laura, but you definitely won. No doubt."

Kate shook her head, the alcohol making her thoughts a little muddled. She didn't feel as though she had won anything. What could she have won? Did she even want to win?

"Can you make me another drink?" Kate said, holding out her empty glass.

"Okay," Moira said, holding up the cocktail shaker. " But I just want you to know that I won't be held responsible for how you feel in the morning."

Kate smiled and nodded. "I'm an adult. I take full responsibility."

"Martha did you witness that? Laura will have me hung, drawn and quartered."

Martha looked Kate up and down. "Well, she certainly looks like a consenting adult."

"And I don't think any of us should worry too much about what Laura thinks." Kate added.

"Hear hear." Martha said, encouragingly.

The countertop was sticky with drink in most places. Kate lifted a bottle she didn't recognize, revealing a circle of alcohol where it had stood. "Kahlua? What about this one? I don't think I've tried this yet."

Martha took the bottle from her hands. "What do you reckon Moira? Black Russian?"

Moira picked up a bottle of rum and tipped it from side to side. "I think we've just got enough, but I'm not kidding—make this one last."

The last of the Kahlua went into the shaker. Kate knew she had drunk too much, and that she should get back to the nurses' home. She felt gloomy and carefree at the same time, as though she could easily do something reckless. She wasn't sure why she still remained, but somehow she felt that to leave was to lose something, perhaps irrevocably.

"Have you seen Laura? We're going to head off now, but I can't find her anywhere." Two women, who must have been in the living room the whole evening, stood just inside the kitchen and called across to Moira.

"Last I heard she was heading for the couch."

"Have you checked the bedroom?" Martha asked with a smile.

"The door's closed."

"I bet it is," Martha said, letting out a knowing, unguarded laugh.

Kate lifted her martini glass to her lips to take a drink, although there was nothing left, and then placed it down. "I'm going to head off now."

"But what about this drink?" Moira said.

Kate stood from her stool. "You're right. I've probably had enough. Will you say goodbye to Laura for me?"

Moira nodded. "How will you get home?"

"Oh, it's only a twenty minute walk. The fresh air will do me good."

"Wait, I'll see you out." The concern on Moira's face was hard to take.

"No really, it's fine." A woman, swaying slightly, had moved over to the counter and was picking up and putting down various bottles. "Looks like someone needs a drink fixing."

"Well, if you're sure. Be careful and don't talk to any strangers."

Kate gave her a small salute and walked out of the kitchen. On the way to the front door, she glanced briefly over at the sofa. The two spaces where Laura and Sarah had been sitting were empty.

The coats were piled on top of each other, but she could see the red cuff of her jacket hanging out to one side and pulled, gently at first and then more firmly. But in finally releasing her coat, the others fell like a colorful avalanche of wool and buttons onto the tiled floor. "Blast."

"You're not going home are you?" Laura stood behind her in the small hallway with two full champagne flutes in her hands. She had the slight sway of a poplar tree. Her green eyes were less clear. "You can't leave yet, I've not spoken to you all evening." She moved further forward, holding up one of the glasses for her to take.

"It's getting late. I need to get back."

"Come on Kate. You've already missed lights out, and Val told me all about the ways you lot manage to stay out late undetected." She leaned closer, lowering her mouth to Kate's ear. "Am I not worth climbing a drain pipe for?"

Kate gave a slight, reluctant smile and this time she took the glass.

Laura tugged gently on her fingertips. "Come on. Just for a little while. I'll give you a tour of the place."

She gave in slightly to the pull, and moved towards Laura. "All right, but I can't stay long."

"I promise." Laura held onto her fingers and led her back through to the living room.

"Where's Sarah?"

"In the kitchen I think, talking to Moira. Why?"

"Oh, it's just that I couldn't find you earlier—to say goodbye."

"We were probably in the bedroom. I was showing her around. Fortunately Moira came and saved me—told me you were leaving. Merry Christmas, by the way."

The large wooden clock on the far wall, with its indications of time just single gold bars, showed it had turned twelve. She smiled and raised the flute. "Merry Christmas."

"Come on, I'll show you the rest of the place." Kate followed her back through into the open plan living room. Laura pointed across to a large table in light oak, in the far corner. The matching chairs were randomly pulled out at angles, and one had made its way across to the other side of the room, next to the sofa. "There's a dining area over there. I don't know how much I'll use it."

"Yes, the kitchen's so lovely it would be tempting to eat in there all the time." She felt oddly formal, as though Laura were showing her around in anticipation of a sale.

Laura smiled. "Yes, that's right," she said, glancing over at a doorway across on the other side of the room. The door was slightly ajar but no light came from the room beyond. "That's the bedroom over there."

"Aren't you going to show me, or is it only Sarah that gets to look?"

"Of course." Laura gave a low chuckle. "Follow me." She pushed the door open wider and Kate walked through. Laura switched on a small bedside lamp that released a low light across the double bed. The darkened corners of the room held light ash furniture, in one a dresser, in the other, a large wardrobe.

"It's lovely. The whole place is lovely."

Kate ran her fingers along the counterpane as she walked across to the other side of the room. A dressing table sat under the window. Propped up on top were at least half a dozen unopened letters, all of their sides perfectly sealed. She recognized the handwriting and remembered the sender's name—Mrs. Gwendolyn Forest.

"I'm glad you came tonight."

She turned and looked at Laura "Yes. I'm glad I came too." She sat down on the end of the bed. "I very nearly didn't."

"Why?"

"I was afraid I suppose."

"Afraid? Of what?"

"I don't know. Afraid of your friends, of you, of what I might find."

"And now?"

She smiled at Laura. "I'm not afraid at all. I—"

"Hey hostess," Moira called from the doorway. "The rest of your guests are leaving. Thought you might want to say goodbye."

"Wait here. I'll be two minutes."

Moira gave a half wave. "Bye Kate. See you soon no doubt."

There was a whole clutter of sounds outside the room; laughter and footsteps, the sounds of "goodbye." Someone said "great party." A door closed, and then nothing—like a shaker suddenly emptying its dice. She looked at the bedside clock. She knew she should go, but instead her fingers held firmly onto the bed covers. Even if Sister Bates were to come to that doorway, she would find it impossible to leave. But it was Laura who stood there, leaning on the frame.

"What are you thinking about?" Laura asked.

Kate gave a small smile. "Sister Bates."

"Oh." She walked across the room. "Are you worrying about the time again?"

"A little. I should go really."

"Okay…" Laura drew the word out. "How about I make you a cup of tea?" She put her hand up as Kate tried to begin her objections. "Look half an hour isn't really going to make a great deal of difference at this stage in the game is it? If you were to get caught, better with a cup of tea inside you and a clearer head."

Kate couldn't argue with her reasoning. She shook her head, but followed Laura through to the kitchen and perched on one of the bar stools, watching her fill the bright red kettle.

"How do you know all those people?"

"Oh, they're mainly Moira's friends."

"And how does she know them?"

"Through teaching, and well…She's an art teacher, so she knows a lot of that crowd. And also from the Gateways—it's a club in town, mainly for women."

"You seem to be good friends—close. I like her."

"Moira and I were a little different from the other girls. ;I suppose that's what drew us together. She was always the brave one at school. She never tried to be anything other than who she was, but it got her into trouble then, and it's been getting her into trouble ever since." The kettle started to whine. Laura lifted it and poured the water into the teapot. "Over here it feels a little more—I don't know how to describe it—sort of, we won't ask if you don't tell." She leaned back against the chrome handle that ran along the front of the cooker. "Anyway. She's learned to keep a lower profile. She's calmed down quite a lot."

Stirring the water, she placed the strainer on the first cup and then the second.

"Come on. Let's sit somewhere a bit more comfortable."

Laura sat down in the middle of the large sofa and kicked her shoes off. Kate stood equidistant from the sofa and the armchair, uncertain where to sit. Laura leaned her head back, closing her eyes. She tapped the place beside her. "Come and sit here. We probably need to talk."

She sat down next to Laura, but leaned forward, her cup cradled in both hands.

"Moira…Is she a…" Kate grappled with the word.

Laura opened her eyes and sat up a little. "Is she a what?"

"Is she a…a com…a communist?"

Laura tipped her head back and laughed.

"I don't see why it's so funny." Kate said, as she watched Laura and wondered if the laughter would ever come to an end. "It's late. I should go." She put down her cup. "I'm not even sure what I'm doing here."

Laura reached for her hand as she began to stand, pulling her back down.

"I'm sorry Kate. I'm sorry. It's just that…" She paused, her face serious. "You're right. What are we doing here?" She didn't look at Kate, but instead stared straight ahead. "And how much is by chance and how much by design, I really don't know." She moved her hand across and brushed her fingertips against Kate's own. "But I do know this…I know that it's Christmas morning, and while most of London's sleeping you're here with me, and you're in this apartment, and you're sitting here on my couch, and..."

"And?" Kate asked, the word catching quietly in her throat.

"And..." She turned and looked at Kate. "And I think it's almost perfect."

Laura lifted her hand to Kate's face and pulled her fingers along the length of her jaw. Kate sat quite still, her only movement the rapid rise and fall of her breast, as Laura traced her thumb along the center of her lips. She could hear Laura's irregular breaths, and, as she closed her eyes, felt the softness of Laura's lips grazing her own. Like reaching for a ball that had been unexpectedly thrown, her hands went up to catch Laura's face, afraid that she might fall away, that the moment might slip from her fingers. She pressed her mouth more firmly and felt the cool tip of Laura's tongue, as her lips parted.

"I must have left my purse—"

Kate snapped her head away. Moira stood just past the doorway, one foot in front of the other—frozen in mid stride.

"Wow, look I'm really sorry. I should have knocked or something."

Laura reached for Kate's hand, but she pulled it away and stood.

"It's fine. I was just leaving. I should have been back hours ago."

"Well, listen. Don't leave on my account. I just came to find—and there they are," Moira said, as she snatched up her keys.

As Kate moved past Moira and picked up her coat, she felt Laura following behind.

"Don't go like this. Let's talk..."

Kate tried to fasten the buttons on her coat, but her fingers wouldn't cooperate. The buttonholes suddenly seemed too small to accommodate the large red buttons. Giving up, she looked at Laura.

"There's nothing to talk about. It was all a bit of a misunderstanding, too many cocktails," she suggested and turned back to Moira. "Goodnight Moira."

Laura reached out and grasped her arm.

"Please Laura," Kate said, as she pulled away, and Laura loosened her grip. She rushed down the stairs and out through the main entrance door. The temperature had dropped considerably, and she welcomed the cold air as she hurried on along the empty streets. When she arrived at the main hospital gates she hardly knew how she had got there. She went as quietly as she could through the large revolving door, past the sleeping porter, and stole quickly to the end of the corridor. There, she took a door to her left and followed the dimly lit staircase down to the tunnels. She could do the route with her eyes closed and was soon climbing the stairs which led to the nurses accommodation. She tried the door, and to her relief it pushed open. Val must have left it off its latch.

As she closed the bedroom door behind her, she breathed out. Without switching on the light or removing her coat she lay down on the bed. Her body hummed as she lay there in the darkness. She raised her hand to her mouth and traced the path that Laura's fingers had touched earlier and thought of the kiss. Heat rose up her cheeks as she felt a buzz move through her body and rest at her center.

What if Moira hadn't walked in? What would have happened? But she really didn't know. Her mind was as blank as a schoolgirl's September notebook.

***

Laura could hear Moira moving around in the kitchen, probably tidying up as she waited for the kettle to boil. She hadn't said anything after Kate had left, just raised her eyebrows and said something about making tea.

"Tea," Moira said, as she held the cup out in front of her. Laura sat up and took the hot drink. "So... I guess that being friends thing didn't work out huh?"

Laura smiled briefly as Moira sat down next to her. "She kissed me."

"She kissed you? You were seduced?" She took a sip of tea. "Well. They do say it's the quiet ones you have to watch out for."

"No." Laura sat forward on the sofa clasping the warm cup in both hands. "I kissed her, but she kissed me back."

Moira slipped off her shoes and turned towards Laura. "Look. She's a nice girl. It's not difficult to see what you see in her Laura, but she's also very naïve. Her eyes nearly popped out of that pretty head of hers when she was introduced to Terri and Pat."

"She was talking to Terri and Pat?"

"Yep, and to give her credit she actually handled the whole thing pretty well." She put her cup down and turned to Laura. "Listen. There's nobody more than me that would love to see a happily ever after for you two, but I just can't see her giving up her doctor boyfriend, risking her job, her friendships…I don't know what her relationship is like with her family, but I wouldn't imagine they'd be too thrilled either. You've got to start being realistic about what people are capable of, and I just don't think she's capable of all that. It's asking an awful lot Laura, too much, and God knows we've been here before. I mean at least this one's not married, but even so… Just don't let her make a fool out of you."

"She wouldn't do that."

Moira shrugged and took another drink of her tea. "No, not intentionally."

CHAPTER THIRTEEN

The hospital's theme for Christmas was 'Under the Sea', and what Sister Thomas had described as the pièce de résistance for the Dickens Ward was finally finished. A life size King Neptune stood tall, if slightly over to one side, on his bright blue and green tail. Nearly every member of staff, and a number of the patients, had contributed to the construction of this papier-mâché god of the seas. Someone had been let loose with the red paint since Kate had last been on the ward, so his lips gave a ruby pout and his cheeks appeared blushed crimson, leaving it hard to tell if he was actually male or female. Only the foil trident held aloft in his right hand showed for certain that he wasn't in fact a mermaid.

There was always a hum during the weeks of December, with the ward to decorate, the carol service to rehearse and the dinner to plan. This morning the excitement and fun had culminated. Nurses flitted about with handfuls of paper seaweed, and hung brightly painted fish from any available surface they could find. But her feeling of knotted anticipation was not from waiting to see Mr.

Clarkson dressed as Father Christmas or watching Dr. Evans carve the turkey, or the carols that they would soon be singing.

When she thought of Laura, she didn't know whether to smile or frown. She felt as though she had been given a magical, unexpected, but quite impractical gift. Like being handed a crown or the sword Excalibur, and then left to wonder how it could possibly lend itself to her ordinary life.

"Morning sleepy head. I see you didn't make it for breakfast," Val said, as she reached up, pinning the end of a paper chain firmly into the wall of the long corridor. Kate held the ladder as she carefully stepped down. "Just to warn you, Patsy had one of her fits last night. There was such a commotion. Everyone came out of their room. Sister Bates even came up. I'm not sure, but I think she might have noticed you weren't there."

"What time was it?"

"Just after midnight."

"Did she say anything?"

"No, but I'm pretty sure I heard a knock at your door after we'd gone back to our rooms. I could be wrong, but—"

"Come on. Matron wants everyone to come now." One of the student nurses called.

Kate went back quickly into the ward to fetch her cape, and noticed that someone had given Neptune a long black beard. Strands of knitting wool fell from his chin. A man, most definitely a man, Kate thought. A rosy lipped, rouged, man.

They congregated out in the large stair well. Matron stood on the half landing below with Sister Bates, while the nurses stood up and down the stairs.

"Oh, I've forgotten my cape." Kate watched Val fly back up the stairs, two steps at time, weaving between the other nurses. As she turned her attention back to Matron, Kate noticed Sister Bates' eyes meet and hold hers. Kate gave a slight smile. The Sister's stern look didn't alter, as a student nurse handed her a cardboard box filled with candles.

"Come on girls. Let's have a bit of order. One nurse on every other step, right and left." They all followed Matron's instructions.

"Sister Bates will be handing out the candles in a moment. Just be mindful of curtains and bedclothes."

Following the Matron's cue, Sister Bates worked her way up the stairs. The same student nurse that had handed the candles to her followed behind with a box of matches, lighting each candle the Sister handed out.

When it was her turn, Kate held her hand out, but Sister Bates paused. She held the candle up, slightly out of her reach.

"Did you have a nice time last night Nurse Ford?"

Kate looked straight ahead. "Yes, thank you Sister Bates."

She grasped the candle as the Sister moved it towards her. "Not too good I hope," she said, as she slowly released the waxy stick and walked up to the next step.

Kate stared at the candle as the nurse lit the wick, watching the flame flicker and fan in the open stairwell.

"Everything all right?" Val asked, returning to her step. Kate gave a small nod. "Could you hold this? I need to turn this blasted thing inside out."

Kate took the candle as Val refastened her cape, the festive red lining on display.

"I can't even remember what we're starting with," Val said, taking the candle back.

"Silent Night, I think," Kate said quietly, as she looked up the staircase and followed Sister Bates, wishing each nurse a Merry Christmas, before handing them a candle.

They started with the Medical wards, following a route that ended in the nurses' day room. Kate had tried to sing along with the others, but her attention kept going back to Sister Bates. When they had stood on the wards to sing their carols, she would glance across and see the Sister, singing the carols, occasionally smiling at the patient's or Matron. She looked around the dayroom, and found her talking to Matron, smiling at Mr. Clarkson's red velvet suit, seeming to enjoy herself. Kate blew her candle out. For her, all the fun of the day seemed extinguished. The doctors handed out mince pies to laughing nurses, but Kate bit down drily on hers, the pastry sticking to the roof of her mouth and the mincemeat cloying around her teeth.

"One of the nurses on your floor became unwell last night." Sister Bates stood by her side. Kate dropped her hand down, her fingers tightening around the mince pie and causing the foil case to crumple. "It led me to discover that you weren't in your room, and it was after midnight. I know you were granted a late pass, and being qualified I will make some allowances, but I would ask you kindly not to take too much advantage of your position." She talked methodically as though she wanted Kate to absorb the gravity of every word she spoke. The mince pie still sat stubbornly in her mouth, and she tried to swallow it before answering.

"I'm sorry Sister Bates. I forgot the time. I promise it wont happen again."

"And do you mind me asking where you were?" She blew out her candle and handed it to a cadet, as Kate tried to gauge the innocence of her question.

"With David," she said with as much assurance as she dared.

"That's odd. I bumped into Dr. Richards this morning on Bronte ward. I suggested he should be more of a gentleman and get you back before your curfew."

Kate stood silently, as the Sister unbuttoned her cape, turned it the right way round again, and draped it back over her shoulders.

"I suppose you can imagine what he said to me?" She began to refasten her cape.

"I *was* with David, but I left him a little earlier than I'd anticipated." She paused, wondering how best to continue. "There was a party…Dr. Harrison's house warming party." Sister Bates lifted her attention from the top button. "I hadn't planned to go, but I had the late pass…so I decided to go along, just show my face, but I got rather caught up and lost track of the time. As I said, it won't happen again. You have my word."

"Dr. Harrison?" Sister Bates widened her eyes. "What an honor, considering she seems to keep herself to herself so much with all the medical staff here." She stepped closer to Kate. "You two have been spending quite a lot of time together—days out, trips away. Be careful. I feel as though she's maybe seen and done more than someone of her age and sex should."

She nodded along with the Sister's words and leant forward to place her candle in the box. "As I said Sister, it won't happen again."

"You're right. It won't," she said, brushing her hands down the front of her cape. "All your privileges are removed, including late passes, until I tell you otherwise." She reached up to check her cap was still straight. "There are always consequences to our actions Nurse Ford. You're a clever girl. I'm sure you know that."

***

Kate had to push hard against the force of the wind as she slowly moved the revolving door. Dead leaves and an old cigarette wrapper blew at her feet as she stepped outside and saw the familiar figure under the lamplight. As soon as David saw her, he threw the end of his cigarette to the ground and stepped forward to stamp it out, but a strong gust took hold of it and pushed it away. The orange end glowed vigorously as it rolled from his feet.

"Hello—Merry Christmas. I thought you'd be at your mum's." Kate shouted over the bitter blows of cold air.

Pulling her in close, David spoke in her ear. His breath was warm against her face. "I wanted to speak to you." He pushed his hair back. "Come over here." He pulled her across, nearer to the shelter of the building. "Last night things were so queer between us, and then when Sister Bates came and spoke to me…None of it makes sense." He nodded briefly at a small group of doctors coming from the hospital and then turned back. "And then I started thinking. It's not just been last night. You've been a little strange with me for a while. Things have been a little off kilter between the two of us."

"I'm sorry. I've not been fair to you."

"What's going on Kate? Where did you go after you left? Sister Bates said you didn't get back 'til after midnight."

"To a party—"

"A party! But you never said anything about a party. What party? God Kate you're so secretive these days."

"It's not a secret. It was a house warming party." She was tired of explaining herself, and annoyed at David's right to know where she was and with whom. But she knew he did have that right and he wasn't being unreasonable, and somehow that irritated her even more. "When I left yours I just decided on a whim to pop in. I hadn't planned it. In fact I'd told her I wasn't going."

"Who? Whose party?"

"Dr. Harrison."

"Dr. Harrison? I might have known. This is getting out of hand."

"Out of hand?"

"Look Kate, I think you've well and truly fulfilled your duties as far as she's concerned."

"Do you want to end it? Call it all off?" She felt a sudden release as she said the words, unsure if it was guilt or anger that had spun them.

"God, no Kate. That's the last thing I want to do. I love you." His grip tightened, but his voice softened. "Look. Let's not ruin the holidays. That's not what I wanted to do. Just clear the air, that's all. Make things right between the two of us."

Kate relented a little, sorry for the small look of shock on David's face. "I'm sorry. I have been a little distracted." She took his hand, which was as cold as hers. "After the holidays, why don't we try out that Chinese restaurant Val and Johnny were talking about the other day?"

David looked up from where she had placed her hand and smiled. "That sounds good," he said, taking a firmer hold of her hand. "Come on. I'll walk you home."

They stepped away from red brick wall of the hospital and the wind slapped hard against the side of her face. Her cap momentarily lifted. She pulled at the grips and loosened it off until it finally came away, and she reached for the last few pins that remained in her hair. They pressed on together hand in hand. David tried to tell her his plans for Christmas, but gave up, as his words got carried away on relentless gusts, and it hurt too much to try to lift her head to listen. She had to push her head down and look at the ground.

"Well, talk of the devil." Kate looked up at David's words and felt his grip tighten a little. Laura was walking down the steps from the nurses' home, her hands pushed firmly into the pockets of her heavy wool coat.

"Hello Dr. Harrison. Merry Christmas," David said.

She stopped in front of them both, pulling at the corners of her collar, bringing them closer around her face. "Merry Christmas."

David nodded towards the doors. "I thought you'd moved out?"

"Yes, yes I have." She looked across at Kate. "I've just dropped the keys back with Sister Bates. I've been meaning to do it for a while now." There was the crack of a side gate as it swung back into its iron frame.

Kate tried to pull her hand away from David, but he clasped it tighter.

"Merry Christmas Kate."

"Merry Christmas." Her words felt mouthed rather than spoken, hardly making a sound.

"Come on." David gave Laura a quick nod and pulled Kate away and towards the nurses' home. "What?" He said, as he continued on and up the steps. "It's hardly the weather to stop for a chat."

Once in the shelter of the porch, he released her hand. "It's cold. You'd better get inside. I'll see you when you get back from your mum's." He leaned in and kissed her forcefully, pushing her lips hard against her teeth and holding her there. He dashed down the steps, head down, not looking back. The sky was as dark as ink, and the clouds above were low and white. They blew across the sky so fast that they seemed to follow him, like an army of phantoms above his head.

CHAPTER FOURTEEN

Kate looked up and down the neat row of houses as she stepped out of her uncle's car. Even though it was winter, nearly all of the gardens had been tidied up, and the soil turned over ready for spring planting. If she were to look in the cupboard of the back bedroom, she knew she would find Dahlia tubers wrapped in newspaper, waiting patiently for the months of June and July. Every year she was surprised by their unashamed boldness. The bright pinks, reds and yellows shining out like lollipops on sticks. But at the moment there were just the wallflowers and the shoots of tulips and snowdrops coming through. Kate smiled. Even in December there were signs of new life. How could such tender shoots survive the bitter frosts and snow that were sure to come?

"I'm off to meet George at the club." She turned to her uncle as he spoke. "Tell your mum and Aunt Mable we'll be back about three."

She nodded and turned back to the gate, feeling a sudden fondness for the house. No more than ten years old, it still felt fresh. A few of the other properties in the street had started to show some wear, with the paint on the window frames and the gates beginning to peel and flake slightly, but most still had a feeling of hope—of a future better than the past.

She swung lightly on one of the two metal poles that held up the short, flat porch, and stepped up to the door. The door was on the latch, and she could hear the scraping of dishes and the sound of a knife chopping against wood, as she placed her small suitcase down and wandered through to the kitchen. Aunt Mable was in the middle of a story about one of the families from St Mary's Church. Her mother hadn't attended since she had moved away, but her aunt still liked to keep her up to date with the comings and goings of all the parishioners.

All three women were busy basting the ham, chopping the sprouts and peeling the potatoes respectively. Condensation pooled on the metal window frames, as the pudding steamed in a pan below. The smooth lines of the fitted cupboards and Formica worktops were lost behind pans of uncooked vegetables, yesterday's half eaten turkey, and crumpled shopping bags.

"Hello Everyone. Happy Christmas."

Her mother, sister and aunt all lifted their heads form their tasks and put down their utensils. The room became full of the business of welcoming hugs and kisses.

"Hello love. Where's your uncle Harold?" Aunt Mable said, as she pulled back from her embrace. "Down the club no doubt?"

Kate nodded. "He said they'd be back about three."

"Kate will you take over from Janet. She needs to get changed," her mother said, giving her a brief hug and returning the ham to the oven.

"I don't know why I can't just stay like this." Kate looked at Janet. She wore a close-knit wool jumper and jeans, and it reminded her of the two girls on the train. Except, although Janet wore jeans and a jumper, just like one of them had, it was different. The ways that her clothes hung, and tucked, and fell, were all quite different.

"Get those off. I've just finished making you that dress. I've hung it in the hall. Now get along and put it on. No arguments," her mother said.

***

Uncle Harold leaned over the table to take the sprouts, holding his tie back with his other hand. "So Kate, how's everything going at the hospital? I hear you've moved up a little?" What will it be next? Matron?"

Kate smiled and passed the carrots along to her aunt "Not quite yet. I've only just qualified. The next step would be a Senior Staff Nurse."

"But you could be a Sister after that. That's the next step isn't it Kate?" Janet said as she took the dish of carrots from her aunt.

"Oh, I'm not sure if Kate's going to need to worry about such things. How is David? Is he at home with his family?" Her mother said, taking her seat at the far end of the table.

"Yes. He sends his love."

"He's a good lad that one."

Kate registered her mother's words and smile as she swallowed a mouthful of food. "There's a new registrar"

"Oh yes. Is he nice?" Her mother asked absently, opening out her napkin.

"She. Yes, she's very nice."

"A woman? Goodness." Her mother shook her head lightly.

"She's from America. Her parents are English." Kate watched her mother stand and reach for the stuffing.

"Harold, you've not had any stuffing."

"Which part of America?" Janet asked.

Kate turned and smiled, grateful for her interest. "California, but she worked in New York.'"

"California? New York? Why on earth would she want to be here?" Janet leaned back in her seat and tipped her head back. "Those words just feel like sunshine." She leaned forwards and placed her elbows on the table. "England's so grim."

"New York is freezing in winter," Aunt Mable said, wiping her mouth with the white cloth napkin.

"But I bet the cold is sharp and crisp. Not like here. It's so grey and dank." Janet pushed a sprout around her dinner plate, mixing it with the gravy. "And I bet the sun would dance off the Empire State Building—even in winter."

"Vera, you're going to have to stop giving this one so much pocket money," Uncle Harold said. "She's been to the pictures filling her head with all these fancy notions."

"How old is she?" Janet turned back to Kate.

"I'm not sure, probably in her late twenties."

"Isn't she married?" Aunt Mable asked.

"No." Kate looked down at her napkin as she said it, and then up into her aunt's curious eyes.

"Doesn't she have a boyfriend? A fiancé?"

"No."

Aunt Mable screwed up her mouth. "These women who press too hard. If they're not careful they just end up on their own. They forget how to be women. Men are put off by that—too pushy, too smart for their own good—like your friend Margaret."

"Maybe marriage isn't for everyone." Kate said, trying to sound casual.

"Only if you're not quite right," Aunt Mable said, tapping the side of her head.

Her mother jabbed her fork towards Kate. A small boiled potato, covered in parsley sauce, bobbed in front of her face. "I'm not having you end up like Evelyn." She thought of Sister Bates, and how she would be spending the holidays. Working probably.

"Don't you think that she's happy in her own way? Besides, she had a fiancée. She's not really to blame for her situation. There are lots of women like her, whose husbands and fiancés never came back."

Aunt Mable let out a small snort. "Strangest engagement I ever came across."

"Mable." Her mother spoke with a warning tone.

"Well come on Vera." She turned to Uncle Harold. "What did you make of James? That fella Evelyn was engaged to. You met him a few times."

Her uncle shrugged. "Bit of a fairy."

"Not in front of the children." Her mother spat the words quietly.

"Exactly!" Aunt Mable smiled triumphantly. "Weren't there some rumors about him and…now what was his name?"

"Billy Jameson." Harold said.

"Exactly, just rumors. I saw the ring. He was just sensitive. A quiet lad."

"I'm not saying they weren't engaged. I don't know." She shook her head. "It all just seemed not quite right somehow."

"Well, that's enough about that." Her mother turned to her sister. "Janet, tell Kate how well you've been doing at school."

"I won the Progress Prize."

"She's been given a Thesaurus."

"That's wonderful Janet. You'll have to show me after dinner," Kate said.

"Sarah Scott won the Year Prize. She says she wants to go to university to study Geography, but Liz says how's she going to manage that? Her father only works at the Co-operative."

"Maybe she could get a scholarship—if she's bright enough," Kate said, as she pushed her fork into the last piece of ham on her plate.

"Or maybe she needs to be a little less bright and have a little more sense," her aunt said, stabbing a brussel sprout and pushing it into her mouth.

They came through from the kitchen, their hands pink and clean from the washing and drying they had shared after dinner. Her stepfather and uncle Harold were fast asleep in the two armchairs.

"Come on Harold. Time to get moving." Aunt Mable stood over him and he jumped slightly at the sound of his name, looking around, as though he was slightly unsure where he was for a moment. Her aunt walked over to the mirror above the dresser and fixed her hair.

"That's a nice dress. Is it new?" Kate asked. Her aunt ran her hands down the sides of the colorful belted dress.

"Yes, it's from a pattern I bought the other day."

"I meant to say it looks nice on you," her mother said. "Doesn't it look nice George?"

Her stepfather looked up and stretched. "Yes—nice."

Her mother rolled her eyes. "Sorry Mable, that's about as good as it gets around here."

"Harold's just the same. I sometimes wonder why I bother."

Uncle Harold came forward in his chair and stood slowly. "Well, like I always say—women don't dress for men, they dress for other women."

"I thought my father said that," Kate said out loud, but to nobody but herself.

"What dear?" Her aunt asked, and her mother turned towards her.

"Nothing, sorry." She shook her head and spoke more quietly. "It was just something that I thought dad had said in our parlor a long time ago. It must have been uncle Harold."

Kate lifted her case onto the nearest twin bed and started to unpack the few items she had brought. She hung her coat on the back of the door, changed into her pajamas, and took her wash bag through to the bathroom. When she returned, Janet lay on top of the other bed, reading the back cover of the book Kate had brought with her. When Janet was younger, she would often come and ask to sleep in her room, waking in the night—afraid by a nightmare, or just the dark. Watching her, with her head propped up and her crossed leg swinging backwards and forwards, she didn't seem as though she could be scared of anything. These days, when she came to her bedroom, it was to talk of school, friendships, music, films, and more recently, boys.

As Kate pulled back the covers and climbed into bed, Janet put the book down on the bedside table between them.

"What you said earlier, that marriage wasn't for everyone." She turned to lie on her side, propping up her head with her hand. "Did you really mean it?"

"I don't know. No, probably not," Kate said.

"Well you certainly got a rise out of Aunt Mable. Her face was a picture." They both laughed. "So…do you think you will marry David?"

"I don't know."

"Really? But you've known him a while now. Do you love him? Are you in love with him?"

"I don't know. It's hard to know what love is."

"Well then. That's your answer isn't it? You can't marry someone if you're not certain you're in love with them."

"No. I don't suppose you can."

"You have to follow your heart."

Kate lay back on her pillow and smiled at the simplicity.

***

"Would you mind if I went back tomorrow?"

"Tomorrow? But I thought your leave was until Thursday?" Her mother looked up from the wool cardigan she was knitting.

"It was, it is…it's just that Sister Bates asked if I might be able to cover tomorrow's night shift. The timetable got a little messed about and its left them short."

"I see…well I suppose there's not much going on. Aunt Mary and Uncle Stan were going to pop across, but you can catch up with them another time." She put the cardigan down on the arm of the chair, resting the needles carefully on top. "Kate…is everything okay?"

"Oh, yes fine. Why do you ask?" She took a mouthful of tea.

"I don't know. You just don't seem yourself. You've hardly said two words about David. Is everything all right between the two of you?"

"I'm just not sure mum."

Her mother picked the knitting back up, shaking her head as she separated the two needles from the tangle of wool. "First Derek, then Kenneth, and now David. I don't know what you're hoping to find. He's a nice lad. You could do a lot worse."

"You're right. I probably could."

CHAPTER FIFTEEN

The carriage was almost empty. A young mother sat with a baby on her lap. A small boy sat next to her. Each time the train came to a stop his young face would look up hopefully at his mother and she would shake her head. "Not this one Bobby. We've still got a little way to go." Kate smiled at the little boy and then the mother. She looked above the young woman's head to the underground map. Three more stops, or seven. Seven if she followed through with her intentions; the ones she had had when she left her mother, slightly disgruntled, earlier that day. But now it seemed easier, much easier, to just step off at the Monument and go back to the nurses' home; to sit with the others in the day room and share their stories, read magazines and books. She had some new piano music—a present from Aunt Mable. She pictured her and Val picking out the notes. Val singing. In half an hour she could have that—as easy as that. But she knew she wouldn't. She would stay on the train.

She would like to have gone back, just to return her case and freshen up. But then she would risk the ordinariness of conversations about holidays and work schedules. She was afraid that she would stay, sitting on Val's bed, or in her own chair, or on the piano stool in the day room. Besides, how would she answer their questions about why she had come back early, and where she was going? No, it was best to continue on for the four extra stops.

The advertisements that ran along the curve of the top of the carriage were a good distraction. She glanced over the red-faced boy sucking on fruit gums, and a woman cradling a box of soap powder, but was caught by an image of a young couple, perhaps not long married. The woman held a handkerchief in one hand and in the other a burnt offering in a saucepan. The dinner was ruined, but her husband was trying to lighten the moment. The caption read "Don't worry darling, you didn't burn the beer." She shifted her gaze further along. There were images of women holding up soft drinks, packets of cigarettes, bottles of washing up liquid, then a man with a perfect short back and sides demonstrating the 'clean smart look' of that particular pomade. Next to that, almost out of view, a woman embraced a man. Her lips gently touched his cheek. The advert was for razor blades, and her hand rested tenderly on his freshly shaved cheek—a simple gold band on her wedding finger. Kate looked down at her hands resting in her lap and twisted the bare flesh on her own ring finger.

She got off the train and took the steps up into the chill December air, concentrating on the short icy blasts that bit the tip of her nose and prickled her cheeks. She continued straight ahead, not looking at the few pedestrians that shared the pavements.

The lights were on, tracing an orange glow around the curtains of each of the three separate windows. Setting her case down on the top step, she stared for a moment at the large black door. Her organs seemed to have travelled—her heart to her throat, and her stomach right down her feet, and as she pressed the bell, her skin rose up and prickled against her clothes. She waited. There was no response. Drawing her bottom lip through her teeth and biting down on the soft flesh, she pressed again, harder and longer this time, but still nothing. She took several steps backwards and lifted her head, searching for some sort of movement—a shadow or a lift of a curtain, but there was nothing. Stepping forward, she rang again, firmly but more briefly than the previous time.

She could come back tomorrow. But she knew that the likelihood of that happening was slipping away. She breathed out the cold air, feeling slighted by the large polished front door and it's unwillingness to let her in. The light from the windows showed no desire to share its warmth. Should she take a walk? But the case, although small, would soon become cumbersome, and there was nowhere nearby that she could think of to stop. The only place she had noticed open had been a pub on a corner, a few streets away. And if she were to return in half an hour, or even an hour, there would be no guarantee that the door would be answered. Laura had relatives in England and Scotland. Maybe she had gone to visit them. But then, the lights were on. Maybe she had company. She pictured Laura and her guest uncomfortably pausing their conversation each time the unexpected bell had rung, waiting for the uninvited guest to leave. She picked up her luggage and went carefully down the steps, sparkling with the beginnings of frost.

"Kate is that you?"

Laura hung out of the window. A white towel, twisted into a turban, sat slanted on her head as small mists of steam lifted from her shoulders and arms.

"Sorry, I've come at a bad time."

"Come on up." Laura pulled down the window frame and was gone.

There was a click, and with one last breath of icy air, she pushed the door and walked up the stairs. One hand rested on the rail while the other carried the small case. Laura leant over the bannister. She had put on a gown. The towel from her head sat round her shoulders, as she rubbed the ends of her hair.

Kate put down her case and looked up, one flight below.

"I thought you were still with your family."

Kate pushed her hands into her pockets. "I decided to come back a little early…Can I come up?"

"Sure, it's a nice surprise."

Laura looked at the case in Kate's hand as she reached the top of the stairs. "I came straight over." She felt awkward. "I hope you don't mind."

"Not at all," Laura said, taking the case from her. "I'll put the kettle on. Unless you fancy something a little stronger?"

"Tea would be lovely." She began to unbutton her coat, as Laura placed the case down and made her way into the kitchen.

"It was trying to snow earlier," she called back to Kate, who remained in the living room, removing her scarf and gloves. "Moira says heavy snow is forecast over the next few days."

Kate removed her hat and walked over to the mirror, tucking back her hair. Through the glass she noticed the slabs and dashes of blue. The airmail letters, all opened, lay across the sofa and over the coffee table. She walked over—the light airy handwriting filled the pages. She leaned closer. The writing was large and looped. It would be easy to read. One letter lay open, flattened out, as though it had been read many times—the fold of the paper no longer able to pull it back and close it.

"Are you hungry?" Kate turned at the sudden closeness of Laura's voice, as she stood in the kitchen doorway. "I think I've got some biscuits somewhere, but that's probably about it."

"Tea is just fine." Kate said.

"Really?" Laura went back into the kitchen, opening and closing each door. "I'm sure they're here somewhere," she said, feeling in the back of the final cupboard.

"Really, I'm not hungry. Laura...aren't you wondering why I'm here?" Kate leaned against the doorframe. Her words slowed Laura's pace, as she carefully placed the kettle on the hob and switched on the gas before turning round.

"Of course..." Her hands played with the tie of her robe. "I thought I might never see you again. I know you probably don't want to talk about it. You probably want to just forget, but..."

Kate pushed herself off the frame. "Actually, I think I do want to talk about the other night." Laura looked up. An uncertain smile formed on her lips. "You have the most wonderful smile."

"Really? I..."

Kate bit her lower lip and nodded, watching the reward of a red blush blossom across Laura's chest and neck. "You make me want to say things like that. Things I've never said to anybody–silly, foolish, heady things. That your eyes remind me of rain clouds, and your hair must be spun from gold." She moved forward and noticed the rise and fall of Laura's chest. "Nonsense really, but with you…" The petticoats of her dress rested lightly against Laura's legs. She had to stop herself from moving in further, and feel her slender thigh between her own. Instead, she reached behind Laura and turned off the hob. The Kettle gave a small hiss as the water inside cooled and settled.

She placed her hand on the tie of Laura's gown. "May I?"

"Of course." Laura lent back against the cooker, her hands resting either side.

It loosened easily, and the chord and gown fell to the side. There was a hitch in Laura breathing.

It wasn't like looking in a mirror at all. She was reminded of the statues at the British Museum; the ones her mother had quickly ushered her past, pushing her firmly from behind by the shoulders, past Apollo and the discus thrower. But it hadn't been those that had held her curiosity. It had been the women—Aphrodite and Venus, with their curved bellies and strong rounded thighs. It was those that she had wanted to study and absorb. But instead, she had turned shyly away, worried about appearing too inquisitive, of looking too long. It had been the same in the changing rooms at the town pool. Some of the girls changed freely, standing naked; their towels dropped to the side or between two hands, as they rubbed hard on their legs and arms. And she made sure that she looked absolutely anywhere else, drying herself carefully under her towel, and slipping her underwear back on as quickly as she had removed her damp red costume.

But now she looked. She couldn't take her eyes away, as she lifted an unsteady hand and felt Laura's skin give, with warmth, over the hardness of her collarbone. Her fingers moved lightly down, between her breasts, and along her stomach. Had she been breathing? She took in a deep breath, and looked where her hand rested on the small prominence of her pelvic bone.

"I don't know what to do now."

Laura cleared her throat and took her hand. "We don't have to do anything." She turned back towards the red pot. "Except have tea maybe." She smiled, her hands shaking slightly as she reached for the kettle. "I'm just really glad you're here."

Kate shook her head and tugged on Laura's hand, feeling like a small child, unable to articulate her need. Laura followed, although there was a slight pull from her—a small attempt to keep Kate there and to have the tea.

It felt a strange distance to travel, as though she were crossing a busy road that required all of her attention to get them to the bedroom safely. She hoped Laura would do something, would push her down or take her up in her arms, but instead she sat on the edge of the bed. Kate sat down beside her.

"Are you sure?"

"Quite sure." Kate said, as though she had been standing in front of a blackboard trying to solve a puzzle, rubbing it out and starting again over and over, and had finally found the answer.

There was that scent, under the fruits and the flowers of her shampoo and soap. Kate was conscious that she hadn't washed away the progress of her day; her mother's kitchen and the breakfast she had cooked; her uncle's car, as he lit a woodbine before dropping her at the station; the gritty tunnels of the underground. Was Laura aware of any of that as she pressed her lips to her neck and then her mouth? Each released button from the back of her dress pushed out a small breath from Kate, but Laura's fingers fumbled on the last few that were lower down and harder to reach. "I guess I'm a little nervous," Laura said quietly.

"Here, let me help." She stood and unfastened the final buttons, and the dress fell to the ground, settling like a puddle, with her at its center. She held Laura's gaze as she pushed off her shoes, bending down, collecting the dress and pumps and placing them on the chair, caught between the desire for order and disorder. She released each stocking, rolling one down and then the other, but the second one wouldn't come as easily. Balancing on one foot, she wobbled and reached out, grabbing for the chair. "I knew I wouldn't be any good at this," she said, standing up straight again and tossing the awkward stocking towards her dress.

"At what?"

"At this. At love making."

"Oh." Laura stood, and shrugged the gown from her shoulders, reaching for Kate and pulling her in. She tugged at each hook on her corset, letting it pop satisfactorily and then fall. The bed caught Kate, as she lay back against the soft covers. She felt the length of Laura. Her breasts, stomach and thighs pressed against her own. Then Laura shifted her weight, and her scent became a taste, a delicious taste; and a touch as well, of warm, smooth flesh. She just caught sight of Laura's face before tipping her head back. Sounds fell around her, moans and sighs, which were only just recognizable as her own.

"Can you stay?" Laura turned on her side and pushed her face into Kate's neck, kissing it slowly. A pale grey light had started to show through the curtains. Strangely, and without sleep, morning had almost arrived.

"Yes, I'm not expected back until tonight." Until then she would be like a surfacing dreamer, keeping her eyes closed to the waking hour. She would have to return to the nurses' home, but for the moment she could forget there was another world, quite separate from this, which she was inextricably a part of.

Laura propped her head up with her hand. "Let's go out tonight. I want to take you on a proper date. I want to show you off."

"But no one will know." Kate looked at Laura, surprised at her suggestion. "We can't tell anyone."

"I'll know." She kissed the end of Kate's chin. "When the waiter takes our order…I'll know." She kissed the tip of her nose. "And when they pour our wine…I'll know." She kissed her forehead. "And when I pay the cab driver his fare…I'll know."

Kate smiled, her lips almost touching Laura's. "Okay, but before that, for the rest of the day. Can we just stay here?" She kissed Laura briefly and then pulled away. "Have breakfast, light a fire, listen to records, watch Take your Pick…play yahtzee…" She kissed her again, but this time Laura pulled back.

"Yahtzee? I don't think I've got any dice. Cards—I've got cards. Will cards do?"

"Cards will be fine."

"And I don't think Take your Pick is on tonight, and my fires are all electric."

"I mean...just do normal things. As though this is just as it has been and always will be."

"Oh, I see." She smiled at Kate and pulled her in closer.

"Besides, we've already been on a date." Kate moved away slightly to see Laura's puzzled expression. "The pictures," she explained.

"Was that a date?"

"I didn't know it then, but yes. I do think it was a date. Our first date."

"And God, I turned up late for it."

Kate smiled and ran her fingers lightly along Laura's arm. "You know how you said that night you felt sure I would have gone? Well, I felt like I would have waited for you all night, forever. It's a kind of madness isn't it?"

"Yes." Laura lifted herself and lowered her weight down onto Kate. "Yes it is."

Hunger drove them to the kitchen eventually, where Laura made toast and tea. Kate sat at the breakfast bar in Laura's plaid pajamas.

"You look beautiful," she told Kate, as she sat the teapot down and reached across to kiss her, before sitting down on a stool. Kate picked up a slice of toast. She caught the melting butter with her tongue and then bit down, thinking toast had never tasted quite so good.

"Do your parents know?" Kate said.

"Know?"

"About your...lifestyle?"

"Kind of."

Kate raised her brows. "Kind of?"

"'Tell all the truth but tell it slant.'"

"What?"

"It's from a poem—Emily Dickinson."

Kate shook her head.

"I've told them in the only way they can accept. I've made it more palatable." Laura poured tea from the pot. First into Kate's cup and then into her own. "The career helps. A woman with a career, particularly a doctor, well she can almost be forgiven for not walking down the aisle at the first opportunity." She put the teapot down and looked at Kate. "I've told them that I won't ever marry. They don't like it, but they can live with it—their daughter, the doctor, too busy to find a husband. At least that's what they can tell their friends. I guess it's not quite as bad as some fading debutante, seemingly sitting on the shelf."

"So, you haven't told all the truth. A half truth really."

She smiled and kissed Kate softly on the lips. "'The truth must dazzle gradually...' Sorry, Emily Dickinson again. I'm a big fan."

She stood and left the kitchen. Kate listened to Laura's footsteps padding through into the living room, and then returning, with a book in her hand. She handed it to Kate.

"I hope over time I can tell them the whole truth, or at least they can come to know it. At the moment it's enough."

The book still had its dust cover, but only just, as it curled over on itself. The spine and the tops of the pages were yellowed, and there was a feint half ring from a tea or coffee cup; as though someone had gone to set down their cup, and suddenly realizing, picked it up—but too late—the damage had been done. She read the title "Bolts of Melody / New Poems of Emily Dickinson." She opened the book, leafing through the pages, catching a sentence here and there.

"Come on, let's find somewhere more comfortable." Laura said, picking up her cup. Kate sat down on the sofa and remembered the letters. They were gone. Laura must have tidied them away at some point. She looked around to see if they had been moved across to another surface—the dinning table or the dresser—but there was no sign of them.

"Those letters, the ones that were here on the sofa before..."

"You're wondering who they were from?"

"It's just that there were so many of them."

Laura sat up a little and looked into her teacup. "Something did happen in America that, lets say, encouraged me to come to London."

"And the letters have something to do with that?"

Laura nodded. "I was seeing someone…She was married."

"Were you in love with her?" Kate shifted slightly so she could see Laura better.

"I thought so…but now…I don't know."

"Everyone says that. It's funny, but out of all the emotions, love is the one we most want to change in retrospect. As though it could be such a deceitful thing."

"Okay then. Yes…at the time...yes I did love her."

"What happened?"

"Her husband found out." Laura looked away and placed her empty cup on the table. "End of story." And with that, it seemed Laura had closed the conversation. But there were all of those letters. How could it be the end? She thought to ask further. But did she want to spend this day talking of difficult things? This day should be kept light, not shaded by each other's pasts or futures. So she took a drink of tea and rested her head against Laura's shoulder.

The waiter pulled the cork and they smiled at each other as he poured the wine. Kate knew that she could have talked Laura out of the dinner date. All she would have had to do was call her to the couch or the bed, and there they would have remained. But there was something about stepping out into the world together that appealed to her as much as it did to Laura.

"Would you ever consider going back to study?" Laura said, taking a drink of the wine.

"No, it's too late now. Besides, I like nursing."

"Because if you did…I would help you in any way I could."

"Yes, I really suppose you would." She looked up as she felt Laura's knee press against her own under the table.

"When can you stay until?"

"My train is due in at eight o'clock."

"And if the train were delayed?"

Kate shook her head as she played with the salt pot in the center of the table. "I can't. I'm walking a very fine line with Sister Bates as it is. I have to be back before lights out."

Laura tilted her head slightly and reached for the salt pot, gently extricating it from her fingers. "So…it could be delayed a little?"

Kate smiled, looking at her empty hands resting on the tablecloth. "I seem to always be breaking the rules for you."

"You won't be breaking any rules. I'll make sure you're back before ten."

She shook her head. "I lied to my mother, and later I'll lie to my friends," she said, taking the pot back from Laura.

"Oh, those rules—moral rules. I'm sorry Kate."

"My choice," she said, firmly placing the salt pot down.

"Come on." Laura stood, collecting her things quickly together from the back of the chair.

"Where to?"

"Home of course, my place."

Kate stood and started to wrap her scarf around her neck. "But what about the food? The bill?"

"We'll pay on the way out."

The snow that Moira forecast had begun to fall and settle. Laura took Kate's hand, as they hurried along the street, their steps caught between haste and caution, as they slipped and held each other until they found a taxi.

They arrived slightly breathless from the flights of stairs. Their smiles were big and easy as they pushed the door shut and came together. This time Kate didn't think for a moment about each button she undid of her own, or the zip that she drew down Laura's back.

***

Laura lifted the suitcase and held it by her side.

"When will I see you again?"

Kate looked up from buttoning her coat "Probably in less than 12 hours," she said, checking her watch. "We're both at work tomorrow."

"That's not what I meant."

Kate smiled. "Of course."

"Maybe I could meet you after? Walk you home, if nothing else."

"Okay." She smiled, this time a little uneasily.

"Unless...maybe that's not such a good idea? A little too public?"

She shook her head. "No. I'll see you then. I'll look forward to it all day."

"Good," Laura said, handing her the small case.

Kate gave Laura one last kiss and a final glance, before she hurried quickly down the steps. She had left it to the very last moment to leave, and it would be tight getting back before the bell. The snow had stopped, but it lay thick outside. She was glad that she had pulled on her boots, as she tramped through the streets, lifting her legs high to pass over the snow. It was a perfect white blanket and the sky seemed caught between day and night—black and orange.

"Oh Kate, you're back. Was your train late in?"

"Yes." She threw her scarf onto Val's desk chair followed by her coat. "Snow on the tracks," she said, pushing off her boots and laying across the foot of the bed.

"What are you smiling at?" Peg sat forward in the armchair, putting her book to one side. "Has something happened? Has David proposed?"

Val looked up from her magazine. Kate shook her head. "Goodness Peg. It's not all about David. No, he hasn't proposed. I haven't even seen him yet."

"Well, you look like the cat that's got the cream," Peg said, sitting back in her chair.

Kate laid her head down, her face warm against the cool sheets. Val gave her a gentle shove with her foot. "You certainly look pleased with yourself."

"I just had a nice time. Much nicer than I expected."

"Lucky you," Peg said, as she stretched. "Uncle John did his usual trick of drinking too much and arguing with dad."

"Well, I hate to dampen your spirits, but Sister Bates wants you to go to her office first thing, before you go to the ward," Val said.

Kate rolled back over and sat up on the edge of the bed. "Any idea what it's about?"

"Not a clue, she asked me yesterday if I'd seen you at all, but I told her you weren't back until today. She came up again about half an hour ago and told me to pass on that message."

"Did she say anything else?"

"No. Is everything all right?"

"I hope so." She stood, picked up her case, and walked towards the door. "I'm rather tired. I think I'll unpack and go to bed."

"But what about your holidays?" Peg shouted out after her.

"I'll tell you tomorrow," she called back quietly, as she opened her door. "Goodnight."

Lifting the case onto her bed, she unfastened the two catches, flicking them back and lifting the lid. It surprised her to see the poetry book, cushioned in against her jumper. She picked it up and smiled, leafing lightly through its pages, and then placing it down on her bedside table. As she brushed her teeth, removed her make up, and undressed, she glanced across several times at the book. Finally, she picked it up, smoothing down the curled corners of its loose cover. She opened the drawer, moving the white box and all the other items that had found their way in there—a writing pen, some notelets, and a ball of string—to the front. She placed the book carefully behind them, and pushed it gently to the back.

CHAPTER SIXTEEN

Kate hadn't slept well, her thoughts skipping from Laura to Sister Bates and back again. She played over in her mind, like a favorite film, the time Laura and her had spent together, feeling anything from the light fluttering of wings in her stomach to the strong beating of her heart, like horses hooves hard against her breastbone. A mixture of excitement and fear, something she always seemed to feel where Laura was concerned. But then she thought of Sister Bates and her request to see her. The thought was there like a dog at her feet, gnawing constantly on a bone.

As she walked to the Sister's office she tried to cheer herself by the thought of seeing Laura later that day, but just as she approached the door, she stopped. Peg was on shift too, and would probably expect to walk back with her.

When David waited for her, Peg would usually make excuses to go on ahead or fall behind with a different group of nurses. But why would Peg do that with Laura? She could never imagine that the two of them might want to be alone. And would she think it strange that Laura had waited? Maybe not this time, Kate could come up with a reason this time; but the next time, and the time after that? And if Peg made other plans or got held back, and she could be alone with Laura, it still wouldn't be like walking back with David. No holding hands, and no kisses as they stood and said their goodbyes. Unless, perhaps they could find somewhere away from everyone, and she thought of how few places there were, and how very public life actually was.

She looked at the door and cleared her throat before quietly knocking on the large oak door. Its polished brass furnishings shone brightly against the dark wood. She listened carefully, but clearly heard the strong call from inside. "Come in."

"Nurse Ford, please take a seat." The Sister looked up briefly at Kate and then returned to her notes. She came further into the room, her steps too loud on the wooden floor. She sat and shifted on the high, overstuffed chair, eventually perching on its edge. A large expanse of parquet zigzagged between her and Sister Bates and she had a desire to pull the chair closer, but instead she sat and watched the top of the Sister's head bob gently as she continued to write.

"I don't believe you've introduced me or matron to your new beau." Still not looking up, she underscored something on the page in front of her.

"I'm sorry sister?" Kate leaned further forward. Although her words had been quite clear, she had no idea of their meaning.

Sister Bates lifted her head slightly and stopped writing. The pen nib rested on the full stop. She looked straight ahead, as if she weren't addressing Kate, but someone over her shoulder at the far corner of the room. It made Kate turn briefly to check that Matron hadn't quietly entered, but there was nobody there. "I would imagine you probably thought that we wouldn't approve. I must say I would find it very difficult to give my blessing," she said flatly, placing the pen down and sitting back in her chair. "Your mother rang."

"My mother?"

"Yes Katherine, your mother." She picked up the pen, replacing its lid. "She rang to check that you were all right. That you had got back safely. She was concerned that you weren't quite yourself. She thought that I might have known if something was the matter."

"I see." Kate watched the Sister's hands tightly twist the ink pen. She could feel her ears and her cheeks warm as the blood swam around her head.

"She also said that you had come home early. That you'd agreed with me to cover a shift." She put down the pen. "Is that right?"

"Yes, yes I did tell her that." Kate could hardly speak. Her words felt as dry as dust.

"And that was a lie, wasn't it?" Kate dipped her head. "Wasn't it?"

"Yes."

"So…you weren't with your family and you weren't at the hospital. And I know Dr. Richards was at work. Would you like to tell me where you were?"

Kate opened her mouth slowly but closed it again, swallowing back all the words that were too impossible to say. She sat and thought of where to start, what to say, but Sister Bates must have grown tired of waiting.

"Did you hear the Queen's Speech this Christmas?"

Uncertain with the change in conversation, Kate looked up and shook her head, slightly relieved that it was a question that she at least could answer. "No Sister, there was a patient I had to attend to—Mr. Gibson. He wasn't feeling so well…" Sister Bates looked at her blankly. Kate tried to recall the short recount Peg had given. "I…I believe she talked a lot about the Commonwealth, and read a passage from Pilgrim's Progress."

Sister Bates nodded slowly and leaned forward. "I'll tell you what she also spoke of, or warned of I should say…She warned of people who would have self interest set up in place of self restraint, of unthinking people who would have morality made meaningless, carelessly throwing away—I think she termed it—ageless ideals."

Any words stopped short of her tongue. Kate looked down at her hands resting in her lap, as Sister Bates continued on.

"I had hoped that you would have been able to show that self-restraint…you were always such a thoughtful girl Katherine, mindful of others. Yet here you are with your mother worrying about you, lying to her, lying to your friends; the start of so many deceits, which can only keep growing. You're lucky I didn't go to the police." She paused. "Katherine, please look at me when I am speaking to you."

Kate looked up and her stomach sank, pushed down by the weight of the Sister's stare.

"Is it all a little mundane for you, living your life like the rest of us?" Kate could hardly bare all the unanswerable questions. Sister Bates let out a long breath and lifted a small glass paperweight, tapping it slowly against the desk. "I've been watching the two of you—her in particular. There was always something that made me feel uneasy, but I couldn't quite put my finger on it. Then I started thinking back to the war, when the world was topsy-turvy and women were given far too much freedom. I joined the nursing core, but other women became machinists and land girls. A few took to those trousers and overalls a little too easily. She reminds me of them. For all her expensive skirts and dresses, she's got that same swagger, the same attitude. Please tell me if I'm wrong. If you weren't with her—with Dr. Harrison." She seemed to struggle with her name, forcing the words out, and then her voice softened. "I've always trusted you Katherine, and I'm happy to trust you now. I would like very much to be mistaken. Were you with her?"

Kate lowered her head, words nowhere to be found. As if her silent admission had released a spring, Sister Bates slammed her hand down. The glass weight slid from her fingers and bumped, rolled and dropped with a shattered smash to the ground.

"How dare you! You have more than most women would dare dream of. A secure future in a good vocation, and also the very real opportunity to marry well to a man who clearly loves you. Yet you want more. Do you think you are entitled to more Nurse Ford? You really are just like your father!"

"No! It's not like that, I—"

"I don't want to know what it's like!" Her breathing was short and heavy as she pushed her hands up against the desk and leaned forward. "What I do know is that these unnatural physical urges need to be controlled, and that it cannot and will not continue. You'll transfer across to The Royal Victoria. They're short staffed and struggling with all the falls from the recent snow and ice."

Kate had been staring at the shards of glass—tiny slivers and large colorful chunks—spread all around her chair and at her feet, but she lifted her head at the Sister's words.

"Matron had asked me to arrange for a few final year students to be moved across, but I've suggested you, and she's agreed. Also, I advise that the moment that poor young man proposes to you, and I have no doubt he will, you accept unreservedly. I've always thought what an excellent Sister you would make, but I think the sooner you marry the better. It seems I will have to be your self-restraint, your conscience as it were. I want you to understand that all of this is for your own good and future happiness."

"It's not like that. It's more than—"

"And if it is a matter of the heart... If she has crept into your heart Katherine, the heart is an unreliable, beating, unsettled thing. Don't look to it for happiness."

Kate lifted her head and felt the whole weight of Sister Bates' eyes resting on her, resting heavier than her words.

"And Dr. Harrison?"

"Dr. Harrison?"

"What will...will anything happen to her?"

"Unfortunately, I have very little say over the comings and goings of Dr. Harrison. I could put in a complaint—speak to Mr. Clarkson about the matter, but that would put you in a very difficult position. I will just have to hope that this is enough for her to keep any such behavior well outside the hospital walls in future. I'm therefore depending on your good sense." Kate nodded. "Unless..." Her voice softened. "Unless, you would like to put in a complaint? If you feel that you were in any way pressured or tricked into this?"

Finding her voice, Kate sat forward. "Oh no—I mean..." She sat back in the chair. "No Sister, there are no grounds for complaint."

"You may go now."

Kate stood and turned towards the door.

"Don't bother with your shift today. I've asked Nurse Jackson to cover for you. It gives you the whole day to pack and get yourself sorted."

"I'm going today?"

"I think it's best. Don't you?" She picked the pen back up and began again to write her notes. "I'll arrange for a porter to help you get your things across."

Kate stood for a moment and watched the top of Sister Bates' head, as it faintly followed the movement of the pen.

"My mother?"

"Don't worry. I've spared your mother any concern. She need never know."

CHAPTER SEVENTEEN

How would she be when she saw her? Should she act as before? Kate would probably want that. She wouldn't want to be compromised. But Laura wouldn't stop herself from watching out for her uniform, different from all the others, filled with her own particular gait and figure. She wouldn't be able to keep from turning her head, even in conversation with Mr. Clarkson or Sister, or lifting her eyes from the care of her patient. She would want the reward of her quiet, uncertain smile. Or maybe it would be bolder now, with shared thoughts and memories.

But also, in the back of her mind, there was another idea, which she tried to discard. That away from her, and with her friends, she might have changed her mind. Her certainty may have altered.

Everyone had already gathered around the first bed—Mr. Clarkson, Sister Bates, and the usual group of junior doctors and students. But their attention wasn't with Mr. Johnson, who sat up with his hands resting patiently in his lap. They had all turned to the clatter and noise further down the ward. The activity came from the nurses, still tidying away the last of the breakfasts. Peg hurried to remove an empty porridge bowl, but the spoon tipped and clattered to the ground. She quickly scooped it up and placed it on the trolley, while Nurse Jackson reached down with a cloth to lift the spilt grey mess from the floor.

Sister Bates bristled and turned back to the group. "I'm sorry Mr. Clarkson. We're running a little late."

Mr. Clarkson tried to give his usual congenial smile, watching the two as they disappeared with the trolley through the kitchen doors. "Well, lets make a start shall we?"

They began to discuss Mr. Johnson's fractured right hip. The kitchen door swung open and out came Nurse Jackson, walking up to the nurse's table and taking a seat. The second bed was empty, but the third contained Mr. Potts. An unfortunate fall from a ladder had led to two fractured heels. It was Peg's turn to come through the kitchen door, although she turned quickly into the sluice, moments later stepping out with a urine bottle, placing it on Mr. Johnson's table and then returning again to the sluice. They moved onto Mr. Awan—another fractured hip. Someone came in from the corridor, a flash of pale blue uniform, but it was a nurse Laura didn't recognize. The nurse leaned down to speak to Nurse Jackson, who nodded down the corridor, and then walked towards the sluice doors.

"Weren't we Dr. Harrison?"

"I'm sorry?"

"We were happy with the x-rays?"

She looked to check which patient lay in the bed. "Yes—and the blood results were fine too," she added, trying to establish with the others that her mind hadn't been elsewhere.

The next patient wasn't in his bed, but sat in the high backed chair next to it, already dressed, the arm under his coat supported by a sling. His suitcase sat beside him.

"Mr. Lynch is going home today." Sister Bates reported.

Out came Peg and the unfamiliar nurse. She caught Laura's stare and gave a brief smile.

"Dr. Harrison."

"Yes?" Laura said, turning her attention to Mr. Clarkson.

"Would you help Dr. Peter's with Mr. Scott's catheter? It's his first one."

"Of course. We can do it after."

She wasn't sure how, but they had arrived at the bottom of the ward.

Each patient seemed to represent the tick of a clock—a passing of time, with no sign of Kate. Could she have missed her? Could she have been in one of the outer rooms all this time? Perhaps washing bedpans, or stacking the linen trolley with clean towels and sheets? It seemed improbable. Was she sick? But she had seemed fine just hours ago, and Laura knew she would have to be very unwell to take the day off. There was a chance that Sister Bates might have sent her on an errand, but it was unlikely at this time of day, with so many jobs to do. And there was a general air of discord, an unsettled feel to the ward—from the dropped spoon, to the strange nurse in Kate's pale blue uniform, stopping and starting in such a nonplussed manner.

"That will be all today Sister. Are you coming Dr. Harrison?" Mr. Clarkson stood beside her.

"I won't be long, go on ahead. I'll catch you up." She watched as Peg went into the sluice, and then followed, reaching the door just as it closed. She began to push on the handle.

"Are you looking for something? Or someone?"

Laura turned. Sister Bates stood behind her. "No—Yes. I was looking for Nurse Ford."

"Nurse Ford isn't on duty today. Perhaps I can help?" Laura turned back into the ward, allowing the door to close behind her.

"I'm sure she told me she had a shift today."

"Yes, she did. But the plans have changed, as they sometimes do. She won't be working here for a while. What did you want? Unless it was of a personal nature, in which case the ward really is not the place."

"No, it was just about Mr. Andrews. I wanted his morphine increased."

"Please come to me Dr. Harrison if there are to be any changes to a patient's medication."

"Yes, yes of course." She looked around the ward. "If you'll excuse me Sister."

"What about the morphine? What did you want it changed to?" Sister Bates called after her.

"It's all right. I'll sort it out later," Laura said, as she walked up the ward, not caring if she had heard her or not.

"And Mr. Scott's catheter?"

The doors were already swinging behind her.

Just a few off duty nurses sat in the day room. Laura glanced in quickly as she passed by. She stopped when she noticed Val. "Have you seen Kate?"

"She's upstairs packing," Val said, looking up from her puzzle book.

"Packing?"

"Yes. There's a shortage over at the Royal Victoria, mainly on the orthopedic wards. All that snow and ice, I imagine. Kate's been asked to go across straight away. I'm going too, but not for a couple of days. Matron wants me to finish my shifts here first."

Laura hardly caught the last few sentences, as she hurried towards the stairs.

CHAPTER EIGHTEEN

Half packed cases and half empty walls. Kate sat on the bed, staring blankly at the mirror, which now stood on the floor, propped up by the fireplace. The rug sat next to it, half rolled up, as though it couldn't quite make up its mind if it was staying or going.

When she had arrived back at her room, she had thrown open the wardrobe doors, pulling out her dresses and coats. Some were thrown onto the bed, while others fell to the floor. She had dragged out the two suitcases from beneath her bed and hauled them up onto the mattress, flinging them open. She lifted the bedside lamp and tugged on the lace tablecloth beneath. It fell and slid along the floor, revealing a large trunk, which she pulled away from the wall.

She didn't fold, just pushed dresses and skirts, coats and scarves into the cavernous trunk. She picked up the framed photographs and threw them in. The books went in. Some landed closed, but others splayed open as though waiting to be picked up and read. She had pulled at the mirror, but the metal chain caught in the hook, so she twisted and tugged until the nail gave up the battle, leaving a small scattering of plaster on the mantelpiece. She knelt down and rolled the rug, but each time it sprang back in defiance, pushing against her will to pack it away. She rattled through her drawers and picked out a ball of string. She tried to break the yarn, pulling with her hands and teeth, but there was no give. Searching again, she pulled out every drawer, each giving up its home and falling to the floor. Then she remembered her apron pocket and looked down at the scissors peaking out. She grabbed them in readiness to cut, but the string had disappeared. It must have rolled away—a cruel game of hide and seek. Spinning around the room she looked, heat rising in her face and through her body. Hot tears rolled and fell, as she pulled on the clothes that lay on the bed, lifting and dropping each one until she gave it all up and lay down, grasping at her pillow, sheets and clothing. She had lain there until her body stilled and cooled, and she had gradually begun to feel the winter chill.

And so she sat on the edge of the bed and stared at the ball of string that sat alongside the rug, ready for its purpose, not knowing where she had put the scissors. Her body felt heavy and her cheeks tight from dried tears.

A rapid quiet knock came. She turned her head slightly towards the sound and then back. The knock came again. "Kate, are you there?" The door handle rattled. "Kate please let me in."

She stood and straightened her uniform, and walked slowly to the door, stepping over the books and clothes that had spilled from her trunk. The pattern of another knock was broken as she turned the handle and opened the door, just enough to see Laura on the other side.

"It's not a good time," Kate said. Laura stood in the hallway, no gloves or hat. Just like the day at the picture palace. Not even a coat this time.

"Not a good time?" She reached for Kate's hand that rested on the edge of the doorframe. Kate quickly pulled it away. "I saw Sister Bates. For God's sake Kate let me in." Kate stood aside and Laura pushed the door wider, sliding past her. "What happened?" She said, as she looked around the room.

"I'm packing," Kate said flatly, picking up a jumper from the bed. She began to fold it. "She knows."

"Sister Bates?" Laura turned to her. "Kate you don't have to go anywhere. She has no right."

Kate shook her head. "Nurses can be requested to transfer to other hospitals if there are shortages." She looked up at Laura. "It's not so unusual."

"Requested, yes, but not ordered." Laura tried to pull the jumper from her grasp. "You don't have to do this."

"She didn't order me to go," Kate said quietly.

"Do you have a choice?"

"No." She took the jumper back as Laura released her hold. "But that's different."

The chair was the only thing that stood where it should, as it should. Laura stepped slowly and carefully as she crossed the room and sat down. "Please tell me you're not going to marry David. He won't make you happy."

"Why not? He's a good man. He'll take good care of me…"

"You're choosing David…Kate, we can take good care of each other."

"How Laura? When I can't even begin to imagine an us? How on earth would that work?"

Laura leant forward in the chair. "Stop thinking Kate. Just for a moment. Don't you feel the way I feel?"

"They're just physical urges that can and should be controlled—unnatural, physical urges." Kate spoke quietly to her jumper as she placed it carefully in the suitcase.

"Physical urges?" Laura almost laughed. "Sounds like those words dropped straight out of Sister Bates' mouth."

"And those letters. What made you suddenly decide to read them after all that time? Will you even be here in six months time?"

"It was just craziness—a crazy moment. It was either open those letters or go up to Chippingfield and knock on your mother's front door."

"Does she want you back?"

Laura gave a small nod. "She says she'll leave her husband."

"If you go back to America?"

"She'll get a good settlement and she has her own money too. She'll be well enough off to live independently." Laura looked down at the floor.

"You talk about David not being good enough for me, but what about her? Don't you deserve better?"

She looked up. She looked straight at Kate.

"I can't Laura."

"At least she knows and accepts who she is."

"What? A bored privileged housewife who prefers women?"

Laura gave a small shrug. "Something like that. Six months of marriage and you'll be bored, stifled. You already are."

"I'm not like her. I wouldn't…I couldn't do that."

"I know Kate." She rubbed her face and breathed out heavily. "I know you'd take those vows very seriously, and that's why it's so important. You're special Kate. If not this…if not us…then at least wait for something or someone better than David. You deserve—"

"How do you know what I deserve? Maybe I don't want to be special or remarkable or any of those things." Her voice was fierce now. "Don't I deserve all the things David will give? Security, a nice home, family one day…" She dropped her head. "It's a kind of happiness."

"Kate—"

"There's nothing more to say."

"Nothing more to say?"

Pushing aside a red coat, Kate perched on the edge of the bed. "Rather, there's no point in saying any more. This is the way things are, and I'm not going to try and change that, and I'm asking you not to either. The world isn't made for this." She waved her hand between the two of them. "For us, at least not my world."

"Was that all this was for you? Just one day?" She pushed her hands along the arms of the chair, knocking a skirt and hanger onto the floor. "You knew. Didn't you? Really? All the time you knew that was all it'd probably be—a fuck, breakfast and dinner, another fuck. A lifetime in one day, unbelievable—"

"Is everything okay?" They both looked up. Val stood in the doorway.

"Yes, fine." Laura got up from the chair.

"Goodness, did someone die?"

"I was just saying goodbye."

"We're only going to the other side of the river, not the other side of the world." Val's words trailed off dully as she looked at them both.

Out of the books that lay across the floor, Laura bent down and picked one up. Kate couldn't see which one it was, but she knew. Laura closed its cover.

She felt awful, even worse than in sister's office. She wanted to say how sorry she was. How she would never have been so careless had she been in her right mind; that the book meant more to her than everything else in the room put together.

"You should take that," Kate said. "It's yours."

Laura looked at her and then at the trunk in the middle of the floor—a mess of belongings piled into it. She placed the book on top and brushed lightly past Val, who turned, her gaze following Laura down the corridor. Eventually, she turned back to Kate.

They looked at each other for a few moments, and then Val stood up straight. "If you need anything, I'll be in my room."

PART THREE

CHAPTER NINETEEN

The orthopedic ward at the Royal Victoria Infirmary was much more established than Dickens ward, which had only recently changed from general surgery. The long nightingale layout, with its dreary row of beds on either side, had been replaced with four separate six bedded bays. There was no nurses' table in any of them, but instead, in the wide corridor outside, there was a nurses' station. Close by was a small kitchen, and also a sluice with an autoclave. Further along, towards the end of the corridor, but before the secretaries' office and the doors to the stairwell, there was the sister's office, and also a day room for patients and their visitors. There was even a small staff room, although habit couldn't stop Kate from going to the dining hall for lunch and the dayroom at teatime. It all made for an altogether more pleasant working environment; something, she supposed, she could thank Sister Bates for.

The patient's were all in their beds as Kate walked down each side of the final bay, tidying their sheets and gently knocking any wayward wheels into alignment. Some of the men lay in plaster, their limbs poking out from under bed sheets. Most of them were elderly, with broken hips, wrists and arms from falls on the winter ice—long gone with the warmer spring air. There was the occasional younger gentleman. One who had drunk too much on New Years Eve and jumped over a wall just two foot on his side, but ten foot on the other; and another, a builder who had fallen from scaffolding. She stopped at his bed and tucked the corners of his blanket back into place.

"Hello nurse. Docs coming round?"

Kate smiled and nodded as she tucked the sheets in tightly around him.

Sister Potts step out of her windowed office, an indication that the doctors must have arrived. The sight of their heads, bobbing down the corridor, confirmed this. One stood high above the others—Mr. Garcia. His head, as brown as a nut, was topped with a thick sweep of dark hair. Before she could turn, his eyes caught hers and he gave her an undisguised smile that caused the Sister to look and then look again at Kate. But instead of an admonishment, Sister Potts gave a small smile and turned to Kate.

"Nurse Ford, can you take your break a little earlier today?" She looked down at her fob watch. "Eleven o'clock should do it."

The dayroom's large metal framed windows let the sun pour in and Kate put down the Nursing Times and closed her eyes, enjoying the warmth without the cool April breeze that lifted the branches outside. Val and a few other nurses sat around the coffee table with her. She half listened to their chat as they tried to complete a crossword.

"Strong in quality," Nurse Hadley read out.

"How many letters?" It was Val's voice this time.

"Seven, begins with an 'I'."

Kate was about to suggest 'intense', when Nurse Hadley spoke again. Although, this time her tone was teasing. "Someone to see you Kate."

She opened one eye and looked at the nurse who had removed her shoes and rested her feet on the coffee table. The paper with the crossword sat in her lap. She gestured towards the doorway.

Standing just inside the dayroom was Mr. Garcia. He waved across as she stood and straightened her uniform.

"Brahms Piano Quartet as promised. Although this one is for you to keep," he said, as Kate approached.

"Mr. Garcia." She took the record from his outstretched hands. "That's very generous, but I can't keep it. I'll return it to you on Saturday."

"You can come?"

"Yes, I'll meet you outside the library at six."

"Marvelous. Saturday then." His smile widened, as he nodded at her and then the group of curious nurses behind.

"Thank you again for the record," she said, as he turned to leave.

"When are you going to put that poor man out of his misery?"

"What do you mean?" Kate said, lifting the Nursing Times from the chair and sitting back down again.

Nurse Hadley put her pencil down and looked at her, wide eyed. "Oh come on Nurse Ford, you know he's absolutely mad for you."

Val leaned forward and took the record from Kate's hands, studying its cover. "She's not long been out of a relationship. She doesn't want to be rushing straight back into one. Do you Kate?"

"Well in that case, stop leading him on and give us other girls a chance."

"Oh sure." Another of the nurses piped up from across the coffee table. "I can just imagine you at all those poetry readings and piano recitals." She turned to Kate. "I don't know how you can stand it. I know he's a catch, but doesn't it bore you to tears?"

"I like it." Kate said, blowing lightly across the top of her teacup.

She had been surprised and flattered when Andreas had remembered her. He had come across when he had finished his rounds and asked her if he was right. Had she been at one of his talks? He knew her face but couldn't quite place her.

After that he would often stay back to ask her opinion, or show her something. It started with X-rays and medical notes, but over the weeks, once he knew that she played the piano, he brought her sheets of music and lent her records. He asked her several times if she would like to go for a coffee or attend a recital, or go to the pictures with him. She declined each time, always finding a reason not to. Sometimes it was the truth that she was working or that she had already made plans, but other times she would make up an excuse. Each time he would smile and say okay, perhaps another time. And it was the way he said it so patiently, that one day made her accept his invitation. At least, that was what she had told herself.

It was to be held at one of the libraries. An evening of readings from a new edition of the poems and letters by Emily Dickinson, he had told her. Would she like to come? He would so very much like her to come. And she had found herself quietly repeating those words. "Tell the truth but tell it slant."

"You know her!" He said, delighted. "I discovered her on a sabbatical in America. How did you come across her?"

"Just a friend."

But she had declined.

It was only later, back in her room that she thought of the possibility of Laura going. She picked up a book and began to read, but put it back down—still on the same page. It wouldn't be as though she were altering the course of things. A thought in the back of her mind wasn't an active move to change anything. Even Sister Bates, God or the Queen couldn't judge her on that. To what end? She didn't know. A cruel pleasure perhaps—a feeling, any feeling; something to dislodge the stone that sat inside her—bigger than a stone—a boulder, that filled her right to her palate; to shift it and feel her heart beat and pulse again.

She thought of Mr. Garcia. He must have asked her half a dozen times to accompany him to one event or another. She should go with him. He was kind and intelligent, a gentleman. He would be good company too, and she was sure she would enjoy the evening.

But Laura hadn't been there.

She had looked around the hall, nervously at first, her eyes darting, afraid to rest them on any single person. But as she began to understand that Laura wasn't anywhere in the audience, and really how silly to think that she would be, she started to relax into her seat and finally pay proper attention to Andreas.

And the more the evening went on, the more attention she paid him. As though he had been a covered statue, suddenly unveiled. She looked at his eyes as he spoke to her, the small creases at the sides, and noticed that they were brown, a deep brown—almost black. His hair was dark and thick, but flecks of grey rested at his temples, and his smile was kind.

At the end, he had bought two copies, one for him and the other for her. She held it in her hands and thanked him, telling him he shouldn't have, that it was too generous. She lifted the book and smelt its newness. Its cover crisp, and its pages impossibly white.

Later that night, she placed it on the small shelf that held a few other books—poetry, some novels, and a bible she had received at Sunday school. Laura's book didn't rest there.

When she had first unpacked, she could hardly bear to look at the brown and blue dust cover, and had quickly shut it away in the bedside cupboard. But every time she opened the door she got such a shock, as though it had been Laura's own body lying in there, or at least part of her—her severed head on a plate, or a hand. She didn't know what to do with it. To get rid of it was impossible. So eventually she tucked it under her mattress, and when she turned at night she could sometimes feel it beneath her. Although out of sight, just like Laura, it pressed on her, a continual reminder that it was there. Strangely, it also seemed to provide some comfort; like secretly burying a body, with only a slight raise in the ground to indicate it existed. When Val lay on her bed, she often thought that she might feel it, and reach under and discover it, and ask her what it all meant. She wondered if it would be a relief to tell her, waiting to hear her judgment.

But the book couldn't stay there forever. She wouldn't be in this nurses' home forever. Things move on. One way or another the present becomes the past. Perhaps, eventually, over the years, she would be able to place it on the bookshelves of a house not even yet imagined. Perhaps one day she would hear those lines again 'The truth must dazzle gradually,' but read by another, her children maybe, or a friend, a neighbor, her husband. Somebody would pull the book casually away from all the others. And she would stop in the middle of what she was doing—laying the table, pouring the tea, washing the dishes—and the ordinary day would turn itself upside down. Or maybe she would pack it carefully away and put it in a dark cupboard or loft. Although, rather like a child with a soft toy, she couldn't imagine it not having a life like quality and struggled with the idea of it shut away and uncared for. But who knew what sort of person she might become? It might be found many years later by nieces, or grandchildren when clearing her home. The book and its coffee stained cover thrown away. Not even good enough to be passed on or given to a charity shop, just a book.

She had continued to accept the invites to recitals and readings, and sometimes to the pictures. At the end of every evening, Andreas would nod and tip his hat before he said goodbye, but after a time he started to briefly kiss her on the cheek. Each time, the kiss became a little longer and the hold a little tighter, but he would always then tip his hat and say goodnight.

She still enjoyed the records Val and the others would play in the evenings; Pat Boone, the Searchers, Doris Day. All singing of love, new love, old love, hearts broken, hearts mended, hearts reborn. She understood every lyric, and knew how all of that felt. But the music Andreas invited her to hear carried her further. When she sat in those music halls and libraries with the soft murmurings of individuals, as they took their seats and waited, she felt comforted. Then the music would start, and when it began in a minor key, she thought, I have lived this note. Sometimes she would think of her father, occasionally her mother, but mostly she would think of Laura.

Kate blew again on her tea. "We're just friends. He knows I'm not interested in anything else at the moment."

Nurse Hadley stopped tapping the top of the pencil against her teeth and pointed it at Kate. "Ah, at the moment. That's what he'll be hanging onto."

"Does he mention his wife at all?" The nurse sitting across from her had returned to her magazine, but looked up to ask the question.

"Occasionally." Kate pictured a woman, although she had never seen a photograph, split by a bullet of cancer—pancreatic cancer—that had splintered so quickly to her lymph nodes, lungs and bones.

CHAPTER TWENTY

They walked carefully back up from the sea. Both wore Capri pants rolled up to just below the knees. Their steps were a little shaky as they repositioned their weight, walking mainly on the balls of their feet to minimize the discomfort of the large, uneven pebbles. They fell with relief into the two deck chairs.

"I went on a date the other night."

"You did?"

"I did." Sarah reached across and jabbed Laura in the arm. "Well you can't expect me to wait around for you forever." As always with Sarah—half joke, half serious.

"And how did it go?"

"Not bad really. She's an artist. We seem to have quite a lot in common."

Laura leaned forward and looked down at her feet, almost translucent from the salt water. "I don't know what to do. Some days I feel I should go back to America, and then others... "

"Surely you wouldn't want to leave all this for dreary California?" Sarah held her hands out towards Brighton pier. The clouds had started to accumulate in the last hour or so, but the sky was still predominantly a cool spring blue. Sarah had been joking, but there was something about the muted English sunshine and the slightly chilly air that suited Laura's mood.

America. She thought of Gwen's letters. The first had mainly been full of relief at discovering where she was, and asking could she please write back? Even if it was just to let her know how she was and that she had arrived safely. The second asked her again to let her know that she was all right—to confirm she was safe. And regret, this letter also spoke of her regret, and how much she missed her. The third asked her to come back—expressing her love. She wrote that that they could work out a way, some way, to be together. The next was pleading, the following one angry, and then there was the one full of madness, where she wrote about flying over to London to find her and bring her back. The final one said that this would be the last letter, but assured her that this would not mean that she did not think of her every hour of every day, or that she would not be waiting for her if she ever did choose to return. What a thing to do, she wrote, to keep you waiting in California—my biggest mistake.

That night, after she had read them all, she had left them lying on and around the sofa and had gone to have a bath. The buzzer had knocked her out of her thoughts. Not about the letters, but about Kate, and what, if anything, she could do. She had hoped that the letters would take her mind from those sorts of ideas.

It was still the same. Her thoughts always came round eventually to Kate. And there it was, that sudden acute pain, over riding the dull ache. Rather like a tender tooth, which could be exacerbated if she chose to poke at it with any notion or memory of her—Oxford, the dance hall, the night at the pictures, or, such as this moment, the night she rang at her door.

Maybe only a wrench, like a flight to America, could remove the feeling. Could she start afresh back in America? Or would she, depressingly, find herself standing on Gwen's doorstep when John's car was gone from the driveway? Sitting in this deckchair thousands of miles away, she had no intention of reigniting any such relationship. But could she trust herself? Did she know herself well enough to be certain not to? Gwen and Kate. How different. Rather like sitting too long in a smoky luncheon club and then, eventually, stepping out into the fresh air.

Laura pulled her coat more tightly around herself. She looked at her watch. It had just turned five o'clock. The sun would probably be around for a few more hours, but its warmth had already gone.

"Come on, let's get some dinner."

Laura noticed her as soon as she stepped into the small café, and turned quickly back to the door, her fingers pulling on the handle. But Sarah was already making her way to a table, and the bell above the door had told everyone of their arrival. So she smiled and waved across, trying not to show any of the reluctance she felt. She made her way to the little corner table where Val sat with Johnny.

"Hi Laura, small world." Laura had always liked Val, and she seemed genuinely happy to see her. "Are you here just for the day?" She was relieved that there was little sign of the awkwardness sometimes felt when two people had spent time together but had then drifted into two separate worlds.

"I'm just here with a friend." She turned towards the table a dozen feet away. "Sarah." The two women exchanged brief nods and smiles. "We caught the train this morning. We're just going to have a bite to eat and then head back to the station. How about you two?"

"Johnny played here last night. I came down this morning to join him for the day. We're heading back later too. It's been glorious weather."

Johnny smiled, moving the cutlery about in front of him. His pompadour haircut and red and black lumberjack shirt made him look every bit the part of a player in a skiffle band.

"Your band must be really taking off, that's great." Laura said.

"We're not doing bad thanks. Things are definitely picking up." Val smiled at Johnny and reached for his hand across the table.

"How's Peg? Did she ever see George again?" Laura asked.

"Oh, she's fine—same old Peg. She saw him a couple of times, but you know…we don't see quite so much of her now, since the move."

"And Kate." She paused. "How's Kate?"

"Okay, I suppose. She's just started seeing a doctor over at the hospital. He seems nice. You heard about David? That they split up?"

"Yes, I heard something…" The waitress pushed lightly past Laura and put a plate of sandwiches and a pot of tea down in front of the couple. A simple question, like a penny dropped into a slot machine had cascaded a hundred more, none of which she felt ready to hear the answers to. But the biggest question, whether she had moved on, had been answered. She wished she could be happy, at least happy for her, like Moira had told her she should, that it was better for Kate this way. Not as she did, as if the weight of a thousand pennies sat inside her. "Well, I'll leave you in peace to eat. It really was great to see you both again."

Val smiled up at her as she stirred the pot. "We must all try to get together some time. You should come and hear Johnny play. He's playing at a few places in town."

Sarah looked up as she walked slowly over to the table. "Do you know them?"

Laura nodded as she sat down. "They're friends…friends of Kate."

"Oh. I see."

"So what do you fancy?" Laura said, as she picked up the menu and studied each line—scampi and chips / steak pie and chips / egg and chips… She continued down the list, trying to concentrate on the different dishes. Glancing over the top of the card, she saw Val watching her.

As they ate, Sarah talked about the play she was writing—she would show it to her once she had finished the first draft. There was the new exhibition at the Tate—she wouldn't recommend it. Oh, and Fellini's new film—did she want to go to it? There was little requirement from Laura to participate with anything more than a nod or at the most a "yes" or "no" or "really?" So she remained distracted, snatching brief glances at Val, where she would often catch her studying the two of them and then averting her eyes quickly back to Johnny, or her sandwich, or her cup of tea.

"Aren't you going to eat the rest of that?" Sarah pointed to the plate in front of Laura. The ham was cold and hardly touched.

"No, I'm not as hungry as I thought."

"So I guess you won't be wanting cake?"

She smiled and shook her head.

"I'll go and pay then."

Laura looked down at her watch. There was still plenty of time to walk via the promenade to the station.

"We miss you, you know." A pair of soft pink hands held tightly onto a white clutch bag. The lightness in Val's manner was gone, as she stood by the table. Johnny waited outside the café, lighting a cigarette. "We all miss you…me, Peg…and Kate of course…especially Kate."

Laura looked up at her properly. "Did she say?"

"No…of course not." She shook her head. "She wouldn't." Val looked outside the window at Johnny and then turned back. Her mouth opened to begin again, but instead she smiled, as Sarah returned to the table. "I meant what I said—about coming to see Johnny play."

Laura nodded. "Thank you."

They travelled back on the train in silence. Sarah had given up trying to make conversation and had pulled out her book, while Laura fixed her eyes outside the carriage, through the glass, paying little attention to the passing fields and buildings.

At first, it had seemed impossible that she wouldn't see Kate again. Every time the intercom had sounded, it rang through her bones, as though the buzzer sat inside her, not across the room, next to the door. And she pictured Kate, usually holding that suitcase, waiting for her to open the door and let her in. Even when she was expecting someone, she still felt a rush, which would instantly drain to nothing when she heard Moira or some other voice coming up the stairwell. After a few weeks she took to just buzzing people straight in, pacing the floor and willing Kate to be on the other side, waiting for the knock. That stopped when she had opened the door to David, looking pale, his usually neatly oiled hair a frustrated mess on his head. He didn't look apologetic about turning up at her door, just slightly desperate. Laura pulled the door wider and he stepped inside.

They stood a little while in silence, and Laura wondered whether she should speak, unsure of what to say.

"Have you seen Kate?" He said finally.

She shook her head. "No."

His face was blank.

"I'm sorry David. I've not seen her since she moved."

"But you were the last one to see her, at your party. And you were spending all that time together. She must have said something—about me—or someone else. God, is there someone else?"

"I'm sorry…I'm sorry I can't give you any answers."

He raked his hands through his hair and down his face to the back of his neck, where he pulled distractedly with his fingers. "If you see her, will you tell her I need to talk with her? Will you try and make her see some sense?"

Laura looked at him. "I don't think I'll be seeing her David."

"But if you do…"

Reaching for the handle of the door, she had given a small nod and then slowly opened it.

Laura wondered how he was. She had seen him a few times since in the hospital corridors, but he had just walked past her, as though she were a stranger.

***

"I saw Laura today." Val said it casually, as she flicked over to the next page of her magazine.

The silence hung between the bed where Kate lay and Val's desk chair, as she registered the words. She looked at Val and then returned to her book. "You did?" She tried to keep her voice steady.

Val put down the magazine and seemed to study her, as she leaned over the back of the chair, her chin resting on her hand. "Yes, down in Brighton. We had a brief chat, but she was with a girl. Not the one from the dance hall, someone else. She did tell me her name." Val paused for a moment trying to remember. "Susan? No that's not it, but I think it began with an S."

"Sarah." Kate offered quietly, the word cracked into the air, her mouth dry.

"Yes, that's it, Sarah."

Kate pushed her book to the side. Wrapping her arms around her legs, she hugged them up to her chest, pulling them tight against her.

Val looked at her thoughtfully. She opened her mouth and took an audible breath, as though about to speak again, but instead looked down as if to study her shoes. Kate held back her desire to ask questions, wanting to pull out every detail of their brief meeting. How did she seem? Did she seem happy? What did they talk about? Did they talk about her? Did she ask about her?

Val broke the silence. "I think they're just friends you know."

"Just friends?" They both looked at each other directly.

"You know…I don't think they're a couple."

"A couple?" Kate parroted, wondering at Val's meaning.

Val lowered her eyes. "Lovers, Kate," she said quietly. "I don't think they're lovers."

Kate quickly picked up her book, trying to hide her face, because she could feel unexpected tears surfacing. She tried to blink them away, but they just quietly toppled and traced a path down her cheeks and along her jaw. She heard Val stand, but she didn't dare look up. The mattress gave slightly at her feet, as Val sat at the end of her bed.

"How long have we known each other Kate?"

"All our lives," she said, placing the book down and wiping her hands across her damp throat.

"Do you remember that day trip to Margate? How old would we have been? Thirteen? The sky was so blue. We had ice cream with devil's blood, waded out into the sea…played on the penny arcades. I think we declared it the best day we'd ever had."

Kate gave an unsteady smile and nodded.

"And do you remember when your dad came back on leave? Surprised you and your mum. We were playing in the street and down he marched. You could hardly believe your eyes. God, how you worshipped him, how thrilled you were to see him… And what about when you finished your exams? You were so pleased with your achievement; you couldn't keep from smiling for the rest of the day. We've shared so many wonderful times, but do you know when I've seen you happiest?" Val pulled herself up the bed and propped herself up alongside Kate. "When you were with her, when you talked about her. Peg thought it was just a bit of a crush, but somehow…I don't know…I saw the way you were with David and I saw the way you were with her…"

Kate swallowed. "You knew?"

"Like Peg, I kept on telling myself it was just a bit of a crush. To be honest I was a little jealous, thinking I might be losing my best friend. But as time went on I noticed that the way you looked at her—spoke to her —wasn't the same as the way you would speak to me or Peg, or any of the other girls. And then I heard the two of you that day, the day you were leaving. Afterwards, I didn't know how to talk to you about it. I suppose I thought if I didn't mention it, it would go away, it wouldn't be real somehow. We could just go on as before."

"None of it was real. It wasn't reality. This hospital, my family, Sister Bates, they're reality. They're real life."

"Maybe it was just a different kind of reality."

"What? Running from everything? Lying to my family? My friends? You?"

"But you're still lying Kate, not just to everyone else but to yourself too."

Kate leaned her head back against the wooden bedpost and looked up at the ceiling. "And what would the future be for the two of us? A couple of old maids…eccentric dears left on the shelf. How would we live?"

They sat in silence for a few moments. Kate looked down and picked at a loose thread of cotton on the blanket's hem. Val cleared her throat.

"Johnny's brother…He's a…a homosexual." She said the word as though it was from a foreign language and she was unsure whether she was pronouncing it correctly. "Johnny doesn't really talk about it. Peter, he's an artist. I've been to his studio a few times, and we've been to a few gallery openings with him. A while back he had a party. I'd thought Laura's friend, Moira, looked familiar. I couldn't place her at the time, but then I remembered that was where I'd seen her, at Peter's party. I think that girl I met today, Sarah, was maybe there too." She bit her lower lip. "I've been rather selfish, wanting the old Kate back, when maybe that's not possible…and not really what you want." Val reached for her hand and squeezed it. "I do want you to be happy." She sat up a little straighter and looked at Kate. "You don't have to live in, now you're qualified. We could get a flat together. In fact I would have suggested it a while ago, but you were with David and, well I thought…"

"What about Johnny? Won't you marry him?"

"Oh yes, but we're in no hurry. There's plenty of time for that. He's busy with his band. It would be fun, more freedom."

Kate blew out a breath and rubbed her face. "It just feels as though whatever I do there will be such a price to pay."

"But your starting point should be happiness. What happens after that who knows? Do any of us know? Look at Peg, desperate to find happiness with someone, to find someone to love and who will love her back. And there you have it all. It just doesn't seem fair Kate."

"Maybe life isn't about fairness. And fair to whom?" She smiled slightly. "I sound like my mother."

CHAPTER TWENTY-ONE

Standing in the corridor, Laura took a breath and was about to knock when the door opened. She was surprised to see Sister Bates out of her uniform and in a twin set and pencil skirt, a light winter coat across her arm.

The Sister remained in front of the doorway. "I was just on my way out. I have an appointment."

"It won't take long." She side stepped Sister Bates and stood squarely in the middle of the room.

"Can't it wait? I'm meeting a friend for dinner."

Laura removed the sunglasses from the top of her head and swung them loosely in her hand. "I don't think I've ever seen you out of uniform. It's funny how the eye can defy the mind. Looking at you at this moment, I find you…" She held up the sunglasses, tapping them against her chin. "almost human, and no, this can't wait."

Sister Bates dropped her mouth, but then quickly regained her composure. She inhaled sharply and stood up straight. "Well then, you'd better take a seat."

"No thank you. I think I'd rather stand."

Letting out a heavy breath, the Sister placed her coat over the back of the armchair. Laura looked around the room, continuing the gentle swing of her glasses, and then turned to the Sister. "Why did you send Kate away?"

"You know why. There was a shortage of nurses. It's quite usual."

"We both know that's not the real reason."

"Well, if we both know, then is there really any need for further discussion?" Sister Bates said, folding her arms.

Laura nodded her head slowly. "I want *you* to tell me."

"Don't you think there are some things that are best left alone?"

"Do you know what I find strange?" Laura asked, perching on the arm of the high back chair. Sister Bates tilted her head. "I find it strange that you had any idea." Laura unfastened the top button of her coat and loosened the collar. "I mean...I know your relationship with Kate is perhaps closer than the other nurses under your charge, but you must be so busy. You must have really troubled yourself to know so much of her comings and goings."

"I'm the home sister. If I didn't know, I wouldn't be doing my job properly." She started to sound impatient. "I really don't follow your meaning, and you are making me late."

"What I mean is." Laura stood and came closer to her. "For most people it'd be the last conclusion they'd come to. Two women together, and particularly Kate, with David, almost engaged.'

"I'm not quite sure I'm following your meaning."

"What I mean, Sister Bates, is perhaps it takes one to know one. Maybe there was something in Kate that you see in yourself, or rather saw in yourself, when you were her age?" Laura slouched down into the high backed chair. "Isn't it all just a little bit too convenient? It's an easy cover. Dedicate your life to this vocation, and you can pretty much come and go as you please. No man in your life? Why, no one will ask any questions. I mean, who is this friend that you're meeting for lunch? That you're in such a hurry to get to?"

"Are you suggesting that there is anything untoward going on?"

Laura looked at her and then slowly shook her head. "No, I imagine not. You would probably never cross that line. Except perhaps in your head. Although, I'm not sure you would even allow that—"

"I was doing what was best for her."

"She's a grown woman. Don't you think she should be allowed to make those decisions for herself?"

"While she is a nurse under my direction, living in my home—no, she does not get to make those choices. And really, you talk as though there was a choice. What kind of life could the two of you have together? No life, that's what. I don't want that for Kate. She deserves to be happy. She deserves that."

"And you think you know what will make her happy? How can anyone understand another's happiness?" Laura said, as she stood. "Look, all I'm asking is for you to let her be. She's not under your direction anymore. She's in another hospital. Just let her get on with her life."

"Are you finished?" The Sister reached for the door, holding it open.

"Just one more question." Laura pushed her sunglasses back on top of her head. "Are you happy Evelyn?"

CHAPTER TWENTY-TWO

The light over the main entrance briefly illuminated each nurse before they descended the steps. Most turned right towards the nurses' home, although a few walked towards the gates, passing Laura as they left the hospital grounds. At first it had been hard to keep track, with so many coming and going. She worried she might miss her, but the numbers gradually diminished to a slower trickle, and then just single drops of one nurse here and there. She looked at her watch and wondered if the student nurse had been right about Kate's shifts.

Laura had been slightly surprised when she found herself standing outside her door, but she also knew that the surprise was a poor lie. Truthfully, she had always been arriving on an incoming tide, moving forwards and then receding, but only really heading in one inevitable direction. A nurse came out from the next room. Kate was at work, and wouldn't be back until at least half past eight. It had only just turned five o'clock. Three and a half hours. She hadn't seen Kate for nearly four months, but three and a half hours seemed such an inordinately long time. She feared that something could come between the two of them in that space of time and that she needed to tell her straight away. Besides, three and a half hours seemed such an odd length of time, too long to wait outside her door. She could have gone back home for a while or bought a ticket for a double bill, or perhaps have gone up to Oxford Street and done some window-shopping. Moira would probably have been at home, and she had thought to maybe find a telephone box, ring her on that telephone she had just had installed, and ask to meet her somewhere.

But she took it for what it was, a waiting game, and bought a coffee from a small café, just outside the hospital. A clock hung above the serving counter, its red second hand ticking slowly round. A young girl moved about underneath it, pulling out scones and buttering teacakes, pouring steaming water into steel teapots and flipping their lids down. Laura tried not to look at the clock or her watch. Only once the coffee had all gone, did she allow herself to look. It had only just turned six o'clock. So she went and bought a magazine and a packet of cigarettes, although she rarely smoked, usually only stealing the odd one from Moira or sometimes at parties.

Once outside the shop, she lit a cigarette and looked at the small cards in the window. They informed her of second hand bicycles and lawnmowers for sale, rooms for rent, and a few local church meetings. After glancing over them, she read each one individually, noting the price of every item and the dates and times of each meeting.

The café she had just come from stood a couple of doors away, but she chose to walk a few more streets to find another. She ordered coffee again and a slice of sponge cake, and put the magazine down by the side of her cup. She seldom read magazines. There was a free pattern for the dress the lady was wearing on the front cover. Laura had never learned to sow, not properly. She had never run up a new blouse or evening gown. Her mother had never encouraged it, and her attempts at school had been poor, her teacher eventually finishing most of her projects. There were also recipes for jam, something else she had yet to do—make jam. She opened out the magazine and found a story. 'All the Love in the World.' Pushing the cake aside, she read, or tried at least, until her watch finally told her it was time.

A couple of doctors from a recent seminar came out through the doors, and she waved back across but didn't approach them. She didn't want to get caught up in any conversations. They stopped to talk to Mr. Grant, as he adjusted a large bundle of papers and journals under his arm. It was Tuesday, journal club day. She ducked away from the lamplight overhead, knowing that if he caught sight of her he would most probably come across. He had made a bee line towards her at every meeting and convention they had both attended, always saying he would have her on board at the hospital anytime, always inviting her to his monthly journal club. She was never quite certain if his interests were purely professional.

She almost didn't see Kate, crowded by a group of nurses. It was the whole movement of her, the swing of her arm, the placement of her foot, the tilt of her head, everything that was familiar, which caused Laura to lift her attention from the group of doctors.

Kate had seen her, and for an awful moment Laura thought that she might just keep on walking, talking to her companions all the way back to the nurses' home, but she turned and caught one of their hands and broke away from the others. Laura held her breath as Kate, head down, ignored the paths and took the most direct route across the grass. Finally, her eyes, with purpose, met Laura's.

"Kate!"

Both turned. Laura absorbed the man coming towards them—dark hair, greying slightly at the temples, handsome even features, and what could only be described as the kindest eyes. She almost wanted to say. "You have the kindest eyes." But they didn't rest on her, at least not initially. The warmth was all for Kate, who stood by his side in rigid contrast. Finally, he lifted his gaze.

"Ah, it's Dr. Harrison isn't it? How wonderful to finally speak properly with you. I keep seeing you at seminars. I've heard so many good things about your work." She felt so tired. She could just close her eyes and let his gentle rhythmical words lap over her, like a warm Mediterranean sea. His English was flawless, with just the slightest trace of an accent.

"It's you…Mr. Garcia," she said quietly, her eyes resting slowly on his perplexed face.

"Yes, that's right."

She nodded and straightened herself up, tried her best to smile. "I'm a huge fan of your research." She extended her hand, and he took it into his, enveloping it with warmth.

"Kate, you never said you knew Dr. Harrison." Laura noted the familiarity with which he spoke to Kate, how easily he used her name. "I was just saying to Kate the other day how we need more female doctors, how you were giving all those old boys a run for their money." He looked at Kate again quizzically, the same smile in his eyes. "You never said, you never said." He turned to Laura. "I keep telling her she should be a doctor. She's so bright. It's such a waste."

"I've told her that too." Laura said quietly. Kate looked away.

"You have? Why then, we must join forces and hopefully she will see sense."

Kate had looked at her shoes, her hands, the stitching around the hem of her cloak, anywhere it seemed but at Laura.

"I'm sorry. Look at me clumsily interrupting your conversation." Mr. Garcia looked from one to the other, finally settling his eyes on Kate. "I just came over to let you know I've got those theatre tickets for Saturday night. I didn't know if you fancied getting a bite to eat beforehand, but we can talk about it later if you like."

"It's okay." Laura spoke into the uncomfortable silence. "I'm actually here to see Mr. Grant. He's got his journal club tonight." She pulled out the packet of cigarettes and half waved them. "Thought I'd have a quick smoke first though. He hates it." She lit the cigarette and snapped the lighter shut. "You two go on."

"Well, we should all go out together sometime." Mr. Garcia said, looking at Kate to show some agreement to his suggestion, but she stood quite still and said nothing.

"Actually, I'm leaving soon."

"Back to America?" Kate said.

Laura turned to her, surprised to finally hear her voice. "Yes."

Kate nodded and looked away. Whatever force that had pushed the question out, gone again.

"Goodbye Mr. Garcia. It was very nice to have met you." Laura took his hand again.

"Goodbye. I'm sorry you're leaving."

She nodded. "Look after Kate, or rather, look after each other."

"Of course." He smiled over at Kate, giving her his full attention. "Now, do you want to get a cup of tea or a coffee? We can talk about arrangements for Saturday night. Unless you're too tired?"

Kate shook her head. "No, I'm not too tired."

Laura wanted to walk away, but there was nowhere for her to go. So she drew on the cigarette. "Goodbye Kate."

"Goodbye."

As they walked, Andreas talked about his day and suggested plans for Saturday. Kate's face felt as expressionless, and her body as hollow, as the Mannequins they passed by along Oxford Street, and she wondered if every future smile would have to be painted on, wiped off and painted on again. She nodded, in what she hoped were the right places, but he might just have well have been talking about the weather or his plans to fly to the moon. She couldn't speak, except to herself, over and over, she's leaving. The vague comfort of them still sharing the same city had vanished.

She thought of the old street map of London that hung in the nurses' dining hall. On her first evening it had struck her how little central London had changed. Despite herself, she had stood purposefully in front of it, until she had found Laura's street. She had then traced with her finger along roads, avenues and lane's, over Westminster Bridge, to where she had stood. There was some comfort, that, at any one time, two pins could be dropped, maybe the Theatre Royal and the coffee house in Soho, or Camden market and Oxford street, or the Regal Cinema and the public library. Their two pins would land on that same map. But now she would need a globe, where her fingers would have to span the Atlantic Ocean to addresses no more specific than New York and London.

The smell of the traffic, the people, the streets, they all felt intolerable. A sickness rose up from her stomach. In a panic, she tried to look at the faces that passed quickly by her. Every one a stranger, oddly hostile, as they moved and jostled past with their shared intention to get to their various destinations, and eventually the final one, home. What kind of home? Who do all these people have waiting for them?

Andreas stopped mid sentence and placed a hand on Kate's arm. "Are you okay?"

"I'm sorry. I don't feel very well."

"Let me take you back."

Kate just wanted to be on her own. She wanted to rush back alone through the busy pavements, pushing and shoving past anyone who got in her way, but she knew protesting would be pointless. "If you could. Thank you."

The feeling of nausea had settled a little as she ran up the stairs to her room. She had managed to retain a measure of composure until she left Andreas, holding on carefully to the swell of tears, the back of her throat tight. She hardly noticed Val on the landing.

"Kate, are you all right?"

She carried on to her door, pushing it so violently that an envelope, which must have been pushed under, lifted and flew up across the room. She went to pick it up, but stopped and stared down at its twisted corners, one slightly torn, and at the writing, drawn from a distant memory.

Slowly, she reached down and pulled out a card. In red curling letters she read the words. "Joyeux Noël." A cartoon fawn stood in the snow, with a little red and white hat perched to one side. A small, plump robin fluttered beside it holding a piece of holly in its beak. She felt the rough glitter under her fingertips as she ran them along the snowy peaks. There was no handwriting in the card, but a single piece of paper sat folded inside.

My Dearest Kate,

I'm not sure how to start this letter. I sit surrounded by balls of paper with beginnings that might encourage you to read on. I will just try by starting with the facts.

I saw Harry Sanders the other day. You probably don't even remember him. He was (and still is) a good friend of your Uncle Harold's. It was quite surreal really. There I was, walking along the quiet lane that leads to the vineyard when a chap comes along on a moped, takes off his helmet to ask me directions, and there is this face so quite out of time and place that it quite flawed me. How funny and small the world is. He's one of those bachelor types, never really settled down, and he was travelling around Europe for a month. We were never close, but seeing someone from a time so remote and missed made him feel like a long lost brother. He came round that evening for dinner and we talked about the old days with wine and such nostalgia. I hardly dared ask about you, and perhaps he wasn't sure whether it was a topic he should broach. But I did, and how glad I was. His news was sparse, but what he could tell me made me so pleased. He told me of your achievements at High school and now that you are a nurse. I am so excited for you, just starting out in life. The war gave women so many opportunities and then took them away again, so I'm glad you have chosen to take up a vocation before settling down.

Life should be seen as an adventure, not something to be got through and survived, and it's important whom you choose to go with on that adventure. I regret leaving you every day of my life. So, why leave you say? If only choices, and such selfish choices I know, were that simple, and we could separate one so easily from another.

There is little I can give you and even less that I should expect you to accept from me, but enjoy this time, you are young, take your time. Your mother and I were too young when we married. We didn't know the people we were going to be.

I live in Provence with Marie. We have a small vineyard, which provides us with enough to live comfortably. No children, sometimes these things just aren't meant to be. Maybe one day you might come out to visit, and we would certainly come to London.

I stopped writing when I heard that you had moved from Oxford. Those letters were to a child, and whether you ever received them, I have no idea. Now you are all grown up, so I write to you as an adult. I don't expect you to ever to forgive me, but maybe you can eventually come to understand the choices I made all those years ago.

With love always

Dad

Kate brushed her forearm across her face, wiping away tears. She smiled and then began to laugh.

"What is it Kate? Who's it from? What on earth is the matter?"

She wiped her hand down her face, pinching the top of her nose with her thumb and forefinger. "My father—it's from my father."

"What does he say?"

"That he's in Provence, with Marie."

CHAPTER TWENTY-THREE

As they came down the theatre steps, Andreas reached for Kate's arm and placed it in his. Kate looked up at him and smiled. He had occasionally taken her hand or arm to guide her through crowds, or when crossing a busy road, but he had always released it once they had passed through, or reached the other side. This was the first time he had pointedly taken her arm and rested it through his. She gently squeezed the sleeve of his coat.

"What would you like to do now? We could get a taxi or we could walk. It's a lovely evening." He said.

"It is." Kate looked up at the clear night sky, although only the very brightest stars managed to shine past the lights of London. "Let's walk."

She thought of the others back at the nurses' home, and how she would tell them all about her night. It had been a lovely evening; the meal, the ballet, the music, and she was quite certain that if anyone asked her if they had kissed, she would answer 'yes'. Soon, she would formally introduce Andreas to Matron, and then they could go to the hospital's spring dance together, officially, as a couple.

They strolled in comfortable silence, turning off the busier roads onto some of the quieter avenues. Andreas cleared his throat and pulled her gently to a stop. He reached down, and Kate waited for his kiss, but he paused for a moment, so she closed the short distance for him, until she felt the press of his lips against hers. There it was, the smooth soft flesh and then a slight wetness as the kiss deepened. She felt the scratch of his skin, and felt his arms come around her and tighten, holding her firmly in place. But that was all she felt, his lips, his arms, and the roughness of his cheek. The sensations seemed to stop just there. And that's where everything stopped, at the flesh, at their coats, her dress, his suit.

She pulled back and lowered her head.

"I'm sorry Kate. Was it too soon?"

She shook her head "No."

"Then what is it?"

"I'm sorry…I wish I could explain."

He lifted her head and moved his thumb gently across her cheek. "I would love to know what went on in that head of yours." He reached down for her hand. "Come on."

But she stayed firmly where she stood, his hand slipping from hers. "It's not fair. It's not fair to you."

He walked back to her and took her hand again. "I can wait. I don't mind waiting Kate."

"But waiting for what? I just…" The cherry trees lined both sides of the familiar avenue, holding thousands of delicate flowers, their softness accentuated by the stiff, somber branches. These were the same branches that had dazzled and shone all on their own just a season ago. It felt like a lifetime.

A slight breeze lifted a number of the petals, and they fluttered all the way along the avenue. Scattered pinks and whites lay at her feet and all around, like carelessly tossed confetti.

"It's already starting to fall," Kate said quietly.

"It doesn't last long does it? The blossom."

"Within a week it'll all be gone," she said, looking up at the branches that still seemed full. But another slight brush of wind came and sent a further flurry.

"Would you mind if I walked home alone?"

"Kate, it's dark. Let me take you back."

"Please, Andreas."

"I'll see you tomorrow?"

Kate shook her head. "I'm sorry."

He blew out a breath, his jaw tightening, as he gave a small nod. Then he turned and walked away. She continued on along the avenue towards the nurses' home.

The lamp buzzed overhead as Kate stood for a moment, watching the familiar faces through the glass front doors. The trill of the bell began, but no one noticed her as they left the dayroom. Only Val caught sight of her. She folded the magazine in her hand and started towards the door with a smile, but Kate took a few steps back. And, as though Kate had told her something, she stopped and gave a slight nod. Kate gave a small wave and Val did the same. She pulled her coat around her and turned back down the steps.

There were no lights, although the curtains were drawn at every window. She rang the buzzer, but knew there would be no answer. Sitting down on one of the steps, she wondered if maybe this was enough. If Laura had gone, maybe it had been enough that she had come tonight. Perhaps she would steel into Val's room, and tell her where she had been, and the next day she could speak to Andreas, apologize and carry on as before. The cold stone step started to press through her dress and petticoats. She reached for the railings to pull herself up.

There was talking and laughter before she saw the two figures at the very bottom of the street. Both were mainly just silhouettes, but she recognized Sarah's dancing ponytail and Laura's tall angular body. She listened to them saying their goodbyes and sat back down. Pushing her hands firmly into her pockets, she stared at the pavement in front of her. The conversation ended, and the footsteps grew louder, and then stopped.

"Aren't you cold?"

Kate smiled uncertainly at the ordinariness of the question. "A little." She shook her head. "Not too much. Will you sit with me?" Laura lowered herself down onto the step. "I thought you'd gone."

"Not yet. I thought you were at the theatre."

"I was," Kate said, pulling her skirts firmly down over her knees. "You were wrong you know?"

"Wrong?"

"When you said I was choosing David. I chose you from the very first moment I saw you…and I'll always be choosing you, over everyone and everything. I know that now…and I was wrong, wrong to say that I couldn't imagine an us…because all I've done since that day is think of you, of us. Other things would come along; work, family, friends—"

"Mr. Garcia."

"They were all just interludes. Things to be got through." She rubbed her hands against the sudden chill of the night air. "Strangely, you became more real than any of them. But memories are so unsatisfactory. I wanted to play you in my mind like a film, but everything kept halting, and you were never clear enough…"

Laura looked down at her shoe as she moved it slightly from side to side. "I'm sorry."

"Sorry? Sorry for what?"

"I seem to be a little troublesome to you."

Kate gave a slight smile. "A little perhaps, but there you go…" Laura still looked at the ground, although, perhaps there was the slightest flicker of a smile. "I got a letter from my father the other day."

"You did?" Laura looked at her properly. "Oh Kate, that's great." She looked into Kate's eyes. "Isn't it?"

"Yes, yes I suppose it is." Kate hugged her legs tightly. "It was strange, but in a wonderful sort of way." She rested her chin on her knees. "He said he'd written before, when I was a child."

"Your mother?"

Kate shrugged. "Perhaps…anyway, he's invited me to visit him—him and his wife."

"When?"

"Oh, nothing firm, just if I ever wanted to go over…"

A blackbird, perhaps fooled by the lamplight, sang it's own song, and a car rolled past at the bottom of the street.

"Well, if you wanted a travelling companion, some moral support. If you wanted me to come with you…"

"Would you?" Kate rocked slightly, her knees clutched tight, as she looked at Laura. "Would you come with me?"

"Of course I would," Laura said, taking Kate's hand into hers. "Don't you know that?"

Kate looked out across to the small park on the opposite side, enjoying the soft warmth of Laura's hand. The breeze had dropped, and the trees stood solid and still behind the iron railings. She tried to find the blackbird.

"It's one of those evenings—a little unreal." Laura said.

"Perfect."

"Almost." Laura shifted closer, and Kate felt the press of her shoulder and thigh against her own. The beat of her heart almost masked the sound of footsteps that approached and made them both look up. A man passed by and tipped his hat.

"Come on." Laura said. "It really is too cold out here."

Kate felt the chill as Laura moved away and began to stand. "Moira's got a new record player. It can play six records, one after another." Laura helped Kate to her feet, keeping hold of her hand. "That's where I've been this evening, to have a look at it. Have you ever seen one?"

"No," Kate said, and shook her head.

"If you like, you can see it next weekend. Moira's having a party to show it off. You know Moira—any excuse to mix a few cocktails."

Kate smiled, and as she climbed the steps, her hand in Laura's, she began to imagine a player that could do that, and how it might work.

"Of course, we'll have to take some of our own records. Unless you don't mind listening to jazz all night."

Reaching into her bag, Laura pulled out a set of keys. She put the key in the lock and the door clicked open. "So…do you want to come?"

Kate slowly led her by the hand into the hallway and up the stairs. She gave a small nod.

"I do."

Printed in Great Britain
by Amazon